Gravedigger

The Lord Impaler Series

ARIELLE. LYON

DEDICATION

For my beloved husband who loves me despite my twisted mind and dreams. For you maman, who inspired me to follow my dream. To you, grandpa, an angel in heaven, I love you.

This novel is dedicated to all who believed in me. I also dedicated it to those who doubted my will power, as it pushed me to prove them all wrong.

THE LORD IMPALER

The Gothic Series

1	Mrs. Blackwood	2018
2	Gravedigger	2019
	Annex	
3	My Tongue Of Old	2021
4	Wladislaus Dragwlya	2021
*	The Lord Impaler Companion	Coming Soon

COPYRIGHT

CHAPTER 1
READ MY BLOOD

"I told you not to drink from strangers!" He growled through his teeth, where a strong impact resonated from the wall when propping his guard against it. "We have givers and VitaL for a reason!" he let go of the body as it fell on the wooden floor of the French mansion, and with his smoky voice, he added, "Wipe that blood off your face and put away those fangs, before I smack them off your mouth."

The vampire used his sleeve to wipe the sanguine liquid dripping from his mouth. He looked up toward the tall and dark lead vampire and said, "It's strange hearing those words from the one who used to have a forest of impaled bodies…remind me how many were there, twenty, thirty, or was it—"

"A hundred thousand, and don't make me add you to that list!" He shouted through his smoky voice, adding with a carved frown as he pulled him back up against the wall by the collar of his shirt, "Don't think for one moment that because you're part of Matthias' House, I won't hesitate to impale you and turn you inside out, you filthy piece of shit!"

"I was sent by Corvinus to keep an eye on your doings, Vladislav. The High Council is doubting your loyalty to our people." His voice, reminiscent of a snake, crawled up Vlad's skin and so he stared at the bloodsucker with his vampire's eyes, showing a red dot in his pupils.

"You're abusing your rank, Frederick."

"Corvinus paid me to be your shadow, and so I shall be."

Vladislav lost his patience and threw Frederick out of the boudoir and closed the double doors. "Piss off!"

As he walked back toward the fireplace, near his friend François, he thought about the many rules to follow as a vampire leader ever since he was turned. His name had him placed on the highest of ranks. His actions had him feared by many vampires that demanded proof of his maker but found none. It had Vladislav seen as a First. In spite of it all, his reputation and life as a human who died over five centuries ago, Vladislav had to comply with The Viper Council.

Frederick belonged to Matthias Corvinus' House, a man who had stabbed him in the back and sold him out to their enemy while he was still human. Vladislav despised the conservative vampires, which were all part of The Viper Council. As he was the leader of the idealists, those who wished to be part of the human world, one female vampire part of the council was the opposite and protected the old ways. There were many cherished traditions, and Frederick was one who enjoyed applying these traditions ever since he had been turned around eight hundred years ago.

Vladislav felt a par on his back and then the hand moved to his shoulder with a firm grip, "Like it or not my friend, if you don't control yourself and start acting with that overly high IQ brain of yours, you'll perish at Matthias' hand once again."

"I lost my token, François. If I don't find it soon, I'll die no matter what."

"Any leads on who took it?"

"All of those I suspected came out clean. I need a witch to help me find it and find the rat who sold me out, again."

All of the conservatives Vladislav suspected of stealing his token came out clean once under his mind spell. He thought because the idealists desired nothing more than to live at peace with humans, that those opposed to it and fighting for the old ways would send someone to steal his one object, preventing him from turning into a puddle of muddy blood. Yet, he came out empty-handed. The smell of burning logs from the fireplace brought comfort to Vladislav's mind, but his problems kept surfacing, and when François showed a grin, he bent over to stare at his computer screen.

"This is Clémentine Roy. She's a Vampirologist and Parapsychologist. She teaches classes at three different universities. She's also the one who found the body of an ancient vampire petrified not too far from the Moosham Castle in Austria. She made the news, and she traveled around until she was silenced."

"Conservatives?"

"Yes. They stopped her from sharing the truth and alienated the body as proof."

Vladislav looked at her black hair going down her neck, hazel green eyes, and fair skin. In her picture, she wore a black tank top with a beaked hoodie and had a subtle smile while standing in front of an iron gate. He couldn't help but smirk when he heard his friend say, "By doing some more research on her, I found that she has a Ph.D. in history and specialized in Legends and Folklore. She is also part of the Life at Dusk web series."

Clémentine showed great talent in the eyes of Vladislav, who sometimes had such a hard time believing how far the human race had come. He had walked through the renaissance, the world wars, and now the modern time. Each period had vampires forced to adapt and change their habits alongside their vocabulary and ways of expressing themselves. Some habits stuck, but his eye for art had never changed, and he noticed a link to an artistic portfolio belonging to her.

With a murmur, and his eyes wide open, he expressed his admiration, "She does love the Dark Ages."

"Especially you, look at all those drawings of your reign." François turned his attention to Vladislav, who stared back, "I think we can have her come to us.

We just need to use someone to feed her intel on vampires being present at the Halloween celebration."

"Take a closer look at her name, Vlad. She's not only important to us because of her knowledge."

Vladislav read her biography in her art section and gasped, "Katharina." He then added, "de Roy...she's a blood witch."

Vladislav stood up straight, surprised by François' discovery, and as he showed him the team working on the Life at Dusk web series, he recognized a Rougarou and an Illusionist, two other beings hiding from humans but also rebelling against vampires. Despite being against bringing other species to the Halloween celebration at the mansion, Vladislav agreed to invite the trio. Every year, some innocent humans would succumb to the bestial nature of what it meant to be a vampire. He hoped it wouldn't happen again.

"She's not just a blood witch, Vlad. She possesses hoodoo abilities. She was taught the ways." He took a deep breath despite not needing it per se and added, "No one has that type of odd resume and hasn't had experience of the *Monsters*. As far as we know, she's most likely the best at what she does."

"Why would you think that about her?"

"She found the body of one of the oldest vampires, hidden meters below the ground close to Moosham. How could she have found it if not from someone from the other side? A premonition, maybe? Something telling her the exact emplacement?" François took a good look around him. "We just need to ask Violette to spit intel to her by reaching out to her through email. If we succeed, Violette can drop your name in the pile, and she'll bite...or you'll bite before she does." Vladislav frowned, "Stop drooling all over
my computer."

"I'm claiming her, François. No one is to touch her but me. Understood? I don't want a repetition of last year when your friends turned the celebration into a fucking bloodbath turning thirty-five humans into vampires because of a fucking bet. We're vampires, not college boys."

Vladislav thanked François for watching over him. However, he feared for a few of his friends showing up to the Halloween festivities. He dreaded an attack from conservatives; Frederick being only the beginning of an infiltration of traditional vampires allying themselves with the conservatives.

"Naten is coming."

"What about, my son?"

"Damian will come alone." François fixed his gaze on Vlad. "Coralie has to stay behind for her own protection and to keep order in the Southern States while Liam is across the northern borders."

CHAPTER 2
WHAT YOU WISH

One week later...

The branches were lit up with little bulbs of white lights. The path she walked on would soon bring her to an old plantation home in the suburbs of Bellerose. The mansion was built at the end of a long path covered in mature oak trees on both sides. Ancient and Romanesque, the house stood tall and proud, with imposing white columns and a large, wooden wrap-around porch. The wide French windows offered a peek into the hugely anticipated by-invitation-only Halloween festivity that was held at the mansion

each year.

The night sky was clear of all clouds, stars were bright like diamonds, and the moon lit up the top of the trees like a spotlight. An imposing and large staircase, shown to be old, with white paint cracking in some places where the wood splintered, brought the young woman to the front door. There, a man stood with a guestbook wearing a black cape and Victoria period suit. He welcomed her with a bright smile showing his fake fangs.

"Hello Mademoiselle?" said the host concerning the guest list looking at her ring finger.

"Roy, Clémentine Roy, and this is my friend, Mika Hunter."

"Yes! There you are. The gold tickets give you access to this part of the mansion, mainly the ground floor. The staircase up is black tickets only."

"All right, thank you, Maxim," Clémentine replied, looking at his name tag on his coat.

"My pleasure Mademoiselle Roy and Mademoiselle Hunter."

Clémentine took off her long silver-gray coat in the hall reserved for that purpose. A man kindly gave her a ticket to keep for the time she would need it back. The clerk was as pale as the moon, his smile very enchanting, and his eyes so bright she thought his makeup was disturbingly amazing.

This is no costume and makeup. I believe this man is authentic, she thought to herself.

The Halloween festivities at the mansion were annual. The mansion was resplendent in decorations of gold and black. The old amber and burgundy wallpaper adorned baroque French curved patterns and embellished the gold framing of old oil paintings hung on the wall going up the grand U-shaped oak staircase.

An immense gold chandelier, decorated with black crystal garlands, lighted the entrance hall bringing the two girls to a corridor on their right where the ballroom was. Stepping in, the two friends immediately saw a six-person orchestra in the back of the room performing music from the nineteenth century, very charming to the ear. Still grotesquely, the notes were somewhat lower and a little more aggressive than the original pieces.

Placed on each wall were fake oil paintings of the main four monsters that inspired the minds of thousands of people through time to change their stories, making sure they would never be forgotten.

The ballroom walls were covered in beige and gold with thick black garland roses coming down the black velvet drapes on each side of the four mural French windows.

In between each window hung a painting. "Clémentine, I can't believe you painted those. They are incredible!" Mika walked around and stared at the talent of her friend. "How did you say the owner found you again?" Clémentine cleared her throat and leaned toward her friend's ear, "I don't think we're here by accident or because he needed those painted. He said he found me on social media. Honestly, I think he was looking for a Vampirologist." Mika cleared her voice, "Right. Let's keep an eye out for what   we   might see tonight."

The first painting shown was Frankenstein's monster with a greyish green flesh tone. He wore a grey suit with an unbuttoned shirt revealing a muscular chest as the character was being hit by lightning. The second painting showed a freshly turned revenant with dark thorn branches surrounding her body. The undead woman wore a white gown stained by her fall, her platinum blond hair flying in the wind. Then, a man tearing his lumberjack plaid shirt open showed his imposing, muscular torso, his arm muscles flexed to its limit showing an undeniable change in his appearance. As he stood below the full moon, it was apparent it was a werewolf in the third painting.

Clémentine kept smiling, but sill asked a serious question to her friend.

"What do we do if we're discovered?"

Looking around, Mika answered, "Surely by now, we've been smelled by old vampires." Mika fixed Clémentine, "But don't worry. I didn't come unarmed."

"Me neither."

On the most impressive wall, above the mural fireplace embellished with a gothic decorated mantle with sizable black beeswax candles, hung an imposing gold frame. The painting of a picturesque man wearing an old dark green linen shirt, his large neck beautified with a large gold cross with garnets, and his long, black, wavy hair was hanging down both sides of his neck, down to his pectorals. His eyes were as piercing as a wolf and red as wine. His mouth slightly opened, showing the specular reflection off his fangs as drops of blood dripped from his luscious bottom lip on both sides. It was obviously the incarnation of Dracula.

"I know we went over this already, but do you think they're 'lifestylers' or vampire wannabes, role-play people?"

"Violette's letter was too precise. How would she know about the secret military base in Cheyenne County of all places."

"Google map?"

"The base is sixty meters underground, Mika. It's not easily accessible by anything, including internet browsing." Clémentine took a deep breath, "Also, why would she know that a vampire body found in Austria would end up in the States?"

"You got me there."

Clémentine Roys was a reputable historian who specialized in ancient times, legends, and folklore. legends, and folklore. She became a producer of one of the most popular documentary series, Life At Dusk on the Dark Channel. Clémentine used her passion for the unknown to study human history to prove that the evolution of humankind is more than what we thought it was. During her studies, she met a rather strange archaeology student named Mika Hunter, who later became her partner in her pursuit of the truth. She got in touch with the young ginger when a lead to a supposedly alleged vampire burial site was discovered in Austria near the Moosham Castle.

Clémentine and Mika walked to a large table right below one of the paintings and kept a close eye on all activities around them. The table had a beige tablecloth, but on top of it was a black lace net. Black candelabras decorated the table and gold plates of fruits, cheeses, and crackers were placed while large martini glasses were spread across the very long table with red sauce and fountains of shrimp coming out of them. There were bowls of bread, baskets of black candied apples, dried fruits, and Cajun specialties went out later on antique trays; serving bites of waffle and fried chicken, bites of po'boys, and other delicious foods that Mika and Clémentine promised themselves to overeat.

"We promised ourselves a good time," Mika mentioned. "Plus, it's not like we're unarmed if they happen to all be real vampires." She sneered, "Those wannabes don't know who they're fucking with, and that might promise to be good."

Clémentine chuckled, "But what if they happened to be real vampires?"

Mika gulped, "Then we're fucked…well, we still have our silver chokers and jewelry. That should slow them down...wait, I forgot, which metal takes them down?"

"Silver, wooden stakes, mercury, ultra-violet in any capacity, setting them on fire, decapitation even, ethylenediaminetetraacetic acid."

"Wow, say that three times fast." Mika stared at her friend, "Please don't. It was rhetorical." She then added, "Also, we only have silver because we're sure a thousand percent that these are wannabes."

Clémentine took out a small little jar, "Ethylenediaminetetraacetic acid."

"Damn...I guess that's why you have a Ph.D. and I have a Masters."

"Nope, it's nothing but fourteen years of acting and reading."

"I only read music."

"You live in my bachelor suite."

While the mansion was luxuriously decorated, the guests were all dressed in the fashion of the 1800's. Black and silver, or burgundy and gold suits were worn by men while most women seemed to have opted for either purple or black dresses adorned with corsets and crinolines, but without the typical hats. Many costumes seemed very accurate to the last details. So many looked old and even the fabric seemed to be out of   a

time capsule.

Clémentine wore a moiré forest green French silk dress patterned with leaves and blossoms. The ball gown had short, tight sleeves decorated with puffs, black French lace, and a silk ribbon tied in a subtle bow. It had an elongated bodice and was tied in the back. It had a soft sweetheart neckline embellished with black lace and a ribbon. Her jet-black hair was tied up in a loose bun with a crystal pin and, although long bangs were not famous at the time, some locks fell down

her forehead.

She wore a silver and garnet necklace with matching earrings and black silk gloves going up past her elbows, showing a small part of her blue roses tattoo.

Mika wore a more eloquent red and gray silk bustle dress with fantasy patterns. She had black gloves, and her dark purple hair was curled and held up in a tighter bun than her friend. In front, the dress buttoned at the neck, where she added an oval gold medallion that could be used as a watch. Mika had more womanly curves, while Clémetine was blessed with a larger chest.

When they both disposed of their plates, they heard the orchestra playing a minuet. Mika offered her hand to Clémentine, who laughed, and both joined other dancers on the ballroom dance floor. Their dresses moved with every turn following the music. Clémentine tried to locate Violette LeBlanc but couldn't see her anywhere. Over the last few weeks, Clémentine received many emails concerning this particular festivity. She proved herself to be a trusted source when she revealed she knew about the discovery of the real vampire. Her presence was not a coincidence. Clémentine could feel something from the crowd that was intoxicating, something often associated with vampires.

"Maybe François St-Arnaud will show up later on tonight," Mika said while holding her hand high, so Clémentine could twist underneath before the song ended. "I don't know. Our tickets are only good until midnight. I heard after then there would be a party for elites only. They are the black ticket buyers."

The music changed, and Clémentine watched as Mika fanned herself in desperate need of cool air. Her friend pointed at the bar and left. After a few minutes, a drink, and a short rest, they were ready to hit the dance floor again. The sound of the music, magical to Clémentine's ears, had her and Mika swirling around the dancefloor.

She turned around abruptly but was hit by a large chest. She was face to chest with a man in a completely black three-piece suit. She lifted her eyes until she was forced to move her head up and saw the face of a man with the most mesmerizing eyes she had ever seen. Clémentine was five and a half feet tall and wore black ballerina flats yet was barely up to his chest, so she guessed the man must've been about six and a half feet tall. His hair was ebony black cut in long layers down his neck. Yet, her attention was drawn to his eyes. The iris was of a dark forest green color while the inside was as bright as emerald.

"I'm sorry, miss?" he said with a smoky voice that sent shivers down her spine.

"Clémentine, Clémentine Roy." Her voice was so soft-spoken, she thought he never heard a word.

The man had a smile in the corner of his mouth, just enough that she could see a bit of his arctic white teeth on the side of his grin. His neck massive and robust following his squared jawline, and Clémentine noticed his shirt was opened two buttons down. She could see an old gold chain reflecting from the light of the room.

She then heard his soft-spoken and silvery voice asking, "Would you dance with me?" Clémentine agreed, still weak in the knees at the pure sound of his voice. The orchestra was playing *All I Ask of You* from *The Phantom of The Opera*.

Clémentine couldn't help but smile as she danced in the arms of a tall man that possessed all the traits that she always dreamed of. He was tall, dark, and irresistible. Somehow, as crazy as it seemed, she could've sworn she did see him once in a dream. He led her all around the ballroom dance floor, and as he smiled, she wondered if there was someone special in his life. Then she realized she had given him her name, but he never said his.

They both stopped dancing as the melody changed and as they walked away from the ballroom dance floor, he said with a calm tone of voice that Clémentine would have listened to all night long, "My name is Razvan Bucur, but you can just call me Razvan."

"You have a foreign accent I know, and your name…are you Romanian?"

"Yes. I was born in Romania but traveled around and ended up settling down here for a while."

"Romania…I've always wanted to visit such a fascinating and historical country."

"Thank you for the compliment on my native land, but may I ask why such an interest over other more popular sites?"

It was so strange, Clémentine could have sworn she heard a whisper in her mind, but she soon forgot about it when she began to daydream about the country that had inspired her work for so many years. She even became a professional vampirologist due to all the legends guiding her back to the mysterious past of Romania. Her passion for the legends and folklore had her study history, and anthropology, to finally be specialized in the paranormal. Yet, to this day, she had not seen the homeland of Razvan.

It was in an attempt to answer Razvan's question that Clémentine saw the mountain on the horizon in her mind. As she got closer, the bright stone walls of the castle were crowning the top of the cliff where it was built, but slowly giving in to the five hundred years that passed, leaving it in ruins after an earthquake that took place in the early nineteenth century.

Clémentine tried to imagine the castle back in its glory days, but the only images she found on

Google were there to remind her there was no way she would ever see it otherwise. Brick by brick, she saw its reconstruction. For a split second, she contemplated the castle tall and robust like the fortress it was meant to be, back when it was built to defend and protect the people one man swore to uphold to his inevitable end.

"I would love to see the Poenari Castle for once," Clémentine finally answered after lowering one eyebrow, trying to understand how she had been able to see the castle in such precise details.

"Why is that? Although I do believe I know the answer."

"Vladislav Tepes III Dracul...sorry, I mean—" replied Clémentine as she knocked her forehead with her right hand before Razvan cut her short.

"You meant right. Although Vlad Tepes would've been just as right.

CHAPTER 3
THE TWELVE STROKES

Clémentine wanted something to drink but didn't want to walk away from Razvan for a reason she refused to confess to herself. She was attracted to him. She lowered her head and swallowed her saliva, hoping it would be enough for the time being. As if Razvan just read her mind, he showed her the back of the room on the opposite side from the dance floor with a gesture of his hand. He guided Clémentine to the bar where he asked for her drink choice, and with her crystal and small voice, she answered Razvan while looking down.

"A bottle of water, please."

"For you, sir?" the bartender asked with what Clémentine could tell was nervousness as if he knew him, almost trembling in his presence.

Razvan's voice was smoky, yet authoritative, "A glass of the red I brought. My name is written on the label. Thank you." The bartender bowed to him before reaching for the bottle; "Yes…" then the young man cleared his voice "Of course, sir."

Clémentine lowered her brows paying attention to the bartender's every move. He seemed very uncomfortable around Clémentine's new dance partner, mainly after he used a more commanding voice to have a drink. Brushing this peculiar moment out of her head, she looked at Razvan, who some would probably say was the only alpha male around, but to the point of fear, she wondered who he really was when he held out the drinks and ordered the bartender to put it on his tab.

"Here is your bottle of water, Clémentine."

"Thank you, Mr. Bucur." She answered with a shy smile, trying to keep her thoughts to herself as she stared at his chain around his neck.

"Please, call me Razvan. I don't want us to be formal." It almost sounded like an order, but she guessed it was probably his usual tone of voice and answered practically right away.

"Alright, Razvan, what was that about?" pointing at the bartender who still seemed shaken by the encounter.

She could see the sheer embarrassment on Razvan's face as he lowered his head to look at the drink that had been served to him in a metal flask. He took a sip and tried to move the conversation away from what just happened by asking her to explain to him why she wanted to visit the very famous Poenari Castle
in Romania.

Of course, she revelled in her fascination with history. Her favorite parts were the mysterious sections past where the real and fiction met and created legends that would feed one's imagination for centuries. She was fascinated to the point where a name could be immortalized both in what was known to be real and the realm of dreams and fantasy. Clémentine noticed a spark in Razvan's eyes. He seemed enchanted by her passion for his country's history. He somehow got her to talk more about her apparent fixation on the one historical figure until he stopped her shortly and asked where her accent was from. He mentioned that he knew French, but it wasn't from Louisiana nor France and so he was curious as to know where she indeed was from.

"I'm French Canadian. I'm from a town north of Montréal called Mont La Bellerose. It is located in the province of Québec. Like many towns in my province, we share the same name as ones here in Louisiana."

Razvan brushed a lock of her hair away from her face; his fingers followed her neck down her shoulder to her hand he raised to his mouth as he said, "A young history of valor and dreams...*ma belle*." He ended as he kissed the inside of her wrist. The tall, mysterious man showed her to a table and took a seat by her side as he mentioned how much he enjoyed the company of a woman so passionate about ancient history. "I must admit I have a weakness for French women." Clémentine timidly smiled as she felt her face warming up. She looked down and somehow knew Razvan noticed her blush as his smile widened when staring
at her.

Thinking that they had talked enough about her, she tried to make him say something about himself. She was curious about what his occupation was. Razvan avoided every question she ever asked by moving the exchange into another direction. Clémentine could tell he tried to make it all about her, but she wanted to know more about him. Clémentine took a good look at his appearance. His body gently leaned forward as he rested the weight of his upper body on his arms, which were crossed on the table. She noticed small delicate wrinkles that were caused by smiling, and subtle little lines beside his eyes. He must have been in his mid-forties. His posture said a lot about him. Razvan inspired respect; there was no doubt about it. His job must have been something that would put him in control, a leader, or a CEO of some sort, maybe.

They both stayed silent for a short while, and then finally, his right arm moved away from his left, and Clémentine was able to take a good look at his hand. She saw no ring on his finger, forbidding her from moving forward, although she knew her shyness would always prevent her from doing so.

"Is there a special someone in your life?" He asked with a low, charming voice as if he read Clémentine's mind.

"No, you?" she answered, hoping he would say he was alone and single.

"No. There hasn't been anyone for a while, like you, I assume," Razvan replied, one eyebrow lifted and a grin that Clémentine found irresistible.

Clémentine moved the straw from her water bottle in between her peach lips and swallowed the liquid, trying to avoid Razvan's gaze that seemed to have a mysterious hold on her as if he could read her mind... *How does he know it's been well over two years that I've been with someone?* When his eyes met hers again, she expected him to say something to keep her by his side. However, the deep streak of a violin was heard, followed by notes given by the contrabass. Clémentine turned around and saw her friend, Mika, coming back.

All of a sudden, both Clémentine and Mika jumped out of their skin. Heavy and low strokes of bells rang. Soon it would be midnight, and Clémentine and her friend would celebrate Halloween with a bunch of vampire wannabes—or so they hypothesized if they could manage to find a way to stay. Both of them wondered why they decided to give a shot to this Violette LeBlanc character.

The woman, according to the letter, was a vampire herself. However, once they tried to find her online, they came in contact with a society of vampires. Not exactly what they were looking for, and once they kept looking, they found role-playing games taking place in historical places. Again, not what they wished to see.

"I didn't find Violette anywhere. I don't think she's here." Mika said, still shaking from that loud sound.

"I guess it was a scam or something. At least it didn't cost us anything since they paid for our tickets and invitations." Clémentine said as she moved off the chair.

"Why is it that you have to leave so early?" Razvan asked questioningly.

"Mika and I were given tickets by Mr. St-Arnaud to come to this Halloween celebration. It was supposedly a place to meet 'vampires' as we both are from a documentary show. I guess we were wrong to follow the lead without more information. Now, since those are golden tickets and not black, we have to leave."

Clémentine noticed almost right away how Razvan turned around. She could have sworn she heard him whisper, "They were supposed to be black tickets." The violin and contrabass struck yet again.

The guests were allowed twelve strokes to leave the mansion. Clémentine feared she would never see Razvan again, so she took his hand as he seemed now hypnotized by the people going. He quickly looked down at her as she said, "I guess this is goodbye. Have a nice evening, Razvan." The moment she was about to withdraw her hand, she heard him say with a fierce voice, "No, you're staying." Clémentine gulped, but saw Razvan's eyes soften because he seemed to have less tension on his face when he said, "Please, come with me."

Clémentine and Mika followed Razvan, who let go of her hand, to the grand dual staircase situated across the ballroom in the entrance hall. As they started walking up, bodyguards asked to see their tickets while Razvan kept going up, and stopped the two ladies. Clémentine tried to explain that she was with Razvan Bucur, yet the guards didn't seem to know who she talked about until one of them answered, "Mr. Razvan Bucur is not present tonight. He refused the invitation."

Clémentine wondered if two men were sharing the same name, and both invited to the same Halloween festivity when she heard Mika's voice whispering in her ear, "Weirdly detailed. Do those guards know the names of all their guests like that?" Clémentine glanced at her friend and shrugged. "I mean that was quite unsettling." Escorted to the entrance as Razvan still had his back turned to the staircase, Clémentine and Mika decided it might be best not to fight the guards and leave the mansion as they were supposed to in the first place.

"Leave them." Clémentine recognized the silvery voice, and she felt her skin tingle when turning around. He said, "Come, Clémentine." She asked for Mika to follow, as she wouldn't go anywhere without her that night, for a few reasons she tried keeping between her and her friend. "As you wish. She may come as well."

Razvan gently took her by the hand. His skin was somewhat warm to the touch and covered her own quickly. She lifted her dress with her other hand, and as she stood close to him, she could smell his musky cologne in the air. Moving to the top of the staircase, she felt Razvan stop. She looked up and saw him standing very close to a guard as he growled through his teeth, staring down in the man's eyes, "Never will you interfere with my evenings again. Have I made myself clear?" The guard, ashamed, made a quick and repetitive nod, and then stared down at his shoes as if he were too embarrassed to look anywhere else, especially at Razvan.

Clémentine passed before the guard, and as she was about to say thank you to the man out of pity, she felt something strange and heard Razvan say, "Never mind him. He needs to learn his place." She smiled at the man, but he looked away very quickly, and she felt a stronger grip on her hand. She turned to face Razvan, who said, "Don't."

Clémentine quietly followed Razvan to the back corridor on the second floor where people were dancing, very pale people with eyes as red as wine. She heard Razvan assert, "You might not have the black tickets, but I run this place with François. If someone comes to you and says you don't belong here, it is essential that you answer the *printul* and *voivode* granted your presence here for the both of you. Say that you are my own personal guests. If they don't grant you your right to stay, you will tell them that they   will   suffer the consequences."

The man had his hands on both Clémentine's shoulders; his head slightly tilted to the side as if he tried to make sure Clémentine understood what to say. She nodded, somewhat uncomfortable, she decided to avoid his gaze, but he lifted her chin with his index finger and said, "Now if you'll excuse me for a short moment, I need to find someone before they close the entrance doors. Do not venture down the corridor alone. Wait for me."

Mika used her hand fan to cool herself down and said with a laugh, "Wow, what a tall drink of yummy." Clémentine agreed, but said; "Something about him scares me, but I can't help myself, I want to stay and find out what it is."

Mika's expression changed from a light smile to a frown as she moved in front of Clémentine. She took her hands after letting go of her hand fan attached to the belt of her dress. She looked at Clémentine straight in the eyes with a splash of tears; something that Clémentine had never seen her do. Mika, at first, was a schoolmate in graphic design, but quickly became more like a sister when they developed a strong bond and Mika had agreed to work alongside Clémentine   as a photographer.

When Mika had stayed the night with Clémentine one night, as they were to go on a ghost investigation the next evening, she revealed that she was a Rougarou. Because of how Clémentine was raised, it didn't surprise her as much as her friend thought it might. She explained that she was a descendant of a strong bloodline of witches from her grandmother's side while on her grandpa's side Shamanic blood was common. It had Clémentine grow to be very sensitive to the paranormal and had her study not only science but pseudoscience as well.

"I can smell werewolves, Clémentine. There are quite a few walking around." Mika admitted while a Rougarou was stronger than werewolves, by numbers, they were still quite strong.

"I'm also sensing undead people. I can't stop all the flashes I am getting." Clémentine always described everyday people's thoughts as easily brushed off, while ghosts and undead, she would see images. The images were harder to ignore because they wanted to be heard. "This is a gumbo of people. I feel so many different presences."

Clémentine and Mika both knew the event could be a live-action role-playing game, a lifestyle type of party, or an actual vampire gathering. They had prepared themselves for the occasion. Mika had a small device, which she would hold in her hand. It would take pictures to then send to their HQ, where a team could investigate the attendees. As for Clémentine, she granted access to her web series' team into the database software, which she had copied from her former place of work.

"Does the biotech department of RunwayLAB know you cloned the software?"

"Nope." Clémentine said, "They're too busy covering their asses from 2014."

In 2014, Clémentine and Mika made the cover of a reputable and accredited scientific magazine. They went on to give conferences around Europe and North America about their historical findings concerning the petrified vampire body. They were invited to comic and book conventions and many other events. Ever since the discovery, a few more people in the field added their names to their research, and Life At Dusk rose in popularity as a documentary series. At least until the scientific council shut it down and Clémentine decided to walk away from RunwayLAB.

"Our lives have changed since the vampire body discovery," Mika said, adjusting her bustier to look more like a dignified Victorian lady. "I can't believe I'm earning my living from photography."

"I can't believe archaeologists and anthropologists knew about vampires and kept their mouth shut about it. It raises the question, 'how many times did the little green men visit us?' Is the Fairy Tooth real too?" Clémentine remarked while looking around the ballroom and entrance hall. While her show received high ratings, her reputation as a scientist had taken a dive.

The magnificent, imposing plantation house named after the owners of the land, Comptois de Jirondelle, was a three-story high chateau. Before coming to the event, the two friends and their team had researched the property. They had discovered that from the day of its construction to the current date, it had remained in the family. St-Arnaud was part of the original house of Comptois de Jirondelle. The house had a bloody history, and credited paranormal researchers and investigators from all around the globe tried to demystify the many mysteries surrounding the property that hid deaths of the most brutal kind.

"Welcome to the real Halloween Celebration, where vampires are free to be themselves!" One guest shouted behind Mika and Clémentine.

"Clémentine, should we be concerned right about now?"

"Not yet."

Blood poured from a man's throat when one 'vampire' female plunged her teeth in his jugular. The red liquid splattered all over the few people circling as the man slowly went down to his knees.

"Now?" Mika asked again

"Yes." Clémentine answered.

CHAPTER 4
THE MIDNIGHT HOUR

Clémentine closed her eyes for a moment. She moved her head forward, trying to isolate herself from the rest of the mansion. She heard screams and many ghostly voices crying coming from below her feet. Something was hidden in the deep concealed basement of the ancient manor. It was something ugly and leashed to protect people, so the truth would never come out. Unexpectedly, her mind got colder, a soft breeze ran past, and she heard, "Not now." Clémentine then felt a push, and her eyes jerked wide open. She stared at her friend and said, "Someone felt me."   Mika   shouted, "Da fuck?"

The two ladies jumped when hearing the two giant heavy wooden entrance doors closing. A voice coming from an old microphone placed before the orchestra was heard asking the general guests hiding among the crowd to show themselves. No one moved, looking at one another as if the owner of the mansion asked a ridiculous question until a handful of the general guests were brought up to the front of the ballroom.

"They will be prepared for all of you to enjoy, but in the meantime, let's dance!" Heavy black velvet drapes fell over each French window to camouflage the glass. The electricity was shut off. For a moment, everything was pitch black. Clémentine forcefully grabbed onto Mika's arm, who did the same. Clémentine's eyesight was superior to an average person, and she kept her friend close until she heard her say, "Please tell me you have more than one jar of that ethanol-electric acid?"

"Ethylenediaminetetraacetic acid." Clémentine replied, "I have two."

"Really? You're correcting me now?"

The lights went back on but stayed low. Both women looked around and realized the chandeliers were lit with what seemed to be an oiling mechanism.

The four mural fireplaces were burning logs of dry wood, leaving an enchanting smell with every piece of bark crackling. No artificial source of light was on. The entire house was plunged into a warm, but low lighting, as the fire and flames were burning bright. It would have been harder for anyone with regular eyesight to walk down the darker corridors, but not to Clémentine, whose view allowed her to see in a more extensive visible range and a broader color spectrum. She never feared the darkness and embraced it as she found comfort in the night.

Something was going on. Both ladies wished they had gone with the usual crowd as their tickets had indicated. Clémentine saw an older woman walking toward her and Mika. The strange female must have been about ten years older than Clémentine. Bleach blonde hair was pulled up on one side and loose on the other. She wore a light green shorter period dress with a garter. Her bustier was so tight that one could have sworn her breasts would have popped out. Apparently, the woman was going for a courtesan look. When she was about five feet away from Clémentine, she said with an arrogant smile moving her hand above her head, grabbing the attention of two tall security guards; "Hey boys, these two don't belong here. Take

them   to
the host!"

In the meantime, Clémentine took a good look around and realized the people on the floor were all dressed as courtesans. Some guests, elite members she presumed, walked by her, and grabbed the hand of a man or woman and dragged them down the corridor. The body from earlier, still on the ground, had Clémentine pay attention to her senses. Vampires. Clémentine looked up to face the two guards wearing black suits, Bluetooth earpieces, and walkie-talkies around their belt. They both had ashen skin, grey eyes, and were bald. They appeared to be twins. "Okay, follow us quicklives."

Clémentine was not about to let strangers touch her. She frowned, but suddenly felt a current going through her body. She was about to say something when she heard Mika state, "You smelled me a mile away, I know you did." Mika reinforced, "My people are part of the treaty. We are just as strong as you and just as influential. Beware, my wolf." Her eyes glowed gold, and sharp claws came out of her nails.

There was a breeze taking over Clémentine's sensitive mind. It felt as though for the moment, she was inside her head while experiencing the outside world. She knew the voice, but she refused to accept that it could be possible for her to hear him inside her head. He was not dead, and the only ones she could communicate with were on the other side. Yet, she heard him say loud and clear, *"I'm coming."* Clémentine walked in front of Mika, feeling assured that whatever happened a moment ago would end soon. They had wanted the proof that vampires were real, and they sure had it now.

"The *printul* and *voivode* asked us to stay. I believe you know who I speak." Clémentine was a great body reader, and by the pupils of the guards dilating, she knew she caught their attention. "Unless you want to suffer the terrible consequences which would occur if you removed us, which I would watch with my own eyes witnessing glorious history in motion, I suggest you walk away from us. Now."

In a whisper, she heard Mika say, "Ba-bam!" then she complimented her acting, reminding her it was not a waste of her time. "Well, someone like me needs it. I hate people."

The two guards moved away, bowing. Clémentine doubted it was her introverted personality that inspired such a change of heart. A warm musky wind wrapped around her as a very imposing shadow grew behind her back. Clémentine did not need to turn around to know who stood behind her. He softly touched her arms, and as he made her look at him, he asked who caused her trouble. But she kept her mouth shut, somehow worried about what would happen if she would confess her fears.

"Ladies and gentlemen! Feast your eyes on the fresh red velvet bar!"

CHAPTER 5
GET ON YOUR KNEES

"Oh hell no!" Mika shouted, covering her mouth instantly with her hands.

A large curtain was pulled back, and, on a stage, placed in a row, were the men and women that were brought forward earlier to the host. Clémentine recognized some of them from earlier on the dance floor. "My friends," the voice said, "here are the intruders." They were all in lingerie, wearing what seemed to be porcelain Venetian masks. Clémentine could see them shaking and trembling. They were alarmingly afraid, holding each other's hands.

The atmosphere was a mix of excitement and anxiety. Clémentine's stomach crawled up her throat, leaving a sensation of burning from the inside out. The crowd was enjoying the terror emanating from the people on stage. The people in the group were hungrily licking their lips, drooling over those exposed, vulnerable, and terrorized.

"Shit, shit, shit!" Mika repeated, "Is this is a fucking vampire making ceremony?"

"No...I think those people are going to be drained by vampires and eaten by werewolves," Clémentine said as she recalled Mika mentioning the presence of her kind.

"Maybe it's a super elaborate role-playing game?" Mika asked as she tried to fake a smile.

"If it is," Clémentine said, "lots of it seems to be improvised."

Clémentine noticed a woman smiling widely, and she saw two incisors piercing through her gums and coming out, sharp and bright white. Another in the crowd joined and then another. "Those aren't cheap fang-smiting. It's quite elaborate if you ask me." Mika pointed past Clémentine to a possible exit through a back door. "I mean, we wanted to see vampires in action. We did. Now we should go and write it all down, so that we never speak of it again." Clémentine nodded, "Yes. Those aren't the types who want to be out in the open."

There was an exit sign at the end of the corridor. It was situated where Razvan had told Clémentine not to go, but there was no way she would stay and be part of whatever was going down on the main floor. Her hand deep in Mika's, they started pacing through the other VIPs when she felt a firm grip on her other arm. She would have recognized that touch anywhere. It was robust, unique, and...warm.

"I have told you not to go down that corridor. It isn't safe." His voice was wrapped in smoke, and he was soft-spoken as he let go of his grip on her arm. "Nothing here is safe tonight," he added.

With a frown, trying to hide her fear that he would try to abuse her that night, she said with a loud voice, "Then why would you want me and my best friend to stay?"

"To protect you," Razvan said, as he looked straight into Mika's eyes. He continued, "She knows what I mean."

Clémentine moved further away when Razvan tried to reach out for her hand. She saw a change in his eyes, and his face hardened as he listened to her statement. She almost regretted saying it the moment it slipped from her mouth.

"You imply that we know anything about what is going on tonight?"

"Aren't you both sharing intel to your HQ, which is part of the Belvoir Coven? Aren't you here to spy on vampires that are willing to join the coven?" Razvan's tone was harsh and cold. Clémentine almost feared it would freeze her flesh. She looked up, feeling her eyes betraying her and then hugged herself, uncertain of how she could now leave the mansion.

"You fools," Razvan said. "You, Clémentine, you call yourself a vampirologist. What is it about tonight that has you so scared? Shouldn't you be grateful for the scenery?"

The more Razvan said, the more Clémentine regretted falling for his charisma. She looked over the railing and heard an auction taking place on the stage. Clémentine gasped, and tried to move away, but felt Razvan's arms tightening around her body to keep her away from the stairs. Clémentine feared for her life and her friend that she held onto tightly, not letting go of her hand. There was a freezing wind passing through her head at the very moment she was about to break down in tears. *Do not worry. I won't let anything happen to you. I need the ability that was given to you by blood.*

She raised her head and looked into Razvan's eyes. His posture was straight, his arms around her, and without moving his head, he looked down to meet her hazel gaze. No words were spoken, yet she could've sworn she heard his voice inside her mind. Clémentine wondered how that was possible, and how he knew of her bloodline.

"You need to stay away from curious eyes as long as you can. Your smell is obvious, but from up here, you might be safe for a while." Razvan said aloud, "You will be discovered, but just whisper my name if someone does something, and I'll come to you. Do you understand?"

Clémentine nodded, but wouldn't let go of Mika's hand. "She's coming with me. No one will dare touch her." Despite Mika nodding, Clémentine held on to her when her friend crouched, "It's time we come out."

Clémentine slowly let go, hesitant to entirely see Mika following Razvan toward the stairs as Clémentine walked behind an antique wooden credenza. She feared what was now real, wondering if it would've been best to accept the false reality exposed to the general public. Mika was a Rougarou. She shared all a pack of wolves possessed: their strength, their keen senses, and skills. Without the need to transform, she could grow the claws, share the eyes and teeth along with the power of the bite. Rougarou alone could match the strength of vampires. The downside was that Rougarou people were solitary, just like Mika that night.

In the shadows, Clémentine had her back against the wall, and her eyes closed. She wished she was anywhere else. Then, she heard her friend's crystal voice speak aloud, and she moved her head toward the railing and saw her standing on the stage. "I am Mika Hunter. I am a Rougarou of a French bloodline. As part of the Order of the Dragon, you are not to touch me, or I am allowed to order your death."

Through shrill screams and hollow echoes of what sounded evil, Clémentine tried to focus on her friend's voice as her skin turned cool grey, and her eyes glowed gold like a wolf. Clémentine walked toward the railing, "These people are nothing but curious about your kin. The world is awakening to the paranormal, and we are to accept the possibility of an eventual civil war. Drinking from them will resolve nothing but bringing in what we do not want to be awakened, the *Firsts*."

Mika knew more than she stated. Clémentine thought her friend was too enthusiastic, but that night proved her wrong. Clémentine remembered all that was taught to her by her grandparents. She decided to let her ability come forward. She wouldn't hide anymore. Clémentine was part of the Belvoir Coven, assembling all people like her under one roof to protect themselves and find a way to come out into the light. To make that task possible, they needed to be proven to be true, one creature at a time, in a slow manner such as archeology.

The best creature to come first would be a vampire.

"You are the owner of this place, and I know you as an idealist vampire. So, keep your word and make those people forget this entire experience and send them on their way. The world is not ready for an entrance as brutal and barbaric as this." François laughed, but Mika pointed at the people on the stage,

"Do as I say or suffer the consequences." Clémentine saw Mika's eyes glowing brighter, her veins turning black as blood dripped from François' eyes and nose when she noticed Mika looking at Razvan. "Terrifying consequences."

The host showed resistance, and Clémentine feared for Mika becoming part of the unwanted guests when Razvan walked forward. She heard gasps and gulps among the crowd. "François, you will obey Miss. Hunter. The Rougarou people are the arbitrary people. They are part of the Belvoir Coven and, therefore, shall be respected and treated with honor."

"Yes, *printul,*" François said, bowing to Razvan before proceeding with his guards to move the unwanted guests away from the stage.

Clémentine witnessed vampires for the first time. They were well concealed and capable of hiding themselves well. They knew when to kill and when to hide. Razvan addressed the crowd, then forcefully grabbed François by the arm, "I am very disappointed, my friend." Clémentine had perfect hearing way above a normal human range so, hearing Razvan's whispers to his friend had her wonder about the vampire population and hoped for Mika's sake, that they were both safe.

Grabbed by her shoulder, she was thrown into the side wall next to the staircase. Clémentine's head knocked against the beige brick wall, followed by her shoulder. As she tumbled down a few stairs, it became harder to breathe as a cramp caused her to feel pain. Everything became blurry, and Clémentine had a hard time breathing, and a throbbing pain going up her arm had her build up tears. Following the unexpected fall and wounds, Clémentine tried to focus on Razvan's name but found herself unable to think. Then, she felt someone picking her up, and a scream began to build, but the pain of her ribs expanding and stretching with every breath choked her voice. Still unable to concentrate, she felt something warm dripping down the side of her head.

Unexpectedly, Clémentine's body slowly slid into a man's arms when she saw his fangs coming forward. It couldn't be real. Clémentine refused to believe she just stepped into the vampire reality her grandmother was talking about when she was growing up. It couldn't be. She tried to reach for the acid jar in the pocket of her dress, but it was too late.

"I found her upstairs. I think I just found myself a new toy for the night," her kidnapper said in a whisper to a few people around him. "I'll have my way with that blood bag, and then if she's good, I'll make her
my slave."

In tremendous pain, still in shock and unable to move on her own, Clémentine turned her head to the side, incapable of fighting back after such a hard impact. Her right arm might have been broken because, despite all her will, she couldn't move it. She feared for her safety, and she saw people moving away, trying to make a passage for one man to come across.

The smell of burning candles, the low lighting, and the symphonic band suddenly seizing the music had Clémentine believe someone famous was coming forward. All she wanted was to know that Mika was all right, and that everything would be alright, so that her friend could leave. Clémentine braced for the worst when finally, the shadow of the man came forward. Clémentine recognized him. *Razvan,* she thought to herself, before noticing his incisors coming through as he spoke.

"If you do not hand her to me at once, I will personally see that you are moved to my basement, where I will introduce you to each and every torment that I was put through. I will make you my toy for the night and then my slave." There was a cold silence before Clémentine's kidnapper found the strength to say that he wished to keep her, as she smelled very different than all the others in the room.

"Even the witches smell more common than her. Besides, I found her first."

The guests gasped. It was apparent they knew something that particular vampire didn't. When Clémentine crossed Razvan's glare, she saw him strongly exhale from his nostrils, and then a loud growl was heard. "Don't you know who I am?" he shouted before he added with a sharp frown, "Look at me, you shithead." Clémentine saw Razvan's eyes, not green anymore, but turned a deep red with a crimson glow inside his pupils.

The man holding Clémentine trembled, and she heard loud cries, as drops began falling onto her neck. He cried blood. He screamed louder than her ears could take when he cried, "Stop! Stop!" Still in his arms, Clémentine wondered how much longer that vampire could endure her weight before he would drop her to the ground. Clémentine wanted to move, but everything in her mind was still foggy. Her arm felt as though it was dislocated from the shoulder's socket, and it was sending a shooting sting up and down her arm. She then heard her kidnapper's shaky voice, "Here, take her, my Prince. I'm sorry. I didn't know who you were." Clémentine then heard Razvan's commanding voice, low and masterful, "You shall pay for your ignorance." He then moved his head, a signal to the guards to remove the abductor.

Clémentine's body hit the ground when the vampire let her fall. She wanted to scream, but no sound could escape her mouth as she was still struggling to breathe. Clémentine heard loud cries coming from the vampire, begging for his life. But the music started again as François said, "Please, now, let's enjoy Halloween as we are meant to my friends!"

The moment Clémentine tried to lift herself, something watery dripped from her nose and went down her face. When she looked up, barely able to move, she saw Razvan's arms wrapping around her body. His eyes were fixed on her mouth, where her blood dripped. His eyes were a dark red and reflected the light of the flames coming from the back of the room in a very romantic, yet fearful way of a predator looking down on its prey.

"Help me." Clémentine managed to say with a broken voice, barely capable of letting the air in.

"I am. Trust me. Your aggressor will be severely punished."

"Help." She repeated before she felt Razvan moving her arm sideways, and gasps were heard. She saw him move his eyes down and said, "You are a Tolkien fan…how poetic."

Clémentine knew he was referring to the elvish symbol of her favorite author tattooed on the inside of her forearm. She might not have understood why it was so poetic to him; the only wish Clémentine had was to be taken to a doctor who could take care of her ribs, so that she could breathe.

"It's okay, Clémentine. I will take care of you. Look into my eyes, *ma belle*."

Clémentine moved her head to look into his dark crimson eyes. The glow was now gone. She should've been scared. Instead, she felt as if a grip held her pupils into place, and it was impossible for her to move away. Her body heave and her mind still foggy, she wanted to run but was unable to. "Sleep now and all will be okay." Her eyelids were suddenly responding to Razvan's soft-spoken words, and Clémentine closed her eyes only to find herself quickly falling asleep.

CHAPTER 6
A HEROE'S VALUE

Clémentine opened her eyes, and they slowly adjusted to the light in the room. A comfortable mattress beneath her brought her comfort, as well as the bed sheets and duvets that enveloped her body. The sheets were all white and gold, and many pillows were placed under her head and around her shoulders. The walls were creamy beige with many oil paintings hung around. The French windows were open, their framing as white as snow, as were the crown moldings around the apartment. She could see across the French doors that separated the bedroom from the rest of the sumptuous suite.

The light by her bed was dimed, but bright enough that she could recognize the face of Mika. Her friend smiled once her eyes familiarized from what she thought must have been one hundred years since she last was awake. Clémentine lifted herself and placed her back against the wooden headboard. She did a sweep of the room only to realize that she had been in someone else's bed. She was now aware enough to know that this wasn't the room they had rented at the hotel. Nothing was a dream. All of it was real. Either that, or she had lost her mind.

As Clémentine talked to Mika she could hear someone else walking around. From the corner of her eye, Clémentine thought she saw a shadow. Alarmed, she turned to her friend, who held her hand.

"Mika, where am I?"

"You're in one of the Comptois de Jirondelle mansion's bedrooms Clémentine. You've been sleeping for the past fourteen hours," Mika said with a soft-spoken voice.

"I broke my ribs, Mika. Did someone bring me to a doctor or did one come here?"

"There was no need for a doctor, Clémentine. You're healthy now."

By the look on Mika's face, Clémentine could tell there was more to the story than what she was willing to admit. The shadow was approaching the room, and Clémentine's eyes widened. She recognized the broad shoulders, the strong posture, and the silhouette. There was nothing about him Clémentine could forget. She felt as if a bond somehow attached them one to each other. Like the cool breeze of a northern winter swirling in her mind, she heard his voice, *"I am relieved to know that you are awake."*

Clémentine's eyes turned to her friend, "Mika, remember when you asked if we should feel concerned?"

"Yes?" Mika answered, slowly with a trembling voice.

"I think we should've left when you asked."

On the bed beside her friend, Mika nodded, and when both held each other, despite their strong abilities, the voice of Razvan asking for Mika to leave had Clémentine looking deep into the bright aqua of her friend's doll eyes. Mika lifted her pillow a few centimeters, and Clémentine saw the two jars of acid. They both fixed one another with a long look, knowing that they understood each other without words having to be spoken.

Clémentine tightly held the sheets in a fist and asked with a robust disapproving voice, "I believe I can leave now." She was about to move from the bed, wanting to understand why she needed to stay in a bedroom when she felt a tingling in her skin that set it on edge.

The tingling ran up her spine to the back of her neck, and it was something that she could no longer ignore. It was from within her that the connection to Razvan became real. She couldn't deny it. He was one of the vampires, and he was a very powerful one at that.

Clémentine stared at Razvan, walking in wearing dark washed jeans and a V-neck silver-grey sweater with the sleeves rolled up to his elbows. His black hair was loose and a little wild, and it was cut just below his jawline. His eyes were like bright emeralds, just like she remembered them. His nose, fine and straight and rounded at the tip, led to his heart-shaped upper lip and the thinner bottom one. His cheekbones were not too high yet pronounced, with a distinctive line that showed he hadn't shaved from the night before.

Clémentine tried to look away, but every fiber of her body guided her stare toward his crotch for a split second. It was a long enough glance to notice he was gifted. Embarrassed, she quickly looked up and could have sworn she saw a smile crossing his face. He brought his thumb to his lips and bit the tip as if her glance had him shy. "Did you see something you liked?"

Clémentine kept her mouth shut, unaware of what the correct answer was. She looked into the emerald of his eyes, and as though a movie was playing on fast-forward, she saw glimpses of what seemed to be someone else's life. She saw splatters of blood, a leather whip, walls of stones, and she heard the cries coming from a young boy. The moment the vision blurred,

Clémentine took a deep breath and looked everywhere but at Razvan, who sat by her. His hands were warm, and they touched both sides of her head as he asked with a soft voice, "Does your head hurt?"

"Not my head, but the memories you are sharing with me." Clémentine's hand wrapped around his wrist.

"I am sorry, I didn't want to share those with you…you pulled those out of me."

"I guess I wanted to know who you were and went too far back."

Razvan let go of her head and slumped. His elbows resting on his thighs, he stayed by Clémentine, and as both his hands came together, he looked at the ground. Clémentine wondered what he was thinking about. She recalled the events of the Halloween party and couldn't help but question what would happen to her and Mika, as going unnoticed was completely unthinkable.

"You and Mika are staying here for the moment." Razvan said with his silvery voice as he lifted his head, "I will not let harm come to you or your friend. You are too important to our cause."

"So are you," Clémentine said, and she got a quick glance from Razvan.

"Who do you think I am?"

"A vampire, and we need one to join the Belvoir Coven to help us come out in the open. Of all the creatures out there, vampires are the ones who will gain the best results from the human population, and you are strong enough to protect us from harm if any comes at us. We both know that it can, and it's a real possibility."

When a cool breeze settled within her thoughts, Clémentine answered aloud, "No, I do not mind you inside my head. I've lived all my life with ghosts coming and going. At least with you, I know you are here."

"You are not reaching for a cross or the Bible by your bed."

"Why would I? From the little I've seen from your past as a boy, you are Catholic yourself. Assuming that it hasn't changed, what good would a cross do me if we're both God's children?"

He smiled as he lowered his head, and his words had a lighter meaning, "I am so grateful François
found you."

He asked for her to come out of the bed and accompany him to a room where there were other vampires gathered that were wanting to join the Belvoir Coven. Because Clémentine and Mika stayed somewhere else than Bellerose, their belongings were being brought to them but had not arrived yet. "I'm in my underwear wearing...um." She looked at the grey shirt, which seemed to be for a man. "Yes, it's my shirt. I thought you'd be more comfortable with something on, and Mika took care of you. Alone." Clémentine nodded but mentioned she had no pants. Razvan handed her a pair of black yoga pants that someone who assisted him had bought for her.

Under the covers, Clémentine was capable of slipping into the pants before she jumped out of bed. She quickly placed her hair into a bun and followed Razvan from the room. Mika remained in the room. They passed by the upper balcony and walked around a large solid oak table holding a crystal vase with a full bouquet of black flowers and cotton branches. Right next to the staircase was a door, but instead of going inside, Razvan turned her to walk down the corridor. On her left was a large double door that Clémentine guessed was linked to a boudoir by the look of the room. She wondered why they didn't just go through the entrance back in the other room as she loved books and old shelves.

"This is a quicker way to go, but I'll show you the book collection another day. Also, the mansion is holding other activities today, and I don't want us to be stopped and asked questions."

"What kind of activities are they holding today?"

"Some players are reenacting a book series or a show? I don't know. They're telling a story and then acting it out? Is that a thing?" Razvan asked, and it made Clémentine chuckle.

The doors opened to an extensive ballroom. The walls were the color of cream, with shimmering drapes on each side of the tall and wide French windows, which looked over the backyard of the mansion. The caramel hardwood floor was waxed to perfection, and it reflected the light coming from a chandelier above. Displayed in specific corners were statues of remarkable historical people from Joan of Arc to… "Wait, isn't that?"

"Yes, Pocahontas," Razvan said with a smile. "She…she was a hero."

They were martyrs of their time. Clémentine walked around until she noticed a group of people standing and looking in her direction. Mika, standing by Violette's side, blinked once. Clémentine knew what it meant; it was their signal to each other, a warning. Clémentine looked for vampires that might be undercover scouts of the opposite party, the conservatives. Based on her body language reading only, Clémentine tried to find an untrustworthy face in a pool of people. The lights dimmed and Clémentine notices they could no longer hear any noise from outside of the room. A melody was being played softly.

All the vampires present were dressed in casual clothing, a little better than herself, yet she loved the smell of Razvan's shirt. Clémentine wondered if she was out of place in many ways that she couldn't explain herself. Mika wore a sweater and yoga pants too. At least she wasn't the only one that was less than casually dressed.

Red velvet armchairs were dispersed around, and Clémentine noticed a few people sitting and talking. The group of people seemed to have lost their interest in the two girls and returned to their previous activities. Violette interrupted their silence; "Vampires must hide from society in order to survive. It was only until recently that either some of us were in power or fully exploited. This behavior has us now divided into two clans. An ancient Egyptian nobleman leads the conservatives. The idealists are being led by an orphaned vampire, and one of the greatest monsters of humankind's history, Vlad the Impaler."

Violette's hand pointed toward Razvan, who Clémentine saw close his eyes slowly. Clémentine held his hand tightly, thinking of how he had guided her through the mansion. He had presented himself as Razvan Bucur. Was there even a vampire named as such? Oh yes, there was. The two bald twins from the Halloween party said he couldn't come. She mumbled, "You…you're…you're Vladislav Tepes?"

"Yes."

Mika ran to Clémentine and was about to shout, "Wait. You're Drac—" Clémentine put her hand over Mika's mouth just in time. She thought the Prince of Romania might not want to hear the romanticized name created by the nineteenth-century British author, Bram Stoker. Clémentine did well as she noticed gasping in the crowd present as they all rose when Vladislav, a tall man of about six feet in height, stood taller and smiled.

His almond hooded eyes were the color of emerald green now had a red dot on each pupil while his skin was paler than it should've been. Clémentine knew by the past it would have been tanned. Clémentine noticed a square jawline leading back to upper cheekbones, and just like that, she met his gaze. Despite wanting to let him know she was offended that he had lied to her, she suddenly felt even more attracted to him than ever before.

"Please, Clémentine let me present myself again now that we're away from prying eyes." He said with a soft smoky veil embracing his voice, "Hello. I am Vladislav Tepes." His voice was silvery, and he had a smile that carved in a few masculine wrinkles around his eyes and showed through his few days' beard.

"Yes. Um." Clémentine managed to mumble through her admiration for her hero standing before her. She was lost in his smile when she heard him shyly chuckle.

"Yes...um, why don't you present yourself too?"

"Oh!" Clémentine exclaimed, feeling her body trembling in his presence unable to think straight, she heard Mika taking over in her best interest.

"Clémentine Roy here is a fan of your...um, quite dedicated work." Mika pushed Clémentine, who guessed she meant, 'girl, get your shit together!' She heard her adding, "Her name's Dr. Roy, she's the historian who found a...um, one of your kind. In the ground. In Austria." She took a deep breath, "I'm just Mika Hunter, the photographer who is not a doctor, but owns a Master's in visual art. I follow Clémentine everywhere in very inconvenient situations like this one."

Clémentine heard Vladislav chuckling again, and as he shook Mika's hand, she noticed a red dot in his pupil. "You're a strong Rougarou from a strong bloodline. You command all werewolves and possess all that a wolf possesses, at the exception of its appearance. You can speak to them and will always be an alpha. I've never met a Rougarou in person." Vlad bowed and added, "Nice to meet you. Again."

Mika looked at Clémentine, unaware vampires could detect another one's abilities to that depth. He then took Clémentine's hand with a smile, and she voluntarily gave in to his gaze as she heard him say, "You have...some shaman blood in you as little as it is." She nodded, yet she felt he knew more about her than he said. Not many knew her deepest secrets with the exception of very few, including Mika. "So few know about what you are truly capable of, and sometimes it is better that way."

Clémentine sat by Vladislav in a red armchair next to a wooden table filled with VitaL black bottles of cloned blood. Mika seemed quite busy chatting with Violette and taking notes of some stories. She couldn't fight it; Clémentine's attention was on Vladislav, the one man she had dedicated her life's work to. In a book she wrote about her findings and questions, love and pain, tears and sorrow. She never wanted him to find out about it, but it was too late. One vampire walked in and gave him the book, "Are you the L.K. Roy, who wrote this book?" She so wanted to shake her head, and she started to when she felt his hand softly holding her face by the chin, "Do not lie to me, Clémentine. Please."

Clémentine felt a strong wave of warmth spreading through her body from her core to her extremities and nodded. He whispered, "Thank you." He added, "For not lying to me." He smiled as he turned the pages, moving his eyes around the lines she thought he hated and quickly her fingernails started scratching her lips as she pulled dead skin away. Then, she heard gasps from the crowd present again. She raised her eyes to look at Mika standing by a white column, her index finger on her bottom lip. Clémentine knew a drop of blood bubbled.

Vladislav's eyes, fixed on her drop, his hand reached to hers, and he lowered it to his knee. "This is a bad habit. Your mouth shouldn't bleed unless I want it to in a manner so as to pleasure you." Clémentine, despite her eyes staring at Vladislav, could manage to see from her peripheral vision Mika over articulating in silence, 'what the actual fuck!'

All of a sudden, her eyes closed when his tongue came in contact with the drop of her blood. Strangely, she felt like another drop sealed upon her lip and had her opening her eyes and look to his. It was a kiss.

"What just happened?"

"One drop for another."

Clémentine subtly licked her lip, and with her fingers softly touching her mouth, she asked, "What is happening?" Vladislav smiled and closed the book, "Never before has someone come this close to me in my entire life and now in this existence. I never let anyone come to know me this well. You found my life and wrote it down. You have found secrets about me that no one else throughout the centuries has discovered. You even walked to the place where I met my end as a human. What was I to do if not at least thank you for this?" He held the book, a broad smile upon his face. Clémentine couldn't believe that 'a drop for another' was his kiss and his way to thank her for her work, which to her was a blessing.

She was not oblivious to what vampires were. After all, she was a witch herself, and Mika was a Rougarou. However, when it came down to the bloodsuckers, very little was known. But Clémentine was not just any historian. She was a vampirologist. She knew Vladislav could feel her emotions. She had known from the moment he spoke to her. He heard her heart beating faster, and most likely saw her cheeks reddening, her pupils dilating, and it was enough for him to know she would welcome and cherish his kiss.

His head still close to her own, "I—"

Clémentine put her hand over his mouth. She heard gasps from all vampires around. No one ever touched the prince. But in the distance, at the opposite side of the room on the second floor of the ballroom, she heard a trigger being pulled. There was only one person worthy of such bullets, and if what Violette said was true, Vladislav had to be the target.

She said, "Trust me." Vladislav nodded silently.

CHAPTER 7
EVERYOBDY WANTS
TO RULE THE WORLD

As if time had slowed down, in a blink of an eye, Clémentine violently pushed the wide and tall solid oak red velvet armchair Vladislav sat in. The chair toppled around and tipped over to the ground. She then turned and used herself as a shield to protect the historical Romanian hero. The bullets tore through her flesh, hitting her liver and, most likely, her small intestine and possibly her kidney, as well.

Every scream and cry was muffled by a moment of denial, as Clémentine's right hand rapidly filled with a warm liquid, which covered it entirely. She looked around, but it was as though everything played in slow motion. Her vision blurred, and the moment she glanced at Mika, she saw her nails morphing into and her teeth elongating as she propelled herself to the second floor. Mika's eyes glowed like a full moon on a cloudless night, tears pouring as she howled. She would make those who killed her best friend pay. Because at that moment, Clémentine knew she would die that night over two wooden bullets.

Her body suddenly heavy, and as the floor slowly moved closer, it became harder to hold herself up. Her body now weighing a metric ton, she didn't possess the energy to keep it up straight. Even closing her eyes seemed like a heavy lifting task. She tried to speak, but no words came out. Lightheaded, she couldn't tell where she stood and then her knees bent, and she crumpled to the floor. Vladislav rushed to her side. She had heard him shout to the vampires earlier, but it was in Romanian. At that moment, she couldn't rely on the brain function that was capable of translating his words.

"I'm dying, am I not?" Clémentine asked him, "Is that how you felt?" Normally, she would've thought the question to be insensitive. After all, Vladislav Tepes III was stabbed and died bleeding during a battle. His voice was lost in a whisper as he said, "Well, the blades were coming in and out, but I believe it could be similar." He paused for a moment, and Clémentine felt him holding her head up,

"Except, no one will die today, or at least, you won't. I won't let it happen to you, *îngerul meu mic.*"

Violette, with her vampire strength, tore the bottom of her skirt and pressed the fabric against Clémentine's wounds. A moment after feeling better with Violette's strong pressure on her side, she heard Vladislav's voice. He asked everyone to step away. He gently moved Clémentine near the wall against one of the French windows. Her back was against the cold hard glass, and her hand was trying to press against her side, but it wasn't as strong as Violette's. She looked at Vladislav and again heard his voice, "Do not close your eyes. Look at me, *îngerul meu frumos.*"

As Clémentine's blood was draining, a frightening sensation of being emptied spread through her entire body, as coldness enveloped her flesh. She kept her hand pressed against her wounds, but instead, Vladislav took her hand and moved it away from her body. She would soon lose her life to the puddle of red forming around her. The piece of clothing had absorbed all the blood it could, and as she faded into nothingness, she heard his whisper.

"Trust me." Vladislav murmured. "I won't let you die. I promise."

Clémentine felt his kiss on her forehead. "I know it's scary. I know because I felt it once a long time ago." Both his hand on each side of her face, he lifted her head, "But you're with me now. You don't have to be scared anymore."

Clémentine could hear mutters and a little farther, like an echo, Mika's voice filled with anger. Her eyes were cracked, and through her pain, she saw Mika slowly fade into the night. She couldn't keep her eyes focused, and her consciousness was escaping her. Soon, nothing but a shell would remain. She was afraid, cold, and wished she had taken her medication with her, but there was nothing her pills could have done now as it would not have magically stitched her wounds and brought her back to life.

"I do trust you or I will trust you."

Would he turn Clémentine into a vampire? "No, I would never do that to my *ingerul meu mic.*" Then what would he do? About to close her eyes, he shook her a little and was given a knife by someone dear to him as she heard him say, "Thank you, *fiu.*" She couldn't think clearly, but *fiu* meant son, or so she thought from the little she could still grasp.

Her eyes opened as her lips parted and emptied all of the strength she had, and breathing was almost out of reach. With her brain lacking oxygen, hallucinations began of a time where her body lay against the fresh grass of an early evening. The smell of green and resin in a cool breeze surrounded her. Her body broken after a long and hard fall reminded her gravity was not common knowledge at the time. "Clémentine. Do not sleep!" She heard him yell.

Her eyes opened by the movement of her brows lifting. She watched Vladislav hold a knife pointed at his throat, and she saw the blade flash as he used a confident stroke to puncture his skin and pierce through his jugular. Rapidly, her body was held forward against his chest, and her head leaned against his neck. "Drink. Drink everything you can. Bite into the flesh and keep the wound open until I tell you to stop."

Clémentine, only half alive, obeyed Vladislav without a second thought and did as he asked. She could hear a subtle growl the moment her mouth came in contact with his skin. The thought of hurting him briefly crossed her mind, but a chuckle interrupted her thoughts and came out vibrating from his flesh through Vlad's throat.

"Beloved. This is a tingling of the skin for someone like me." He added, "I would recommend you go harder on me."

As she drank his blood, the objects from her insides were being moved through her organs, and a hollow sound came in contact with the wooden floor. It almost had her gag, but the taste of Vladislav's blood kept her focused on his neck. Her vigor was regenerating as she strengthened her grip on him, and it felt as though her life moved back within her. She grabbed on to Vladislav and dug her teeth into his neck. Nothing else mattered to her then the next gulp of his blood. She wanted more and could feel how wonderful it left her body glowing. Clémentine then felt his hand gently caressing her black hair. "It's okay. You are healed now." She ignored his words.

All of a sudden, she heard vampires shouting, "Let go of our Prince, blood bag!" and "Obey him, quicklife!" Whispers were spread throughout the entire ballroom the whole time Vladislav held her against his neck. She heard them speak of her like she was nothing but a mortal meat sack. But quickly, Vladislav's hold on her intensified, and he retorted with a strong, commanding voice, "Do not address her as a mere mortal! She's...mine. I will claim her as mine tonight."

Clémentine moved her head away from his throat as his words pierced right through her heart. She didn't know what 'mine' meant in the vampire dictionary or in Vlad the Impaler's language. He smiled, "It's okay. Do not be afraid of me."

Her hands were holding onto him with a strong grip, and she feared to let him go. His smile showed wrinkles on either side of his face. Signs of the years he once spent alive in the fourteenth-hundreds across the Atlantic Ocean in Romania. He ran his fingers through her hair, every movement like a caress as his fingers went down each streak along her dark pitch-black hair. She saw a subtle red light in the middle of his pupils, and for a moment, she wondered what it was when he said, "Come with me." His hand holding her own, she tried to lift herself up but still felt a little weak. She thought that the power of a vampire was greater and would've healed her faster.

About to move her foot upfront, she shifted her weight so that she could stand up. All of a sudden, as she was about to fall to the ground, strong arms wrapped around her and lifted her back on her feet. Vladislav moved her right arm around his neck and moved his other behind her knees, holding her tight against his chest. "Let's do this right." He started walking, and when she glanced at Mika, she could read her lips, "What the fuck is happening?"

Lost inside her mind, Clémentine wondered how it all happened. How did she end up in a mansion in one of her favorite places on Earth? How was it so perfect that she even met a man she had admired for years, one who was supposed to be dead? Her eyes fixed on him, her brows curving as she asked herself how it was possible that he was so kind-hearted and gentle to her. It couldn't be so perfect. Something had to counterbalance this insanity. Was it just a dream?

On the third floor, away from the gathering and activity, at the end of a long corridor decorated with old oil paintings, two wooden doors opened with the help of guards. Inside were Vladislav's chambers. He had a king-size bed with gold and cream comforters. The walls were painted in rich tones of greens. Tall French windows with opaque cream curtains were open, but Clémentine noticed the thick

automated   rolled-
up blinds.

He lay her down on the bed, "You will go through an adaptation."

"What do you mean?" Clémentine asked as she stared at Vladislav, taking off his long sleeve grey shirt. He had his back turned, as he reached for a white t-shirt. She looked at his large muscular back, every muscle moving in harmony as he raised his arms to let the shirt caress his skin as he pulled it down to his hips. His long layered black hair, now a little wilder at the moment, was brushed back from his face as he turned around to face her.

"Will I turn into a vampire?" She asked as her vision blurred, afraid.

"No." He replied with a firmer, hurt voice, "I said I wouldn't do that to you. Weren't you listening?"

Clémentine didn't like his tone, frowning she replied with a clearer voice, pointing at her middle where the two wooden bullets had punctured her skin. "I did, but pardon me for asking again. I might have missed a word or two when I feared what might happen to me. You know, after taking two bullets for a man I considered a hero and of a superior intellect genius!"

"Vampire."

Clémentine tried to swallow her tears, but nothing rolled back up her cheeks and instead wet her face down as it left a trail on her face, which she felt warming, "Excuse me?"

"I am a vampire. The man you speak of gave his life for his people a long time ago."

His voice was soft spoken, yet so masterful, and cold. It almost felt distant, like an echo of what it once was. Clémentine feared he lured her into trusting him, guiding her to his bedroom. She had fallen for the oldest trick in the book, a charming bad boy going after the innocent school girl. Wait, Clémentine wasn't that innocent…well, not in that way, but her friends knew her to a big-hearted woman, always ready to help a stranger.

"He only died if you have let him. You killed that man yourself. They didn't. They stabbed the shell, not your essence." She stood up, "Now, if you'll excuse me, I'll take my leave." She then heard a murmur from him, "You are right."

Clémentine used the back of her hands to wipe her face, and noticed all the blood. All of the sudden, moments of her past resurfaced. Not the moments before where she was bleeding to death, but passages of her teen years where everything was lit like spotlights on her for everyone to see and judge. Her nerves exposed, her hands began to shake. She raised her eyes, and as the contact of warm skin touched both sides of her face, she heard a voice coming through the thickness of her memories, "Clémentine. Look at me."

She shook her head and stepped away, not about to give in to him and fall for his…name, stature, history, and everything in between. She whispered, "I thought they were right, but even choosing to have a dead hero can disappoint you." Wearing her sport bra after someone attended to her wounds, she placed the grey t-shirt Vladislav handed her pulling it down over the yoga pants she was wearing and was about to walk out. However, his grip kept her immobile.

"I said, look at me."

Her heart was sinking deep down inside her chest, with tears blurring her vision, as Clémentine tried to fight her urge to shake. She met Vladislav's dark green gaze and gave him a chance to explain himself. She wanted to know why the man she saw in the ballroom wasn't the one standing before her that moment, but all he repeated was, "Vampire."

"So, being a vampire makes you bipolar?" Clémentine said.

Vladislav's chuckle had her pay more attention to his facial traits. His head lowered, the tip of his thumb against his mouth, it was as if he sought a way to explain to her what was happening. His eyes met her own, and his voice was now all she could hear and focus on because, in her world, nothing else mattered.

"I'm the same as I was in the ballroom, Clémentine. I'm just worried that what I started, I might not be able to finish." He paused, and as his smile widened, she could tell it was caused by discomfort by the way he brushed his hair back. "This…all this around you. You, standing here with me, all of it, it's not a coincidence." She listened carefully after asking what he meant. "You are more than a blood witch to me, Clémentine. You mean more to me than all the gold in the world. Nothing could ever separate us, Clémentine. They tried, but they failed. I promised you then I'd find you, and I did. I'm not about to let you go."

Clémentine looked around her. She felt her heartbeat quickening, and that was never good as she battled cardiophobia. She stepped away from Vladislav, thinking maybe, after all, perhaps the psychiatrists were right, and he was psychotic. After everything he had gone through, it could explain his behavior. The song explained it best; *Everybody Wants To Rule The World.*

Clémentine tried to see what she could use to defend herself when she suddenly remembered the acid she had brought with her. She reached in her yoga pants pocket and retrieved the small vial, where she held it firmly in her hands, "I don't want to use it on someone I have devoted my life to for so long. My admiration turned into an obsession, and into a love for a being, I do not know. Someone who died more than five hundred and forty years ago." She could read the confusion on his face as his brows arched, "This is Ethylenediaminetetraacetic acid. It will reduce you to a puddle of blood mud."

"Please." Vladislav said as he opened his arms, "Do not hurt me. I swore I would never do anything to hurt you, Clémentine. Let me explain."

Clémentine remembered her grandpa's advice from back when she was a little girl. Never put yourself against a wall or a corner. Stay away from walls. Always analyze a room and locate all exits. Then, have a plan to kill everyone in the room except you. Everything is a weapon if used with logic and efficiency. Clémentine made sure Vladislav would stay near the bed, giving her enough room to throw the acid vial at him and run for the door, the windows, or use the fireplace gas lighter to set fire to the chamber. Her heart rate slowing, "You have five minutes."

"Your name, tell me, isn't it, Clémentine Katharina Roy?"

"Yes…how do you—"

"Your eyes, your fine little nose, your lips…when I saw you the first time on that web series, something awoke in me. I had to do research on you and your ancestry. I was able to link you back to my Katharina."

Clémentine knew the story. Well, she knew the story as well as anyone else capable of performing a search on the internet. Nothing about Vladislav was a hundred percent sure. It was all speculations and deductions from historians trying to tie pieces of history back together. Trying to know the truth about Vlad the Impaler was as hard as trying to catch one needle right in the middle of a tornado. One would have more luck at winning the lottery.

"Every woman in your family bears the name Katharina as a tradition, do they not?"

"Yes. I asked my grandmother why, but she said it was just a tradition. How would you know from one name that I am that woman from your past?"

"Your history is written in your blood." His smile was trembling as he added, "I wasn't a vampire when I shared time with her. But once we become a vampire. we can taste one's history and see moments of their lives. You share a strong connection to your past lives due to your gift as a witch. Your blood is richer than most and all was confirmed to me the moment I tasted one drop from your lip."

Clémentine lowered her arm, still holding the acid vial as her smile trembled. Her eyes moved away from Vladislav as she realized she was nothing but the reminder of a dead woman he had loved. She let herself fall onto her knees; hardwood beneath her she covered her eyes with her hands. She wished she could go back in time and miss the first time that she pulled a history book from the shelves of her local book store and read his name.

"Clémentine, that's who you are to me," Vladislav said. "You carry her blood, and yes, you reminded me of a time when I was happy." Both his hands touched her shoulders, then began moving up and down her arms. "Do not mistake my emotions for you as one for a ghost. I know Katharina is long gone. What you remind me of is happiness. When I look upon your face, I feel happy. Something I haven't felt since the moment she was taken away from me and killed by one of my enemies."

Clémentine raised her eyes to meet his, that wasn't written in any books or websites. She lifted her head, "I don't want to be a ghost. I don't want to be any man's ghost of a woman he once loved. I am alive. I'm me. I'm Clémentine, Dr. Roy, the Vlad Lady…shit." She heard him chuckle. After all, it was her nickname from the time she turned thirteen years old to the moment she fell to her knees on the floor crying. "You are," Vladislav said with a smile. "You are Vlad's Lady if you want to be."

Was it this easy? She knew him but didn't. He knew her but didn't. Those feelings were a mix of fantasy and pain. Clémentine dreamed about a reality where she would meet Vladislav, and he would be the one she thought he was—a hero. Now, she didn't know. He was a mystery to her, just like he had always been to all historians.

All of a sudden, a stabbing pain pierced through her middle, and her body fell forward. Blood was coming out of her mouth, and she firmly closed and opened her eyes only to see a veil of red and blurs. She dug her fingers into the wooden floor and tried to cough in the hope of letting more air inside. "What is happening to me?" She asked with a voice fighting through blood, choking on her words. "How do vampires...exist?" She fell on her side and held her stomach when she noticed Vladislav lying by her side, reaching for her hands.

"Your body is adapting to my blood," he explained. "You will not become a vampire, Clémentine. What I did was let you lose about a third of your blood and you replaced it with mine. It is enough for the...symbiote's egg to attach itself to your heart and have you regenerated and live as half-human, half-vampire. Before you ask, you are the only one because it takes a *First* to do it, and I wasn't sure if I was but, as it turns out, I am."

Confused, Clémentine raised herself on all fours and asked Vladislav to explain the part where a parasite's egg got into her body and was attaching itself to her heart. The truth was that all Vladislav knew was vampires existed due to a symbiote living while attached to a human's heart. The creature itself was intolerant to ultra-violet rays and had a violent allergic reaction to selected metals. It nourished itself with blood and continually relied on it to live.

"Because the symbiote nourishes us of everything else we need, the only requirement is to drink blood which keeps us young and somewhat alive. The symbiote acts as our heart, and its constant regeneration has us regenerate as well. It provides us with overly developed senses and abilities over time. That's why the older the vampire, the stronger it becomes. Every symbiote duplicates itself, and when the time comes, we feel it through an urge to reproduce and create progenies. Due to our battles, being killed, and hiding, often vampires just purge themselves of the 'egg' by vomiting. I used the one I had to save you."

The taste for blood. She already had it by drinking Vladislav's and she remembered how good it was and how strong it made her. How was she not a vampire?

"To become a vampire, you'd need to be almost emptied of your blood. More precisely, two-thirds of it. It causes the symbiote to be in survival mode and ready for when the vampire blood pours in to mutate the hemoglobin and use it to multiply their own effects to morph humans into meta ones if you will. I didn't let you lose enough blood, so the egg, when it attached to your heart, wasn't in survival mode since it could already drink your blood."

"Will I crave blood?"

"Yes."

"How do I get rid of it?"

Vlad sneered, "You either drink mine or I will introduce you to the VitaL products."

Clémentine embraced the gift being part vampire could mean, but despised Vladislav for having put a living parasite inside her. She didn't know if she should be angry or thankful. After all, Vladislav did save her life after she used herself as a shield. Her fingers digging into the wooden floor, her entrails twisting and turning as flames seemed to be spreading through her insides. With blood pouring from her mouth, she managed to reach Vladislav's hand with her own and squeezed it so hard that when turning her head, she saw him frown. "I don't know what you thought you were doing. I don't know if you thought I'd love you as that woman did over five centuries ago, but right now, at this very moment, I feel death, and I smell death, and it's coming from you."

Her eyes, covered in blood, everything she saw had a red veil covering it. She tried to lower herself closer to the floor, but it only hurt her more. She stayed on all four, blood foam in the corner of her mouth, and she thought she'd turn into a dragon soon when she heard his voice. A voice that once had her weak now hardened her heart.

"All I thought about was saving your life," he said with a soft smoke to his voice. "Hate me as much as you desire, at least my conscience will be at peace because to hate one must be alive."

CHAPTER 8
ONCE A PRISONER

The sun was slowly going down in the sky. Clémentine sat on the bed and touched the cross with her fingers on the bedside table. She had spent a night and a day with hell coming out of her mouth and nose. Unable to swallow or ingest anything, her throat was dry and so was her mouth. With each of her body parts aching with a throbbing pain, still adapting to her new gift from Vladislav, she looked at herself in the mirror and noticed a unique change in her eyes. Just like Vladislav, she shared the dark green hazel color, sometimes turning lime green when watery. Now, when in dimmed lighting, her eyes would glow.

Suddenly, Clémentine heard the door cracking open. An average built man walked in wearing a grey suit, his platinum blond hair and grey eyes so bright she thought they would light up the room. She recognized him from the night before. He had spent hours with other people at the Halloween festivity dancing
and laughing.

"My name is Frederick. I'm one of Vladislav's guards. He asked me to take care of you and look after your needs."

How formal. She might have known what Vladislav was, but now she needed to find out who he truly was. Not the historical figure, but the real him that no one else knew but those around him. "Um…well, my name is Clémentine, and one of my needs would be to know who Vlad is."

"I am afraid I cannot answer that. It is for him to tell you who he is. All you need to know is that I'm here at your service."

Clémentine stood up and looked around the room before she walked toward Frederick. The vampire moved out of her way, either to avoid contact with her or just by politeness, she couldn't tell. She saw across the bedroom a gigantic mural fireplace and a very inviting, but empty, living room. It was a beautiful chamber that Vladislav had given her.

"Where is my friend, Mika?"

"She is with Violette. They are discussing you both returning to Montréal."

"But my trip here was not just for Halloween. I'm one of the guest spokespersons for the—"

"I understand your concern, but Vladislav felt your safety was more important than an appearance at a paranormal research convention."

Clémentine frowned. She was not about to let a stranger order her life around like she was some sort of object to be toyed with. She demanded to see Vladislav. Frederick warned her, "Mr. Tepes is indisposed   at the moment."

Immediately Clémentine felt something strange and heard a faint voice. She pushed Frederick aside and walked outside of her chambers toward the end of the corridor. On her left, there was a door leading to a dual staircase. She remembered the disposition of the building. She remembered it from walking with Vladislav. She wasn't about to stay because some vampire told her to, despite that 'some vampire' being Vlad the Impaler.

She ran up the stairs and just when she thought she had lost Frederick, he appeared before her. She guessed he was a paranormal—vampire as she thought. It only proved to her that there were more vampires who desired to be out in the open, and that was good for her cause. Yet, there was something off about Frederick. He was a bloodsucking creature; she could smell it, something the symbiote must've woken in her. Her anxiety level rose drastically, and if she could feel it, so would all vampires.

As she walked over to avoid the vampire guard, she heard him say with a thick Swedish accent, "Please Mademoiselle Roy, it's for your own good. Do not disturb Mr. Tepes…he is…he is very dominant." Clémentine wasn't impressed by his choice of words and decided to walk down the corridor regardless of Frederick's warning. "He can hurt you!" Now, why would he say such a thing? "He is evil and the 'son of the devil.' Do not confront him. Stay with me."

Clémentine turned around. She might have been angry at Vladislav but she was not disrespectful to who he used to be. "He is the 'son of the dragon'. Get your historical facts straight. You should know the meaning of his name. By your appearance and smell, you were most likely there when he was alive."

"What dragon slays and impales innocent people for the pleasure of watching them agonize to their deaths that would take days?" Clémentine stopped and listened to Frederick. "What dragon would let an innocent woman take two wooden bullets for him and then watch her suffer alone the weight of being neither human nor vampire?" He kept going, "What dragon treats a woman he said reminded him of the one he truly loved and then orders her around like a slave. He's no dragon, Clémentine. He's the devil."

Clémentine fought her fears, her anxiety rising as she wanted nothing more than to reach for her medication in her jean pocket. Yet, she still work Vladislav's grey shirt. That must've meant something. Her eyes closed and she thought about Frederick's words. But, a cool breeze took over her thoughts; *"I will be with you soon, Clémentine. I promise I will explain everything to you. It is not my intention to keep you in the dark."* Clémentine was not about to let Vladislav control her thoughts.

"I'm going to see him now," Clémentine said to Frederick. "I've read far worse about him than what you told me." As she strolled down the hall, she noticed enough doors on either side, which would discourage anyone but her. She knew exactly where Vladislav was. She could hear his husky voice and feel his presence. Flames grew inside of her entrails; her transformation was not over yet. Clémentine didn't give in to the pain she was feeling, but she heard Frederick say, "What if he is the one inflicting your pain at this very moment? Have you ever thought of that? Vlad is not a regular vampire. He's what we called the 'orphan' because he has no maker. Somehow his transformation happened without a donor. It gave him abilities beyond all the others. He is unique, and it makes him a thousand times more dangerous than any of us, and he made you his."

"Then he won't hurt me."

Clémentine kept on walking, brushing off Frederick's words. She barely noticed the dated pictures on the old wallpaper and the ancient antique crown moldings that normally would've caught her attention. In any other situation, Clémentine would've admired the architecture because of the history nerd that she was and always would be. The last rays of the sun penetrated the hall through an immense French window that shone on the last door on her left. He was there.

She barged in, determined to give Vladislav a piece of her mind. Once the door opened, she saw burgundy walls decorated with oil paintings, resembling the ones in her bedroom. Two couches facing one another on each side of a fireplace, where her friend, Mika, sat beside someone who she guessed was another vampire. Violette was holding a phone and notebook, taking a sip out of a black bottle with a red and yellow label on it. VitaL She couldn't understand the scene that was taking place before her eyes, but her emotions were no less upsetting.

Clémentine wanted to know why Vladislav thought he was her boss and entitled to make decisions for her. She began to walk up to him, but Frederick sneaked in her thoughts while Violette stopped her promptly. She could still hear Frederick in her head, "Please, you might endanger yourself. He's no typical vampire." Again, she didn't give a crap as to what the guard was saying. Clémentine roughly turned to face the Swedish vampire, but he wasn't in the room. She tried freeing her limb from Violette's grip who had zoomed to her to stop her when his loud husky voice was heard, and Violette let go at the simple words, "*dă-i drumu.*"

The place was suddenly cold, and she felt embraced by a shadow. Her desire to turn around to face him fought with her brain, trying to convince her that running away as fast as she could, might save her life. There was no way to escape him. He was a vampire, and there was no way that she could outrun him under any circumstances. He was too much of a powerful predator, and she was a broken prey. She felt him stepping closer to her back. Clémentine closed her eyes the moment she felt the cool breeze from him moving his hands away from his body to touch her shoulders. His breath near her ear, she heard his voice as he now played with her hair; "I said I would come to   you.   Why   did   you disobey me?"

Although his words sounded warm and enchanting, the meaning was nonetheless one of a master to his slave. Clémentine still had enough strength in her to fight back, or at least that's what she believed when she turned around to face him. His long masculine fingers let go of her jet-black hair, leaving the magic of his touch vanishing in the air. His gold stare and arrogant smile were hard to face. She understood at that moment how his presence was by itself imposing and left a feeling of terror emanating from her skin. He could smell her fear; she knew that much. It took her only a split second to realize how dumb she was - facing a vampire, to give him a piece of her mind, when she had no cross, holy water, garlic, or a stake.

"I do not wish to scare you, although, the simple thought of keeping you in fear of me is very fervid."

Vladislav's fingers caressed Clémentine's cheek and left her face warm. It was something she wished she could've controlled, but his smile reminded her that no matter what she would do or say, it would always be too late since he could enter her mind.

"I wish to let you know that none of the typical vampire weapons will work on me. Frederick warned you; I'm not like any vampire you would come to know except maybe the one who... well, never mind."

Vladislav was about to turn around to guide her toward the couch where Mika was sitting. Clémentine instead grabbed his sleeve. She heard gasps from everyone in the room; growing tired of the vampire responses she rolled her eyes at them. The Impaler turned his gaze toward her, and she saw his eyes absorbing the light like a predator in the wild, they glowed so brightly. She could hardly swallow her saliva, regretting her rough movement. However, she had to show him that she wasn't his slave and he wasn't her master and her physical attraction had to stop.

"I know you are not my slave; neither do I want you to think I'm ordering you around. I'm merely protecting you from a world you hardly know anything about. Wanting vampires to be part of the Belvoir Coven is something we must achieve, yes. But, to what cost? Right now, your presence here and what you and Mika truly are now is out there, out of my control. Conservatives are already talking about your value on the market. You're almost worth as much as I am." His voice sounded convincing, and she caught a hint of emotion she doubted Vladislav was capable of, compassion.

"So, you wish to protect us by keeping us at arm's length for eternity?" Clémentine said as she pointed at him, firmly stating that there would be no way she would be interested in being this close to him.

"I might disgust you at this moment, but you won't feel like that much longer. You already doubt your sentiments toward me. If it means anything to you, I do not wish to keep you close to me if you do not want to be. Neither will I impose it. However, you are mine by the action I've done to you."

"What does that mean?"

"You are mine to protect by whichever means necessary." He added with a disarming look on his face, "And there's nothing I wouldn't do to keep you safe."

Vladislav stepped toward her with his eyes as red and dark as wine. His voice became lower, and his bright, razor-sharp fangs came out. On his irises, she saw black lines forming, and his presence suddenly upgraded from imposing to overpowering. His neck tensed, and his arms rose as a white foggy mist moved around the room, drowning the living area into a bright white environment. Clémentine had no choice, afraid, she used her own ability and shifted her consciousness to Vladislav and shouted, "Stop!"

"How did you—"

"You're not the only one with abilities beyond comprehension."

The mist disappeared, and Vladislav stood straight, his eyes squinting as he seemed to be thinking. Clémentine knew he thought the same that she did; her adaptation to the vampire blood might have enhanced her shamanic abilities. Now, maybe the witch side of her would take over as well and make her one of the greatest assets of the war.

"Vlad, she needs more protection than we thought. Conservatives are not just vampires! We're talking Revenants, the Unseen, Witches, the Sasquatches, and quite powerful humans!" François sounded afraid for their side of the politics, but when she looked into Vlad's eyes, which looked desperate and about to forfeit, she stepped up.

"The Belvoir Coven assembled Rougarous, Moon Wolves, Werewolves, and Wendigos, and we have the Shamans and strong witches too. The Swampers have woken up, and they are coming. You are not alone." Clémentine walked closer to where the vampire idealists were and added, "You have Vlad the Impaler on your side. If this doesn't mean a win, I don't know what does because if there's anyone on this Earth that I wouldn't hesitate to pledge my allegiance to, it is Vlad the Impaler."

She glanced at him now standing by her side and saw a light in his eyes, and a shy grin. She wanted to reciprocate, but her words were meant to encourage the troops and not to make his ego feel better. Either way, it didn't last long when François said, "What about Elizabeth Báthory? Isn't she good enough for a win? She leads the conservatives and has an army of followers more dedicated than those of the Spanish Inquisition!"

"As far as I'm concerned, she's just a psychotic chick taking a blood bath."

"That woman was cheated on by her people, and there's nothing like the wrath of woman scorned."

Clémentine answered Frederick with a sneer, "Tell me about it."

The French vampire turned around his arms in the air, "We're surrounded by crazy chicks, but males are responsible for all the wars!" Violette smacked him behind the head, and the vampire stopped, moving to a chair to calm down. Vladislav guided Clémentine to an old brown armchair, where they could talk quietly for a few minutes. The moment she sat down, he crouched before her, and she wondered what else he had to tell her. Her fears were calming, but there were still many unanswered questions.

"Remember when you asked me how vampires could be real and exist?"

"Yes, you said it was by a symbiote." She smiled ironically, her head tilted to the side, "Now, thanks to you, I have one hatching on my broken heart."

"Vampires are not just alive due to a symbiote. They are victims of a curse from an old witch who had all vampires bound by one token that made them who they were when humans. All tokens are cursed and ruled by one stake."

"The very first vampire stake is the Canta Stake. I know because I'm a witch."

Vladislav ran his fingers through Clémentine's hair, and it weakened her will power. She fixed her eyes upon his mouth as he moved toward her and whispered in her ear, His words had her skin tingling at the sound of his voice. "One person stole my token, and every second that passes by, I am losing my abilities and my strength. Soon, I'll be nothing more than a puddle of blood. What I did to you, I did because I believe that you could be the leader of the war should I die before I find my token again." He added, "I trust you, Clémentine, to be a good leader. You knew everything about me before you ever met me, and with my blood running through your veins, you will now share everything I am. My knowledge of war, of vampires, of everything I have come to know to this day. Use it well. Use it to protect our people."

Clémentine's hair moved in harmony with Vladislav's head moving away from her ear. His eyes were drowning in hers, his brows low, pained by his fate. She, immobile, found herself caressing his face and leaned toward his ear, "I will find your token if it's the last thing I do. I found you, and I will not let this Earth betray you again." His hand closed upon her own with a firm grip she knew opened his heart. Her hero needed her, and by all means, she would help now that he finally spat the truth about his reasons for doing what he did. She would help him.

"You guys, please get a room already!" François shouted. "This isn't a sparkling vampire movie! We're on the verge of a second Spanish Inquisition!"

Mika shouted, "Enough with the inquisition already! We know you were there, stop bragging!" Then she added, "We said we'd help. We just need to find the rat and—"

"What, rat?" Clémentine asked as she brusquely stood up, "What is Mika talking about?"

François explained that ever since a rumor spread that Vladislav weakened due to an illness, the conservatives had been infiltrating the idealist clans around the world. Scouts from the opposite side were sent to spy on the idealist and, of course, Vladislav. He added that his closest friends were being targeted, and stories of their torture were already breaking alliances.

"So, miss 'I pledge my allegiance to Vlad the Impaler' what do you say to that now?"

"Simple," Clémentine said with a grin. "Rats are always the first to leave a sinking ship." With both hands on her hips, she mentioned with confidence, "We give them a reason to be scared and to leave, leading us to their alpha who planned all the infiltrations."

"How the fuck do you plan to do that?"

"They want Vlad ill and weak? We give them Vlad ill and weak. It won't be the first time he's been taken prisoner. He knows the drill."

Vladislav stepped away, "Excuse me?" Clémentine saw a pen and their map of of the all vampire' outposts. She deduced that the blue represented their allies, and the red were the conservatives. She turned the map over and used the back to explain what she meant. Clémentine watched a lot of detective, spy, and action movies. She had an overly developed deduction instinct and narrowed down the rats to five possible places where Vladislav's most trusted allies resided.

"At all times, Vladislav wouldn't be alone. I would be in his head, using him as a puppet." Clémentine explained, "With my shamanic abilities, I can take over his body, and when push comes to shove,

I'll use my abilities if I have to and protect him. He wouldn't come to harm."

"Wait, how can you do the overall possession of my friend here and how the fuck can you pass yourself as him if they ask questions?" François asked with a high pitch voice.

"I simply take over. As for passing as him, I know his life better than he does. With his blood in me, I know everything there is to know, too much even. From his mannerisms to his masturbating rituals. Nothing will get past me."

Vladislav brushed his hair back, and François chuckled, patting Vladislav's back. "I love this gal! She's a keeper."

Clémentine put her arms around herself, trying to muffle the sound of her stomach, screaming for food. She hoped nobody noticed, but she saw Vladislav already asking for Violette to bring her and Mika to the kitchen. Clémentine once again grabbed him by his clothes. His three-quarter sleeve fitted sweater was of dark mossy green, and when her hand touched the fabric, she recognized the feel of high-quality cotton. As her fingers closed on her grip, she partially came in contact with his hard steel abdominals just below his pectorals. She might have stared at his chest longer than she should had. His shirt was a deep V-neck, and she saw a light layer of chest hair that left her wondering how soft it would be. When she lifted her eyes, she saw him staring at her hand with his mouth partially open, ready to say something, but then, why would he say it aloud when he simply could invade her mind?

"Yes?" The Impaler asked out loud. She guessed she was wrong, and he wanted everyone to hear
him speak.

"I'm sorry…I was just wondering if you'd, um, join us to eat." Clémentine hit her forehead with her palm with a trembling smile showing her embarrassment; "Sorry, what a stupid question to ask a vampire. I—"

Clémentine was cut short when Vladislav answered, moving her hand away from his chest, but still rubbing his thumb on her skin, letting her know that he did enjoy her touch.

"I will join you for dinner. We'll eat at ten tonight." Again, an order, but this time Clémentine would let it slide, fearing that she would only test his patience if she opened her mouth again.

"Yes, we'll be there," Clémentine answered.

"No, just you." He simply decreed.

Clémentine nodded, and she heard him say as he slowly moved away, "Thank you, and please, I would much appreciate it if you decide on whether or not you are mine to protect—I want this to be your choice alone. If you'll excuse me, I have vampire business to attend to, as one matter needs my personal attention."

He grinned, letting his fangs show in such a malicious way that she dared not think about what he meant by those words. He walked to the antique bookshelf on the opposite side of the room and moved an ancient Dracula novel forward to let free an old Victorian rotating mechanism. They could hear it roughly start rolling, and it opened a secret entrance to a hidden passage leading to a lower level of the three-floor high plantation mansion. Being on the second floor, she thought they had a long way down, and as Clémentine moved toward the entrance to look over and maybe even follow, she heard him in his mind with a cool breeze. *"Do not disobey me again, Clémentine. Now leave and nourish your body. I feel you will be needing it more than you think."*

CHAPTER 9
NEEDLE IN MY EYE

They prepared to leave and follow Violette, who already left the room to go down to the kitchen, based on Vladislav's advice. She noticed François giving Mika a kiss on her cheek before joining the other vampires to go down the hidden staircase. Clémentine couldn't help but wonder what could be in the basement. She had an idea, a crazy one at that, but knowing Vladislav, she thought maybe it might not have been too far-fetched.

Clémentine noticed Frederick walking in as the hidden door closed. "Frederick, is it possible that there's an old dungeon or antique 'Frankenstein' type of lab where they're going?"

"I'm sorry I cannot answer that question."

"You're a very fun guy, aren't you?"

"If you say so," Frederick answered with the most disturbing smile Clémentine had ever seen. As his smile widened, he showed his fangs like a ventriloquist dummy would open his mouth.

Clémentine had time to notice François disappearing behind the bookshelf door before it closed, she wanted to run after it. She could almost hear Vladislav's voice in her head, yelling no, so she stopped thinking about what was beyond the secret bookshelf passage. She waited for Mika to join her by her side. They followed Frederick toward the door when he stopped Clémentine, "Do not be fooled by him. What else do you need besides his name to prove to you that he is dangerous?" Clémentine asked why he kept taunting her to walk away when it was clear now that she had nowhere else to go. "You could come with me?" Frederick said.

"Where?"

Frederick vanished. A gust of wind followed his disappearance, and Violette showed up, "I was looking all over for you girls. Follow me."

They followed a bright wide corridor, which brought them to the main floor of the mansion. The walls were painted a deep burgundy red, and tall rectangular windows with rich and thick white curtains went down to the floor. The crystal chandeliers were lit, while rolled-down blinds were hiding the exterior view until sundown. Some large and imposing antique gold frames were hung with oil paintings of what must have been important vampires Clémentine figured. "They are the Comptois de Jirondelle family ancestors," Violette responded, noting her gaze.

The staircase they had just went down was made of solid oak with refined carved lines and French curved patterns. The steps themselves were covered by white carpet. When Clémentine focused on the first floor, her friend took her hand. The two friends stood side by side, still disturbed by the dangerous nature of vampires. Mika's hand was trembling, and she wondered why until they stepped into the kitchen and were finally left alone.

"Clémentine, vampires are way more dangerous than we thought. Are we sure we can trust them, even the 'good' ones, especially the one called Impaler?"

"Look, our chance to walk out of this mess disappeared about four days ago. Well, ever since we set foot in Louisiana at the airport. We're in deep shit and over our heads now."

Mont La Bellerose was founded in the year 1689, making it a town celebrating its three-hundred-and-thirty-three years of existence. Mont La Bellerose is a town almost as old as Montréal and shares its French qualities and architecture. Despite it being settled far up, about four hours north of Montréal, Mont La Bellerose still attracted many settlers, except none of them seemed to fit the norm.

Its old, French Gothic buildings and homes dominated the town from all around. Sharing many types of scenery with New Orleans, Mont La Bellerose had tourists visiting its downtown village and resorts, which supported the city and made it a modest place to live. The La Rose Lake overlooked many surrounding mountains known to be its suburbs, and a few were ghost towns—abandoned for mysterious and unknown speculative reasons.

The founding families of the prolific town were the Dascălu, Boisjoli, Roy, Bellefleur, Bourbon, and DeVilliers. Other families participated in the growth of the municipality, such as the Comptois and

Jirondelle, among others. These were all families that had either escaped the witch trials or inspired fear in Europe and needed to start life anew somewhere they would

be accepted.

Mont La Bellerose had welcomed Werewolves a long time ago, along with Witches of all kinds, and Swampers who despised being called Swamp Monsters. The town had its fair share of Unseen, Rougaroux, and even those unspoken from the Indigenous people, such as Clémentine's grandpa, the Wendigos, and Skins. Many other lived in and around Mont La Bellerose, away from humans. Since they were constantly being chased away and afraid, they decided to seclude themselves.

Now, the Belvoir Coven had reached an agreement to welcome humans in their circle slowly. However, to do so, vampires had to be included and show compassion, something not all "monsters" agreed they would. Clémentine and Mika were part of the movement, respected and influential in both 'monster world' and human one. The Belvoir Coven wished them to help open the door to discussions with vampires.

"Mika, you're not teaching me anything here." Clémentine said with a veil of tears because she needed to remember the past, "I went out with one."

"I know, Octavian was a vampire, and that's why I'm freaking out! What if—" Mika stopped and lowered her voice to a minimal whisper knowing in the mansion, the walls truly had ears. "What if Vlad doesn't like it? Did you think of that?"

"Why didn't you stop me!" Clémentine asked Mika, "I was totally 'fan-girling' over him!"

"Because I was being dramatic, 'Look at me! Vampires are so cool!' Honestly, I didn't think of it because it doesn't appeal to me, being attracted to someone who used to impale people as a hobby!"

Clémentine had both her hands holding her head, her elbows resting on the counter, and she tried to fight the urge of tasting her friend's blood when her eyes glanced over her wrist, and she saw the blood pumping through her veins almost like an x-ray type of vision but in full color.

"What I didn't tell you, Mika, is that Vlad wasn't the first one to give me his blood."

For a moment, one could have heard a pin drop in the large and vast empty kitchen. The baroque music in the background, playing through speakers hung in each corner, became silent to their ears. Mika's eyes widened, and Clémentine could see her lips shaking. Her eyes filled with tears as she tried to speak a few words through her breathy voice, demonstrating her fear.

"Clémentine, people like us, if given too much vampire blood orally, we can become much more than we are." Her fear morphed into a frown as her face turned like stone, "I will not lose you to vampires. Do you know how they are made?"

"Yes. If I understood Vlad correctly, it is a symbiote that sticks itself to the heart."

"And how's your cardiophobia so far?"

"Not well."

Many people like Mika were made possible through their genes being different due to a transmitted virus or persistent bacteria. Over time, morphing and evolving had them turn to what regular humans would refer to as monsters. However, vampires were fewer in numbers, careful with those they would choose to join their people. Not only was the reproduction cycle of the symbiote far in between, but not all the humans survived the process. Clémentine now either had one symbiote or two, she didn't know, and that was what Mika feared.

"Why did Octavian give you his blood, and more importantly, why in the seven circles of hell did you let him?"

"I died, Mika." Clémentine dropped on her friend, "I drowned locked in a cage."

CHAPTER 10
DANCE MACABRE

Clémentine's memory…

Mont La Bellerose, Quebec, Canada
Rose Lake, Summer of 2015.

Clémentine had her black hair up in a bun, her black tank-top and cut-off jean shorts were enough on that summer evening. It had been hot all week, and Clémentine was walking with her flip flops in the grass to get near an entrance. She had been invited to meet with some 'real-life vampires' by a not so reliable source.

Ever since her vampire discovery, the shunning of fellow scientists and researchers despite the scientific magazine sticking to Dr. Roy's findings, she had been pranked more than a few times.

While many ranged on her side and wanted to know more, others would show condescension, and each time, Clémentine gave the same answer, "Don't even try burning the few neurons you got trying to find some puns I haven't heard before. I'm un-insult-able. Want to know why? Because I do not care what you think. I don't care what anyone thinks of me for that matter. We are a specter in this universe bigger than your mind can comprehend. We're all insignificant. All we do, all we'll ever accomplish, won't matter once the sun runs out of gas or when the human race finally manages to exterminate itself because one moron thought it would be cool to start a nuclear war. So, do you now understand the space you take in my universe? Yes? Now, piss off."

Clémentine wasn't a people person, and she preferred the company of nature and animals to humans in general. Maybe it was because she had always been unusual. Perhaps it was because she had an IQ above average that allowed her to jump a few grades in school, and so, she saw life differently than others. Either way, Clémentine lost "all the fuck she gave," as she often said, when she discovered astrophysics and the importance humankind had in the universe, i.e., none. Strangely, that study had her turn to the paranormal.

Now at the door of the old town's crematorium, she knocked on the heavy wooden door. It was a humid night, her loose stray hair started to curl, and she had bags under her eyes due to her lack of sleep. Living with insomnia had Clémentine work harder on her shows, blogs, and research, but her body kept paying for it. In an article for a popular UK Gothic magazine, Clémentine even admitted, "My body is powered by peanut butter and decaf because I have IBS and can't process caffeine like a normal caf-junkie."

Music from a Swedish rock band echoed, and Clémentine sang the words in a whisper while knocking. A small rectangular wood plate slid to the side, and the upper face of a woman showed behind the door. "Yes, may I help you?"

Clémentine showed the invitation she had been given by a 'witch' she knew that hung out with a vampire group and said, "I'm 'friends' with a member of your community, clan, house, whatever you are. Her name is Jane Brett." She thought it'd be enough, and the door would open.

"How do you know Jane?"

"Seriously?" Clémentine let out as she slouched over, "Okay. All right, I'll play." She added as she brushed her hair back. "I met her on Facecrap through my Life After Dusk page because you know, I'm the one and only, Dr. Roy, who discovered the remains of a real-life vampire dating back to the fifteenth century."

The door opened, and immediately, Clémentine had her eyes concentrating on one man. He sat across the room on a red velvet chair. He had long wavy black hair, tanned skin, and bright blue eyes. He wore a black tank-top himself and a pair of dark-washed jeans. His eyes met her own and locked. He stood up, and Clémentine quickly guessed he must have been six and a half feet tall. Quite muscular with broad shoulders, she let him come close to her, closer than she ever would a stranger.

He stared down as she lifted her head to meet his gaze again, "Who are you?" He said as he inhaled her scent.

"Dr. Clémentine Roy. I'm here because I was told real-life vampires gathered in the crematorium. Do you happen to know anything about it?"

His full lips moved as he sneered, and his baritone voice caressed her ears, "I know they say they are 'real-life vampires.'" He then leaned closer to her and said, "But I'm a real fang biting bloodsucker who's over six hundred years old, and I can easily prove it to you my precious little AB-. Back in the late Dark Ages, I was infected by the vampire gene while I lay dying in a Hungarian dungeon."

"You don't say." Clémentine replied before chuckling and lowering her voice after pulling him closer by the collar of his tank-top, "I'm a Gravedigger. Not only can I see your life through your blood, but I can also go so far back as when your first ancestor was alive. I revive what you chose to bury, I then take it, and kill if needed." She smiled as she continued, "So, still want to go with that vampire gene infection?"

He sneered, "More than ever."

A few days later, Clémentine found herself in Octavian's arms, lying in her bed under her black and silver sheets. By the Gothic framed window reminiscent of a medieval castle, she looked outside as dawn rose. Her Vantablack walls protected Octavian in the darkness of the room. Developed by Surrey NanoSystems, it is blacker than any black we have ever known. The material properties allow it to absorb the light instead of bouncing it off, therefore, keeping it away from anyone who has insomnia.

Some thought Clémentine to be a little too 'goth' or depressed, even called her weirdo and that she should grow out of her metal-head phase. In fact, Clémentine was only trying to create an environment that would allow her to sleep, relax, and find peace. After inviting people to her house, and receiving all sorts of negative comments regarding her tastes, she cut the toxins off and kept those who saw her beneath the skin and not according to the color of her walls.

Clémentine felt Octavian's left arm closing in on her, hugging her middle until she heard his sleepy voice whisper to her ear, "I never thought I'd see the sunrise again."

"Thank the United Kingdom and science," Clémentine answered as she turned her head to notice his deep amber eyes with a drop of red glowing at the view of the window.

"Thank you, UK and science."

Octavian had his hair loose, longer than her own, she asked why he kept the same hairstyle as when he walked in daylight. His answer, melancholic, broke her heart. "I was robbed of my freedom, my essence, and my people. My hair was cut a hundred times over to humiliate me until I decided I would become the greatest monster of all the Earth." Then, he added, "When I crossed over to North America and met the true people of this land, they understood me. I let go of the ways I've learned from Europe throughout the ages and adopted their own. I let my hair grow, because just like them, to me it was sacred. I cannot recall why or how it all began, but my master knew my hair meant a lot to me, and often to punish me, he would cut it off."

Clémentine reached out to his thick wavy black hair, and once she did, his full honeyed lips parted, and eight fangs pierced from his upper and lower gums. He had not tasted her yet. She was not afraid of the bite, but what it would awaken inside of her once she would be the one tasting his life. He shared so much that she feared to walk in his skin and see through his eyes.

"I won't be able to hold back forever," Octavian whispered as he rubbed his lips against her skin at the base of her neck.

Her arms around his neck, she said, "That day, curiosity might kill the cat."

His kisses on her neck stopped, "Are you that afraid of my life, that you would have sex with me but not discover who I am any deeper?"

Clémentine stared at him, honest and transparent. "There is a reason why not all humans can read minds and lives and layers. We are all hiding a monster underneath. To be honest, yours seem greater than most."

Octavian moved up on her bed and pointed at a sketch she had made a long time ago of the Romanian Warlord, "Greater than your hero, Vlad the Impaler?"

"Vlad sacrificed himself until he had nothing left to save his people. He created a monster for all to remember. The man he kept to himself."

CHAPTER 11
IT IS DESTINY

Clémentine awoke from her daydream about Octavian. Her heart broke when he left. She didn't wish to remember the day he filled her mouth with his blood and so she looked into Mika's eyes, and said in a broken voice, "I can't. Not now." Clémentine recalled burying herself in her work when Octavian vanished from her life. She was often in demand for the anthropological discovery she made about the petrified vampire remains.

Clémentine knew about vampires, but Mika was right; they were more dangerous than any other creature. Octavian, on the other hand, was the one she feared the most. When the scientific council rejected the evidence of the vampire existence, threatening her life in a well-practiced graceful manner, she would understand to stop her research all-together, she agreed but never finished. Clémentine was smart enough to use the warning she was given by manipulating them to fit her agenda. She would not be silenced.

Clémentine set out a case from the Belvoir Coven, which also served as an influential paranormal webzine and blog to expose certain folklore and legends. "Why, again, did you not use Octavian to lead us to the vampires?" Mika asked as they both stood in the kitchen by the bay window. The blinds rolled-up to let in the light of dusk as the built-in bulbs came on everywhere around them brighter than moments before.

"I have his number. I have his name. I believe that maybe I still own his heart." Clémentine babbled, "You know what our favorite song was, Mika?"

"No. I am quite sur you didn't talk about Octavian that much."

"It was, '*The World Is Not Enough.*' Nothing was ever enough." Her eyes were fixed on a blank white spot on the granite table where they sat. they sat. "*No one ever died from wanting too much.*"

Mika reached to hold Clémentine's hand, "I never knew how painful your breakup was. I'm sorry."

A veil of tears covered Clémentine's eyes, "That's because there never was a breakup." She said, "He simply...vanished."

Mika put their plates away and served them some coffee. She moved beside her friend and took her in her arms.

Clémentine was no fool, and she wanted to know what was going on. "Octavian told me that he and I could pull the world apart...it almost tempted me." Mika's arms hugged her tighter than ever. Clémentine had told her before, many of her gifts as a Gravedigger had her fight the desire to destroy anything that hurt her or beings she treasured. "What about Vlad?"

"He has me feel...I can feel his power."

Mika slid out of the booth by the bay window in a hurry, "We're getting the fuck outta here."

Clémentine followed her friend, her stomach in a knot. She asked why when a loud scream reverberated throughout the entire plantation house. It came from below. Clémentine and Mika jumped out of their skin and looked at each other, "Let's get the fuck outta here, now!" They held each other's hands and ran outside the kitchen toward the stairs. They both went down the corridor and entered their chambers. Mika went to the dark oak armoire and took out their luggage. She opened the suitcases, and Clémentine ran to the bathroom to gather their hygiene products.

"If only we had never had that bright idea to investigate the paranormal. If only we weren't born with those stupid useless gifts of shit!" Mika said as she made some space for Clémentine to put their stuff in, not even looking at what belonged to whom, packing as fast as they could. Shoving in the rest of their clothes, and leaving their dresses behind, they closed up their suitcases and started pacing toward the door. Clémentine stopped Mika and said, "They'll be expecting us to run out the front door. We should go out the kitchen."

Mika followed Clémentine, holding each other's hands again, expecting the worst. After all, both had watched too many horror flicks. They flew down the stairs, and once they were near the kitchen, it felt as though freedom was in their grasp when two guards appeared, one of which was Frederick. *How did he know?*

The lights were on, and bright, and the grandfather clock by the kitchen entrance showed it was almost nine. It dawned on her that Vladislav must have entered her mind or felt her terror and warned his guards. How could they escape a vampire anyway? They were at the top of the food chain, and there was nothing Clémentine could do. Her life had changed.

Clémentine let go of her suitcase, her head falling forward as her arms fell on both sides of her body. The moment she let go of Mika's hand, it was like a part of her turned entirely numb. A smoky breeze wafted across the first floor to her nose, and it almost had her wishing she was back home in Mont La Bellerose, where she should have stayed.

"Why is it so important to you that we stay?" Mika asked, aware that her blood was one they wouldn't dare to touch, as it had been shown she was the alpha Rougarou. She put herself between Clémentine and the guards as if to protect her. Clémentine, her head still low, grabbed Mika's hand and said, "Because she's a Gravedigger. She's too valuable for Vlad to lose, because Clémentine can speak and invade the minds of those who have passed. She alone can feel the residual memories of houses and lands. Because she can feel what will come to pass through those that are no more." Frederick said.

Frederick, who seemed to be the leader of the guards, walked forward, "Because she belongs to our prince, Vladislav."

"I belong to fuck all," Clémentine shouted. "Move, or I will make you move."

Clémentine walked up to Frederick and asked him if Vladislav told him where to stop them from running away. He said in his typical phrase, "I can't tell you that." Clémentine's patience grew thin. She tilted her head and imagined a fine, thin bright white thread going from above her eyes to Frederick, who was a few inches taller than her and read something strange as if Frederick wanted something from her, but she couldn't tell if it was good or bad. "He has nothing to say that I don't already suspect."

She walked off and grabbed Mika by the hand to go back to their room. The corridor was wide enough for six grown men standing side by side, if not wider. Delicate, decorative wood tables were placed every few feet with flower vases, resting above them were frames and oil paintings of ancient sceneries of diverse places in France. They both walked into their bedroom, and then Clémentine asked Mika if she

would   be   up   for   a
little investigation.

"What do you mean?"

"Get your Rougarou out. I need you to sniff an Impaler for me." Clémentine, though in possession of Vladislav blood, but not a vampire, her tracking skilled were limited and temporary depending on how old the blood was. As for the one within her, it had been processed by her symbiote and organs and was now 'cleaned.'

Mika's eyes suddenly glowed as her skin tone morphed into greys. Her nose darkened, and she started smelling a trail. Clémentine knew Mika could retain smells of individuals, even more of those who had passed. Vampires had a unique scent, deprived of certain nutrients that would give them an ozone and iron smell. "Above. His room is right above us, leading toward the bathroom."

Clémentine looked up, "Bastard." They both walked out of their chambers and tiptoed their way to the staircase to walk up. Clémentine signaled Mika to place herself against the wall, going in stealth mode as much as they could as the spiral staircase could provide some camouflage. Once on the third floor had a hidden semi-upper-floor, she looked at the wide-open space, painted in dark burgundy. There was a painting on the right wall of the Poenari Castle in Romania. It was an old oil painting placed in an antique gold frame with intricate Baroque carvings of bay leaves and vines. Oil lamps were placed on both sides of the painting, and Clémentine started to question Vladislav's power in North America.

"Our bedroom is below," Mika whispered to Clémentine as she stood in front of widespread double black doors. Clémentine was about to touch the knob when she heard a voice in her head, *"Do not enter my bedroom. I have let you come close enough to my personal life for now. I have shown nothing but respect to you, have the decency to return the gesture."*

Clémentine let her hand fall, and Mika asked why she was stopping since they were so close to know all of Vladislav's secrets. She murmured, "He knew what we were doing all along." Clémentine tossed her midnight black hair away and said, "He let me get to his bedroom door." She pointed at her head, "He's in there." She pointed at her veins, "In there." Clémentine slowly walked toward the staircase and glanced one last time at his door before walking down to their bedroom. So many things crossed her mind while she tried to ignore the fact that her life had changed and turned upside down.

When crossing the entrance to their chambers, Mika walked to the bed and asked her what she would do now that it was almost ten and she would be having dinner with Vladislav. Clémentine barely looked up to Mika and said, "I don't know."

CHAPTER 12
THE DIGGER WITHIN

Crossing to the bathroom, Clémentine brought her hygiene products with her and closed the door. She had her 4th Generation iPod Touch with her, a gift her grandpa had given her a few years back before he passed. He knew how much new technology meant to her, and ever since, she had kept it near her. She hit shuffle, and it played some eighties rock. Clémentine looked at herself in the mirror and wished she would have had stuck to astrophysics instead of being so jaded.

Sometimes, she thought being smart, and having a high IQ was more of a curse than a gift.

Astrophysics showed her humans were insignificant. History and research in the paranormal had proven her right, and as a result, she was rejected. Either way, she belonged nowhere. She was jaded.

Clémentine lived with the knowledge that many would have thought she would be too much to handle. She kept to herself most of the time. Always a silent person, and not doing well in crowds, she found herself even staying silent at school. As a person, she felt she had much to prove, due to the fact that her mother had her young, and her maternal grandparents raised her.

She saw her mother as a big sister, always in competition with each other. Clémentine tried to prove her worth in school, art, history, everything she would touch. The pressure was heavy on her shoulders as her grandmother often pushed her to be better. It caused her to enter a dark period in her life in her late teen years. She coped until she couldn't. Clémentine stayed home with her grandparents, and she took care of her grandpa until the very end. Her grandmother passed away a few years before he did, and she had promised her grandpa she'd stay and so she did.

It put a lot of stress on her, but she kept to his side, and when she found him at the foot of a fir tree, hardly breathing, his eyes closed, and tongue swollen, she called the ambulance and gave him CPR until the paramedics showed up. It was already too late. That morning, Clémentine lost a big part of herself. She was never the same. She moved out of the house that built her. Hours away, she found an old colonial house in Mont La Bellerose and promised herself she would never go back because, like in the words of Thomas Wolfe, 'You can never go home again.' Once you leave, it is over.

Her mother took over the family house, and Clémentine left with the inheritance her grandpa left her. Her life fully changed forever. Of course, she could have chosen the scientific life as she wanted, but once her mind adapted, the world of the night called her back in. Her mindset changed, and she now battled a few problems with it. She couldn't sleep as well, as she had been born with insomnia, it had only gotten worse as the years went by. Her post-traumatic stress syndrome after the year of her grandfather's passing had her wish she had someone else's life. It hurt her so much she wanted someone to take the pain away.

Now on medication, and battling chronic anxiety, she isolated herself for what some thought was the worst idea she had ever had. In fact, it helped her to clear her mind. In the bathroom, Clémentine aligned her hairbrush, strawberry deodorant, and placed her shower gel and razor next to the sink where the vanity was. She turned around and twisted the faucets to start the shower. Her life was flashing back at her and she found herself trying to hide in the dark corners of her mind. Determined, Clémentine pushed it all away. She wanted to forget about the past eighteen years. Many wish they had done things differently, but Clémentine knew that if she believed in infinite timelines and possibilities, somewhere, she made the right decision.

Clémentine didn't live in a science-fiction world, despite her love for it. But it seemed if it had to be classified, paranormal would be more accurate. Not that she wished to be a file on someone's computer. She took her shower thinking about the possibility that Vladislav might need her to stay, that she might require his assistance, and that maybe together they could achieve her dream of having monsters and humans coexist. "Humans and monsters...we need a new word for...monsters."

Once she wrapped a white towel around her body, she walked to the vanity. Clémentine slowly took out her hair dryer, straightener, and hairbrush. She thought about her work with the Belvoir Coven and what she had been hired to do since her career started as a historian and Vampirologist about a decade ago. Never had Clémentine thought about her life changing as drastically as it did from the moment she and Mika uncovered the vampire remains. Her reputation gained popularity with a big crowd, while the scientific community considered her a hack. At the worst, they considered her a danger to society because of her beliefs. Although they knew the truth, they were keeping their mouths shut. "I wouldn't be surprised if a family of Greys lived at Area 51 with Bigfoot as their fucking neighbors."

Clémentine gave seminars and courses on legends and folklores at four different universities. Despite her young age, her IQ had her jump different grades as a child and teenager. Now, near her mid-thirties, Clémentine had a full career, yet, it was all about to burn to the ground once she could convince the Belvoir Coven to welcome Vlad the Impaler into their circle, and find a strategy to make themselves public despite the scientific council's warning.

"If you ever go public with proof of vampire existence again, we will be forced to silence you. This

world is not ready to know about other creatures." "The world isn't ready, or you aren't ready to admit how humans were so cruel that they almost ran all those people to extinction? Because they don't fit your society, your standards, your world, or religion, you want to keep them out of sight? Correct me if I'm wrong, council, but from where I stand, this is the new millennium's inquisition, and believe me when I say that I won't play a part in it."

Those were the last words Clémentine ever spoke to the science council before she resigned. She chose integrity over greed. Clémentine had a scientific mind, and she wasn't working for recognition or money. She simply worked for her own education and the challenges that she set for herself, and one thing she never admitted to, 'helping others.'

Clémentine needed to give Vladislav an answer regarding her stay at his side and accepting his help. He could continue to protect her from other vampires, or she would be on her own and entirely out of his life. Making such a decision demanded a lot of reflection and more answers. Clémentine wished to know just whom Vlad the Vampire was before agreeing to his offer, as her decision would drastically change her life forever.

Clémentine would have to know if Vladislav was aware of her being a Gravedigger, and it had him wishing her to stay or if he knew about Octavian and wanted to know more about her involvement in the afterlife. She needed to know if, by staying with him, it would protect her friends, the ones that she recognized as her family and would do anything to protect. Since Vladislav seemed to be kind enough to answer her questions, all she had to do was pay attention to his body language and observe his gestures to tell if he was being truthful or not.

Clémentine closed her eyes and revisited the memory of standing close to Vladislav moments before he left for the hidden entrance. She concentrated on his musky perfume, the overpowering presence, and the deep green of his eyes. She could almost feel his touch and his breath next to her. That was a Gravedigger's trick. She needed to enter his mind through her memory to slowly possess his body, so that when he went down the stairs, she would be able to see through his eyes what he experienced and lived.

But how would she accomplish such a task, as memory is not alive? Wrong, Clémentine knew by studying astrophysics that time is more than complex and is more alive than we thought possible. Past and future, sharing space, coexist together and therefore it makes it possible for someone like Clémentine to jump from moments to moments outside the space-time continuum.

Using her knowledge, Clémentine decided to listen attentively to all the sounds around her coming from the last memory of Vladislav to see or catch something that would lead her to a link connecting them together. A faint voice, almost like white noise caught her attention, and she followed it. Immediately she felt a cold but distant breeze. Recognizing his signature move through her mind, Clémentine followed the wind, and it brought her deeper into her memory.

Vladislav's eyes moved up, and it seemed to her as if their eyes were connected. With his nonchalant smile in the corner of his mouth he said, "Little Clémentine, your extra sensorial sense to feel the undead can prove to be very strong with the right motivation. You have me quite flattered. Now get out of here before I make you. You have no place here."

Would Clémentine dare let him know the reason she was doing this? Clémentine took a second to herself before Vladislav would push her out and said, *"You asked me to make a decision before dinner, and as much as I desire to give you one, I have nothing to base my decision on. I might appear new to the vampire life, but you are wrong. You tell me who you are, or I walk away. That's right. Because I know that underneath this relaxed smile of yours, you need me. You said it yourself, people like me are nowhere to be found, and you need someone who can track. I'm the best tracker there is on this floating rock."*

Clémentine tried to hide her terror but knew Vladislav could feel her fear. The cold look in his eyes was enough to prove to her that he was taken by surprise with her words and maybe would allow her to stay, but instead he said, *"So be it. I'll answer your questions over dinner. I'll see you there. Now off you go."*

A strong gust of wind pushed her out of his mind and back to the bathroom, where she stood next to her iPod. When she opened her eyes, she tried to stay calm. As the anxiety pill she swallowed spread through her body, she could take a moment to herself as the knot in her stomach disappeared, and her trembling subsided. She feared for her life while addressing Vladislav as such, calling his bluff. Clémentine wondered if she might be the next one screaming from down below.

Clémentine turned around to take a look at the bathroom. She saw the walls and floor covered in pale grey tiles, and one tone was lighter than the rest of the suite. In the back-left corner was a white above ground bathtub, and on her right side, the shower she utilized, which was big enough to hold a party in, had been covered in a darker tone of grey. On the black dual vanity, where her beauty products were placed, were fresh red and white towels. The mirror took a big part of the wall and looked over the shower. Clémentine looked at her reflection and noticed the large black bags below her eyes. She folded her dirty clothes, an unusual habit she'd had since childhood. Her hair needed to be untangled and dried, and despite rarely wearing makeup, she thought maybe trying to hide her fatigue would be a good idea.

She dried her hair, something she would never do. She always let it dry naturally, but time was running away. Once she was done, she straightened it and her midnight black hair looked silky smooth with blue highlights, giving it depth and a magical feel. Her bangs, going down below her brows, perfectly framed her dark hazel green eyes.

She used a few drops of liquid foundation to hide her exhaustion and added mascara to have her eyes look more awake. Her matte velvet black lipstick hid her tendency to pick at her lips until they bled, and she was ready to get dressed. She put on dark jeans, a grey tank top, and a red and black flannel. She didn't intend to look as if she would walk into a five-star restaurant.

Clémentine was a cozy woman who liked wearing comfortable clothing. She always had her nose in a book, or was focused on her computer. She referred to herself as a nerd, not a socialite. She avoided people as much as possible, so wearing anything dressy was playing pretend to her. It was something she had not done for years.

CHAPTER 13
VAMPIRES PAY A PRICE

Clémentine played with her jet-black hair coming down her shoulder. She wasn't too sure about her figure, and despite wanting answers from Vladislav, she couldn't help but think of him as the most irresistible man she had ever met. Clémentine was a very natural looking woman. She wasn't a runway model. She had never had any confidence in her looks, preferring to hide than try to expose her femininity. When Clémentine looked at herself one last time, she was about to grab one of her sweaters when Mika exclaimed, "Stop! You look gorgeous." She wanted to hide behind one of her metal-band sweaters, but her friend reminded her that maybe Vladislav wasn't a superficial type of vampire, "You've always told me not to think for others." Clémentine remembered who they were talking about, the Impaler. "I can't be up to his standards. That's impossible."

Clémentine heard a knock on her door, and she put on black ballet slippers, opening the door to Frederick. He was there to accompany her to the dining room. He mentioned never having seen someone of such beauty among the blood bags, which she had learned was a term adapted for humans. She thanked him, but suddenly felt his hand move down her hip to guide her to the turn for the dining room near the back of the mansion. She looked down and asked for him to remove his hand. "Why?" He asked, but Clémentine simply answered, "Do I really need to express a reason?" Frederick removed his hand and Clémentine noticed he was licking his lips, "Sorry, you're the classiest woman we've seen around here." Clémentine rolled her eyes, "Probably the smartest too." The Scandinavian vampire complimented her once more and wished her a good evening with Mr. Tepes before leaving her in the room alone.

The room was bigger than Clémentine thought it would be. The table was big enough to seat twelve people, and the fire in the hearth roared warming the dining area with its dancing flames. Chandeliers were lit and brought a sense of drama to the room. The furniture seemed to be from the eighteenth century imported from France she assumed recognizing the style and carvings inspired from the time period. She walked toward the fire, intrigued by an oil painting proudly hung over the fireplace. She saw that it was the owner of the plantation, wearing the military costume of a commander from the French Revolution army. The plate underneath the painting stated who he was: "François St-Arnaud, Commander of the Imperial Guard, 1782, Paris, France."

As she admired the painting, she felt a sudden embrace from the shadows of the room. Without turning around, she felt two hands touching her shoulders and slowly going down her arms. "You disobeyed me yet again today. Is this a bad habit of yours not to do what you are told?" He said with teasing in his voice as she turned around to face him. Clémentine knew better than to challenge a vampire. But when he had a tempting grin and such a ravishing stature, she couldn't help but think about her next naughty move just to get more of his time. "You already have my undivided attention, Clémentine. There is no need to defy me any further. I might not be   as   nice next time."

He wore a dark green, scoop neck, long sleeve shirt and jeans. Looking down, she noticed on his right index finger an old silver ring with a red stone. She thought it was a ruby, but he said, "No, it's garnet, and the ring itself is white gold. Vampires are violently affected by silver, but not for the reason you might think." With a shy smile, she retorted, "Garnet is my birthstone." With a smirk, he said, "I would like to believe the universe had us meet, but I do not believe in such superstitions."

He pulled out a chair for her next to his at the end of the table. He signaled with his hand to a man hidden in the dark. He brought a bottle of wine to Clémentine, who confessed she rarely drank and knew nothing about wine. The valet poured a small amount for her to taste.

"Thank you, I actually believe this will be enough for me. May I have water instead, please?" She asked, with a small smile.

She heard Vladislav's snort and asked him why he made that noise. She saw his dimples and a spark in his eyes, as he responded, "You are so charming." The waiter then approached the table with a silver dome covered tray. Once in front of her, she smelled the comforting aroma of Cajun macaroni and cheese, which was then followed by a peach cobbler. It made her laugh, and she heard Vladislav asking if he had made a mistake. She shook her head as she answered, "No, no, it's my favorite food."

She barely touched her dinner, not wanting to look like a glutton. She kept on picking at her flannel until the waiter came to pick up her plate. She smiled, and her fingernails were now picking at her bottom lip as a cup of tea was placed beside her. She felt a sting and looked at her nails, blood.

"You are beautiful, Clémentine. I was unable to take my eyes off you, didn't you notice?"

"I did, I wondered what you were going to do while I ate. Aren't you, um, hungry?" She regretted asking the question the moment the words left her mouth.

"Clémentine, I would never do anything you wouldn't want me to do." She wondered what he meant. Did he assume that eventually, she would let him bite her, or was this biting part of a contract she would have to sign agreeing to his protection and participation for the Belvoir Coven? "I know you want me to bite you." He said, as he stood up from his chair and walked behind her. She suddenly felt a burst of warmth taking over her loins as he whispered next to her ear, "I promise I will, in time."

Vladislav pulled out the chair to help Clémentine up and walked with her around the mansion. He guided her to the second floor, to a large room with two enormous French doors. He opened them to bring her back to the place where the secret entrance was. She wondered if he would show her the hidden passage to the basement, but he quickly reminded her that it wasn't a place for a woman like her.

They were standing next to the balcony door, and as he opened it to let the cold wind of November in, she noticed how warm it felt compared to her town. She smiled and moved outside. Vladislav stood beside her, and Clémentine looked at him. His eyes were as green as an Irish field, but then she instantly saw them turned to red.

"Why do they change so often? What does it mean?" Clémentine asked, confused.

"It either means I'm angry, hungry, or aroused." The vampire replied, letting a few of his white teeth show through an overconfident grin.

"Which one is it?" Clémentine asked, hoping for the last one to be true.

"I am certainly not angry at the moment." He replied as arrogantly as he could, almost as if he could read that Clémentine seemed attracted to that side of him.

Vladislav turned around and started walking toward the corner of the balcony. She followed and heard him ask with a stentorian voice she knew he used when wanting people to listen and obey; "You had many hours to think about my proposition. What is your decision?" Clémentine wished she had the confidence to touch his dark green sleeve, but held back.

It was as if he knew how she felt, and he turned to look into her eyes while he waited for her response. He lifted her head with his fingers, forcing her to look back at him. She finally answered, "You said I could ask you some questions first."

Vladislav closed his hand on her own and guided her back inside the house. He walked to an old desk where he took out an antique metal flask adoned with a symbol she knew nothing about before whispering the name of Frederick. The Swedish vampire zoomed in the room and appeared right next to Vladislav, bowing as he took the flask, "Mlle. Roy." Frederick said with a smile that left Clémentine shyly uncomfortable. When she looked into the grey of his eyes, she felt as if her eyeballs were pushing inward and suddenly felt anxious. She whispered in her mind, *Archangel Michael, help me,* and the pain disappeared.

Clémentine wondered what had happened. Only in her nightmares did she ever have to ask upon the help of the Archangel. She felt he could help her when a strong terror would overpower her. Frederick zoomed out of the room, and it left a cool breeze behind. Clémentine hugged herself, hoping she was able to contain her fright within and pass the cold that suddenly gave her the chills.

"What did Frederick do?" Vladislav asked with a cold voice. It was one she only heard him use with others around the mansion. "I was told he brought you here when Violette was the one I sent for you."

"Nothing, I just stared at him and felt like my eyeballs…wait, how?" Suddenly confused, Clémentine wondered how Vladislav knew about the pain that had happened when crossing Frederick's gaze. She then recalled the way Frederick acted around her, and how he nearly touched her behind when bringing her to the dining room, and how she had to put an end to his act.

"I will take care of him," Vladislav assured Clémentine. She wondered how he could take her word for it, but he said, "I rule my people as I see fit, and that vampire has an addiction for witch's blood. He is known for being a conservative and against the union between vampires and any other creatures. He is not one of mine. He belongs to Matthias' house."

Clémentine knew the history between Matthias and Vlad. Somehow, the once human man found his way to torment her hero even in the undead life. She saw no need to hide Frederick's doing and admitted that he accompanied her and Mika quite a few times around the house. Vladislav shared information with her regarding conservatives and how envious Frederick was of his position and that one of his progeny, Damian Blackwood, was recently married the last of the Orléans descendant, Coralie Bellefleur.

CHAPTER 14
A SILENT BEAUTY

Vladislav walked closer to Clémentine, who tried to hide her true feelings toward him. Even though pointless, her mix of desire and fear was evident and Vladislav already felt it through her veins. Her smile was now replaced with a sad recollection of what she thought of herself when standing next to Vladislav. He was the reason why beauty was invented, there were no equally attractive men or males, and it reminded her that Vladislav would forever be out of her reach. There was a soft breeze in her mind that caressed the darkest thoughts she had about herself, and then she heard his husky voice take over.

"Don't you ever denigrate yourself in front of me, Clémentine. You are one of the most beautiful women I have ever seen, and I've seen more than any other human man. You are one of the very few that entices me and believe me, there were not that many before you and it's been a long while since there has been any." Vladislav said aloud.

Clémentine surprised herself by smiling, and she felt his warm hand moving her hair away from the back of her neck to the side of her shoulder. Vladislav stood behind her, and she could feel him leaning over and breathing on her neck. Her skin reacted to his every breath, and her heartbeat got louder. She bit her lower lip, trying to keep her moaning inside. She wondered if it was the moment he talked about as she closed her eyes and tilted her neck to the side. She could barely find the strength to stand still as his hands closed on both her arms. His lips close to her neck, he softly whispered in her ear, "Nicely played, but not tonight, Clémentine."

He ran his fingers through her hair and inhaled her scent as she turned around to face him. He opened his mouth, and the moment he was about to say something, Clémentine saw his eyes darkening, and his smile changed rapidly to a grimace. His brows lowered, and his voice deepened more than she ever heard, making her swallow her saliva harder than she would have had in normal times. She stepped back as he said, "Looking to be impaled in front of my home?" Faster than she had time to figure out what was going on, Vladislav pinned the poor guard on the brick wall as he shouted, "I said my time spent with Clémentine would not be interrupted."

Frederick's eyes were wide open, and subtle red lines were forming under both his eyes. The vampire held onto Vladislav's forearm holding him up at arm's length against the wall. Clémentine's eyes were on the guard, but when she realized her vision seemed to be adapting to a dimmer environment, she noticed a dark foggy mist enveloping the room. She moved toward

Vladislav to protect herself against the mass when she felt something metallic against her shoulder. She looked and took the flask someone else handed to her.

"Vladislav? Isn't this what you wanted?" Clémentine mentioned as she showed him the flask.

"Yes, thank you, Clémentine." The vampire replied, never taking his eyes off Frederick as he lowered him down the wall. Clémentine watched the poor vampire looking away from her and bowing to Vladislav as a growling sound came out of him like a large beast in the wild.

"Naten, you know what to do." The tall brunette man nodded and shyly smiled before replying, "Yes, Vlad."

Clémentine held the flask with a strange uncomfortable feeling knowing what it contained. She handed the container to Vladislav, who took out the cork and took a mouthful. She stared at him, unable to look away. Her eyes fixed on him, she didn't realize how uncomfortable Vladislav could've been, but when she did, she walked away to let him drink.

"The blood is from a giver. Naten is the guy you saw by Frederick's side. He's one of my most trusted men and, well, he is my best friend. The giver is also a male." She heard him say as he approached her again from behind with a voice that made her understand that he enjoyed her watching him drink the blood that was brought to him.

"A giver?" Clémentine understood what he meant, but were givers his slaves?

"No, they aren't slaves. I have twenty givers in my home. Here François has four of them. They are all people like you aware of our existence and freely giving their blood to us."

"No offense, but why would they do such a thing willingly?" Clémentine asked, wondering if being a blood worker was a thing.

"The rewards," Vladislav answered coldly.

Vladislav explained to her that givers were treated with respect and were cared and provided for. Vampires shared their homes with them. If not, they were given their own place, although most of them found vampire company more pleasing. Vladislav warned her that not all vampires were kind to humans, but he was one of them, and he had been working on having his people treating humans the way he did.

"If I accept to help you and have you join the Belvoir Coven, am I to become a giver too?" Clémentine wondered as she thought about the decision she had to make, but his answer brought her relief, as she knew she had to accept his offer regardless of the outcome.

"No, you will be my guest, and if you remember correctly, I claimed you as mine, which means no one is to come in contact with you in an intimate way." His voice sounded formal and meant business, but she had to make sure he was sincere.

"No small print where it states that I'll have to give you any of my blood?"

"Not unless you beg me to just like you did earlier when tilting your head to the side, exposing your neck to me. I know what you tried to do." His voice so arrogant and sure of himself ignited a fire in Clémentine's lower abdomen down her thighs as she listened to his words. She should have been a tad insulted, but it was all true. She did try to have him caress her neck with his fangs.

Clémentine moved her head teasing Vladislav until she wondered if it was all him mindspelling her into willingly giving herself to him, but his answer proved to be frightful; "You would know if you'd be under my hold. You'd be terrified, and I would want you to fight me off in your head. I would want you to scream in terror until you would realize there's nothing you could do because I'm holding your body in place with my mind, and then you would give up, crying in horror while I would drain you."

He said those words with such detachment she wondered if that was what the givers had to go through every day he had to feed off of them, but the vampire shook his head; "No, I would never do such a thing to humans that give themselves willingly to me. I only mind spell humans that are treating me or my people with disrespect." Vladislav explained to her how he would treat his givers and although she had many questions regarding the matter, she listened to him speak about a little of vampire politics and how he ruled over his district. He explained that the vampire council was actually divided into nine realms, and he was the ruler of one of the most important ones. He ruled over the one that dethroned the first realm back in the fifteenth century.

Clémentine looked away as she tried to fight yawning in front of Vladislav. He walked her up the stairs to her suite, and when he opened the door to let her in the chambers, she smiled. He leaned in to gently kiss her on the lowest part of her cheek right beside her lips. She had so many more questions and he answered one of them as she grabbed onto his shirt by the low scoop neckline collar and moved her fingers to touch the fine layer of hair on his chest; "I am a vampire prince. I rule over a vampire realm, and it means I do have enemies. I need you to help me find them and end them before they end both of us."

He left her bedroom, and Clémentine stood there, watching him walk away. She stared at his broad back, down to his waist and firm rounded buttocks. As she took off her shoes, she imagined him coming back, opening the door to take off her dress, move her hair away, and plunge his fangs into her neck to taste her. She couldn't help but fantasize about the little she saw and the touch of his chest and how hard his abdominals were when she touched him for a split second before he disappeared down the secret passage.

"I will taste you, Clémentine."

"You have to stop invading my mind. There are some thoughts that I would like to keep to myself."

"What if I let you in to see what I fantasize about when I think of you?"

Clémentine agreed, and she felt a gentle cold breeze leading her into Vladislav's mind. Clémentine wished she saw him taking off his shirt, but instead she felt him standing behind her. As he moved her hair away, he caressed her neck with his razor-sharp fangs, and the moment she thought he was about to push them against her flesh, he grabbed her waist and sat her on his thighs on the bed. He gently moved her legs apart, unbuttoning her jeans as he moved his mouth to her neck and as he entered her with his fingers, she felt him bite her neck with such passion she thought she had an orgasm just by watching his fantasy.

"We are clothed in your fantasy?" Clémentine asked a little disappointed.

"I'm not easy, Clémentine. I like to leave something for the imagination."

Clémentine felt pulled out of Vladislav's mind, but his connection to her stayed alive, and it felt like a soft presence in her thoughts. She recalled that his fantasy and hers were very much alike. She wondered what it would be like the night they would give in to each other then she heard his smoky voice say, *"Does this mean you accept my proposition?"* Obviously, Clémentine didn't want him out of her life, so she answered, *"I accept as long as you promise to be honest with me, respect me, and not hide anything from me if it concerns me, my friends, or my coven in any way. Do I have your word?"*

There was a long moment of silence. For the first time, she thought she felt Vladislav's emotion in her mind, and it left her wondering if she imagined it since the emotion she felt from him was discomfort. Since the moment she met Vladislav, he had been nothing but arrogant, sensual, sure of himself, authoritarian, and overpowering. This emotion had to be wrong.

"No, you felt it right...I need to tell you something as I am willing to accept your terms, which is something that I never let a mortal do with me or any monster for that matter." Clémentine was flattered, although she admitted feeling sorry for everyone else. She wondered what her new host, client or friend, was talking about, *"Vlad? Vladislav say something, you're creeping me out."*

She couldn't bear her mind being empty. The vampire prince was right, although it was taking her time to get accustomed to Vladislav's presence in her mind, it was unbearable to feel him entirely out. She looked for a link leading her back to him when she finally felt the gentle cold breeze.

"I am Vlad the Impaler. To this day, I bear the title, and I have done horrible things." His voice sounded hurt and ashamed, among some other feelings

that she thought were strange to someone such as the vampire prince. She refused to believe him.

"You would be surprised at what people can do when they believe no one can dig through their minds."

Clémentine hoped he would come clean and explain himself to her and reveal what was going on that when she heard him say his name, a cold shiver grabbed her spine and the hair on the back of her neck straightened in fear and confusion as she gasped in horror.

"The reason I need you is to find my Donor. The one   who   made   me   a   vampire."

Chapter 15

Pain Without Love

Clémentine looked around the bedroom and noticed she was alone. Mika left her a note on her bedside table saying she was spending the night with Maxim, a vampire she met the night they arrived at the mansion.

Feeling vulnerable and alone, Clémentine's eyes were wide open, and she was unable to move from her bed or think about anything else than what Vlad just said. She didn't know many people whose name was Vladislav, came from Romania and were turned into a vampire. It dawned on her that she spent the night with a man who used to be worth a thousand soldiers. Vlad used to be a man that ruled over

Wallachia and spent years at the side of his father's enemies to learn their ways. He'd witnessed torture from the moment he was a little boy. She feared the man in him died when he was taken away from his mother and was already a vampire when he first witnessed the cruelty men could inflict on others of his kind.

Clémentine finally found the strength to sit up on the bed and breathe. She tried to close her mind entirely, and for a short moment, she thought she did. The sensation of being alone in her head was now strange and almost uncomfortable. Clémentine thought she would hear him say something like, 'Please, don't be afraid of me,' but instead she felt a cold mist inside her mind and a whisper; *"You should be afraid of me."* Fear was only the beginning of the mountain of emotions that rose before her. Every fiber in her body screamed for her to get out, but her mind craved more of his words and presence.

She unzipped her jeans and pulled out her suitcase to grab her white tank top and pajama bottoms. She brushed her teeth and went back to bed to only find herself thinking about who Vladislav truly was. She had the time to process everything that had happened, flipping her entire existence upside down. Clémentine had so many questions, but she wanted to be alone in her head, and Vladislav seemed to have respected her need for privacy from that moment on.

Dawn was breaking, and Clémentine was still awake. Although Clémentine worked as a vampirologist, and with her extra-sensorial perception, she wondered how much deeper in the 'monster world' she would be dragged into. Clémentine grabbed her tablet and opened it to see a reminder of the Belvoir Coven gatherings to come that could have brought her to the Poenari Castle in Romania. "I do not believe in coincidences, but this is sick." Clémentine spent the day answering emails from people who asked for her to visit their class, claiming that they were people who witnessed strange things happening. Many times, Clémentine had gone to seminars where people asked her about her work, about the vampire remains, her beliefs, and often she would have to reply, "The information is classified."

Clémentine's gift allowed her to be in contact with the past and future on another plane of existence. Her scientific mind prevented her from believing in psychics because there was a difference between the evolution of her brain perceiving time as an object that is alive and pretending to talk to one's ancestor. Her capability of entering one's mind and pushing through it far back or far beyond had her being one of the most powerful weapons in the monster world. She knew it, and Vladislav knew it. Whether he was on the good side remained to be seen, and she intended to see it with her own eyes.

It was six o'clock in the evening when Clémentine turned off her computer exhausted by all the messages she had to answer. She grabbed her monitor tablet and quickly drew a man wearing red and gold armor, holding his sword high and proud above his head. His dark black hair flowing in the cold wind of a Romanian winter with snow coming down from the sky. She lowered his dark brows and kept his mouth open to show his fangs ready to defend his realm in a century of brutality and darkness. It was merely a sketch, but she took a picture of her drawing with the mechanical pen she used and posted it on social media. It quickly got a reaction from a few people following her until she wondered if the vampire prince ever saw her illustrations and paintings. As she put her tablet away, she realized she hadn't felt him all day. Clémentine suddenly had the desire to go to him and ask if he wanted her help or intended to use her.

Clémentine put on her favorite white hoodie and was about to go see her friend Mika when her door opened, letting Violette in with a friendly smile and her hair up in a ponytail. Clémentine remembered Vladislav mentioning she was supposed to be the one showing her around. Her joyful voice and thick Irish accent made everything sound charming, but her message was anything but lovely; "Our prince wants you to pack your bags as you will now be leaving for the airport with Mlle. Hunter in about two hours. If you're hungry, someone will prepare you a meal in the kitchen. I'll be back to check on you in an hour." Clémentine didn't understand what was going on. Did 'the prince' withdraw his offer? Was she now nothing but another blood supplier to him and where was Frederick? "Frederick is indisposed at the moment. I was sent in his replacement by our prince, now if you'll excuse me."

Clémentine didn't dare think about what would keep Frederick away from her. She could only recall the moment Vladislav pinned him on the wall so violently she thought the whole mansion was about to fall. She remembered bloody lines coming from Frederick's eyes and nose when he roughly let him fall to the ground and his horrible threat. She thought maybe the guard was now simply uncomfortable around her and decided not to see her. Still, the tone of Violette's voice resonated in her head like a loud warning letting her know that maybe it was a good thing she was leaving to go back home and step out of the vampire world.

When the door closed, Clémentine packed hers and Mika's luggage. Her friend entered the room with a shy smile. Mika sat on the bed and Clémentine smiled, letting her know that she regretted not letting her know about what happened between her and Octavian. She should have known better than keeping passages of her life away from a friend she called her sister. The pain she felt when Octavian left her life was comparable to a sun collapsing on itself. She turned into a black hole where time slows down and light couldn't escape. Everything could go in but nothing would ever come out. Clémentine tried to hide her tears, but Mika asked what happened.

"Vlad wanted me to help him find is Donor, which is the guy that changed him to a vampire."

"Okay, did it occur to him that you're not psychic?" Mika said as she helped her friend pack.

With a big fake smile on her face, Clémentine answered while shoving their clothes in the duffle bag,

"I believe so because now we're being sent on our way home."

"What the fuck is wrong with vampires? I mean, Maxim's fine, he's coming home with us to our coven, but those on top are bat shit crazy."

"You're right. This is bullshit."

Clémentine walked out of their suite to the main dual staircase. She could hear Mika asking her where she was going, but her focus was on finding a vampire that now seemed unwilling to be found. She looked out for the cold brisk link by turning her head around, and once she caught a faint breeze, she followed it to the hidden half-floor, the floor that he shared with his other vampire friend. Clémentine ran up the stairs as if her life depended on it and strolled down the corridor, wrong one. She ran the other direction, and again, she didn't pay attention to all the antiques lying around on old wooden hutches and hung in old gold frames. She saw two large doors and knocked on them as hard as she could. Two tall vampires stood before her when they opened the doors, she recognized them from the ball, the bald twins.

Her brows were low, and so was her head, "Let me in."

"The prince is indisposed at the moment," they both said with their arms crossed over their chests, looking like two comic book characters.

"Take a good look at my face and read my lips, I don't give a shit about what your prince is doing. I want to see Vladislav now, or it'll be ugly." Clémentine spat out, surprised at her very authoritarian voice while she fixed her eyes on both guards pushing through their eyes to get to their thoughts like a drill going through butter. It was easier than she thought.

The two vampires rubbed their eyes and blood came out of their nose. Clémentine was stronger than she looked and more resourceful than most. Nobody in the monster world believed she could dig through people's heads at will, mixing their thoughts, but she always said, *"All is an illusion. Time is malleable for those capable of understanding it."* Her desire to see Vladislav drove her mad because he had played her and she was done being toyed with. About to barge in, a soft breeze caressed her mind.

"I never doubted your gift, Clémentine. I know what a Gravedigger is, and I want to pledge my allegiance to the Belvoir Coven. I will come to you shortly."

Clémentine wasn't about to listen to him. He obviously withdrew his proposition and fired her but didn't know how to handle it. Clémentine wanted nothing more than to see the bitch who took her place because there had to be someone else. She walked into the room, determined, until she gasped and found herself unable to move one bit. Her eyes wide open she saw Frederick on his knees, his shirt torn and all over the wood floor, and the floral patterns on the wall were blood splatters. She had a quick glimpse of Frederick's chest. Covering his pectorals, up to his throat, were severe dark and profound wounds, blood blisters over red skin with black smoke leaving his flesh, which left a smell of burnt hair in the air.

Clémentine stepped back. She understood why Vladislav didn't want her there. She quickly placed both her hands over her mouth right after she asked in a pitiful voice and eyes filled with disgust, "Why are you doing this to him?" Moisture in her eyes, she saw nothing but a blur and a thick black figure walking toward her. She recognized that presence. It was Vladislav.

"If you hadn't disobeyed me, you wouldn't have seen this." His voice was cold, but his eyes were filled with regret that she had seen it, but Clémentine's anger toward him had to be heard. She held him responsible for her w walking in on him in his temporary dungeon, saying that if he hadn't withdrawn his proposition, she wouldn't have been standing before him about to vomit due to the disgusting vampire that he was.

"Withdrew my proposition? Who said I did?"

"Not Frederick, that's for sure. But that Violette you sent said I had to pack my bags to be ready for the airport because Mika and I were leaving."

Clémentine felt his palm rubbing her cheeks as he wiped the tears of terror away. She then rubbed her eyes with the sleeves of her hoodie. She could see his tanned skin, his dark green eyes so hypnotizing, and his smile so enticing she couldn't help but softly hit his chest wanting him to explain why he acted so kind with her only to change his mind the moment he came clean about why he needed her help.

Clémentine hit him again, but he grabbed her wrists and stopped her from moving. His eyes changed from a deep emerald to a darker red, and his mouth opened. A feeling of being powerless before him overtook her, and she bowed her head, "I'm sorry…I don't know what made me think I had the right to ask for an explanation. I will leave. Just don't hurt Frederick any further. He's just an asshole, not a criminal. If anything, I'm the one to blame. It probably was nothing but a headache. I panicked as I struggle with anxiety problems."

She felt his grip was now gone. He had let go of her and so she moved away toward the entrance. As she walked, his voice entered her ears like a song she longed to hear. "I haven't broken our agreement. You are packing because this isn't my home. We are leaving for the town of Stowe in Vermont. I said you were mine, and so you are." Clémentine hid her mixed emotions, and as she turned around to stare at his softened face, she heard, "That's why Frederick is being taught a lesson. He should be thankful that this is François's home and not mine." He grinned, "I don't do my punishments in accessible rooms by disobeying beauties."

His voice was so cold and detached that she wondered what Frederick did to her that was so unforgiving to Vladislav. Was he jealous of the way Frederick touched her hip, or did the flask that was brought back to him accompanied by his best friend displease him? Clémentine let him stand close to her, and when he touched her chin to make her look up, he said, "What I feel for you is irrelevant to his punishment. What I refused to accept was his mind spell that he tried using on you to test your Gravedigger skills. He tried to control you because he could. I do not allow defying me in any way. He knew about my decree of you being mine and decided to mind spell you regardless of my authority, and so his act will not go unpunished."

Clémentine didn't know if she should thank Vladislav or go in there and smack Frederick for trying to control her. Vladislav warned her that he made it clear to his people not to try anything on her, so he made an example out of Frederick. His words, again so cold, left her wondering if she would bring nothing more than pain to the vampires around Vladislav, but he assured her that fear was necessary to best keep his people safe. By the look of Frederick's body, fear wasn't even the top word that came to her mind. Horrifying and gruesome first popped up in her head at the view of his flesh torn apart.

"He will heal, look for yourself." Clémentine saw him motion to one of the bald twins, and one of them handed him a knife he wore in his boot. Vladislav cut the inside of his hand, and almost immediately when his blood surfaced, she quickly noticed the wound closing and the blood dissipating, leaving only a few drops behind.

"We heal. I heal quicker than most, but Frederick will be all right in a few minutes. If you still wish to smack him, I'll allow it. He won't stop you if I order him not to."

His hand all healed, Clémentine grabbed it, moved it around and touched the place where, at the very least, a scar should've been, but saw nothing. Her finger followed his palm line that crossed a blood drop, and instead of wiping it off on her white hoodie or jeans, she licked it and immediately noticed the reaction of the bald twins and others around, their eyes wide open in anger. They all seemed ready to beat her to death, but she saw Vladislav moving his other arm in front of the guards to stop them from moving toward Clémentine, who had seen Vladislav's grin in the corner of his mouth. Clémentine slowly freed her finger from between her lips after rubbing her tongue around the tip to get the blood off and swallowing the red liquid—she wasn't a fool nor was Vladislav. She would see something from him. She lowered her hand to her jeans to dry her finger, leaving a small red stain.

A wind as cold as arctic ice took over her mind and she saw Vladislav walking down the hall, which she presumed lead to his chambers. She then noticed, looking through his eyes, that a mirror was placed in the back of the room, but something strange was looking back. She wanted to pause the moment, but it seemed as if the memory needed to go on as it did when it occurred. The room surrounding him was made of stone, a fire in the hearth still roared, and she looked down as he took off his vest, now only wearing a loose linen shirt. She heard him say, "I know you are here, Judith. I can feel you surrounding me. You are of my people, my own, why have you turned against me? I would've protected you. You know I would've if only you had come to me."

A strong and obscure fog drowned the place in black, as a shadow profoundly scratched Vladislav across his belly. His blood dripped down his abdominal wall, now pierced through, and he heard a strong nasal voice say, "I am a necromancer! Why would a vampire protect me? You would've impaled me in front of your fucking castle for everyone to see! I would've died slowly in agony as you would've dipped your lips in my blood like in the old days of your reign."

Another gust of gloomy wind, another scrape across his back left by a creature that was impossible for Clémentine to see through Vlad's keen vampire eyes. The burning dug into his muscles down to his spine, but still, he found the strength to address the woman.

"Before you were a necromancer, you were Romanian, thus falling under my protection, as the humans willing to acknowledge my existence and the gifted. I would've protected you and made an alliance with you to take down those who have hurt travelers."

Scratches were now covering his torso and back, and Vlad fell on his knees before the mirror, where she saw a black cloud growing more prominent and thicker while red sparks emerged like embers. His eyes glowed in the reflection of the candlelight gold and bright. His brows touched, and his mouth opened, fangs out, and she saw his blood entirely covering his chest. His linen shirt had been torn to pieces by the violent cuts, and his arms were now as bloody as his abdominals, where the shirt showed the biggest bloodstain, drops falling onto the floor.

"It is okay dear, *Voivode*. Now that I've grown stronger, I am able to go after the one possession I wish to own. You, my beloved Dracul." Her voice so small and adenoidal, sounded like a young woman losing her mind, as it moved up in down in rhythm with her words.

"I do not belong to anybody!" Vladislav shouted with a strong husky voice.

The black shadow now covered the entire room, and Clémentine could see nothing, but she heard the voices of the ones who had hurt Vladislav screaming and yelling in foreign languages, which she couldn't understand. She didn't know what the black shadow was, but she knew Vladislav commanded the white freezing fog. The moment the mist dissipated, there was nothing left to see of his attackers, other than a pile of dust at his feet. The moment he looked in the mirror, it was almost as if he looked right back at her, acknowledging her presence in his past.

Clémentine's eyes opened, and when she gained control over her mind and body again, she saw

Vladislav looking at her in the same position they were before she was knocked out by his blood. She then felt a horrible pain on both her forearms shooting to her elbows. She looked down and saw both her hands and fingers strongly digging into Vladislav's biceps. She tried to let go, but her fingers seemed locked down in that position and so Clémentine saw him slowly helping her relax her arms, reminding her that she was okay. When she crossed his gaze, it was of a bright crimson, and she feared he was filled with anger for her to have tasted his blood. Her, a nobody, human blood bag.

"Never say that about yourself, Clémentine. You are not just anybody, you are with me. You are my guest, and as I recall, I could've stopped you from taking your finger to your mouth. I did not, and now we've established that you can taste my life with my blood." He said with much assurance in his voice and control as he glared at his guards with such a forceful look the twins bowed and walked away.

"Then why are your eyes red? Are you hungry?"

"Guess again." It only left her one last option and his voice said it all. Was it the pain of her fingers digging into his flesh or her seeing a part of his life? Clémentine pondered on her thoughts as he helped her to the staircase to bring her down to her bedroom, where she would rest until they would take their leave.

CHAPTER 16
I LOVE ROCK 'N ROLL

Clémentine was now by the door ready to leave when she saw Mika walking toward her, following Violette outside. Mika stopped before the door and wrapped her arms around her friend's neck, and with tears in her eyes, she hugged Clémentine as tightly as she could as if not wanting to let go of her, and it left Clémentine in disarray.

"Keep in touch, okay?" Mika said with many tears building in her eyes.

"But why? I don't understand," Clémentine said, confused.

"You are leaving with Vladislav, and I'm going back home. We must find his Donor. The Belvoir Coven will need to use all the monsters we can spare, and sadly, that means one of us must go. You stay with Vladislav and make sure he stays safe. The conservatives and traditionalists are on the move, and Vlad, well he is in danger."

"How do you know?" Clémentine asked that Mika showed her the text she got from Callie and Jack,

"They're targeting all leaders. It goes without saying that Vlad is the most wanted."

"I don't know about you, but this proves to me that he's on our side. Otherwise, his name wouldn't be on everyone's lips or list to kill." She added, "I'm going home to hold the fort and dig out what I can find about his Donor. No vampire's an orphan, despite his reputation. Someone gave him the symbiote, and we must find out whom. In the meantime, you keep your eyes peeled and call me if there's trouble."

Clémentine couldn't help but let the tears fall as she looked at her friend walking toward a black luxurious car with a chauffeur opening the back door for her. She waved her hand, surprised when a fast gust of wind passed by and shouted, "Wait! I have permission from our prince to leave with Mika. I'm going with her." The vampire, Maxim, had the permission to leave with her best friend, while she stayed behind with his boss. Fair enough, she guessed.

The car left the U-shaped entrance and only the sound of the tires on the asphalt was heard from where Clémentine stood. Clémentine wiped her tears with the sleeve of her black shoulderless sweater and she pulled the hoodie over her face to hide her eyes and took a look at the white print of Joan Jett and the Blackhearts, hoping it would make her look tougher than she was. She felt vulnerable and despised the helplessness she felt. Her entire life she had fought to be strong and relied on her brains, now her fate was hanging in the balance in the hands of the fifteenth-century Impaler.

"She will be safe. She will keep everyone safe at the Belvoir Coven. Maxim is a strong vampire, despite his goofy looks. He is proof of my good faith and he grew fond of Mika." His voice was so comforting and she thought for a moment that maybe he was capable of such an emotion.

"She'll be looking for information regarding your Donor. In the meantime, I'm here to keep you safe and find who might wish to kill you. Me, as a Gravedigger, you, as the Impaler, we're both walking dead. So, let's just say I'm not particularly happy at the moment." She was looking for reassuring words.

"Yes. Neither am I." His voice, cold as ice, was anything but reassuring.

Clémentine saw his hand stretched out to help her up on her feet. Once up, she looked down but felt both his hands on both sides of her hoodie and he pulled it down. He moved his head to look behind him and a valet zoomed beside her to take the luggage and put it in the trunk of the second car. "We are running late."

Clémentine followed Vladislav to the car. The chauffeur opened the door but Vlad stepped aside to let Clémentine in. He sat beside her, and she stared at him in a pair of jeans, a grey V-neck sweater, and a black leather coat. His hair was a little wild as if he only just awakened, and a five o'clock shadow showed that he had not shaved. Clémentine concluded that hair kept growing way longer than she thought after death. She kept her chuckle to herself. Then again, she realized that it made him more attractive than before. Her eyes going up and down his body, she undressed him with her imagination. Looking outside his window, he spoke to someone on the phone in his maternal language with a tone of voice that he used with his friends but not his staff, "*La revedere.*"

The moment he hung up, Clémentine looked out her window not wanting to cross his gaze and letting him know that she had admiring him all this time. For a split second their eyes crossed, but Vladislav's face seemed grave and preoccupied, as his brows were lowered and his mouth closed, without the subtlest sign of one of his arrogant smiles he always had while looking at her.

The sky was dark grey and overcast. The day was full of heavy rain. Clémentine was reminded that she was alone with a man she barely knew. But she trusted that he could protect her from people she didn't know. The man was Vlad the Impaler, but Clémentine wouldn't dare acknowledge his last name, as it would prove to her that he was the one who tortured hundreds of thousands of people. The Romanian warlord had special 'forests' that scared other kingdoms to the point of giving him a frightening name that made his reputation one of the most dreadful ones.

"So," Clémentine asked, "Vampires can walk during day hours?"

"Only when the sky is heavily overcast. Then again, only a handful of vampires can do it. The valet you saw is a werewolf, and Maxim is too, not a vampire—not entirely anyways."

What was she doing? Clémentine braided her hair on one side and placed her hoodie back over her face, not wanting to show her sadness while staring at the rain hitting her window. They were on their way to the airport, the same one she and Mika had landed at.

The chauffeur took an exit that brought them down a dirt road, where she admired the vegetation and the magnificent weeping willows. The weather mapped her emotions so well and she thought it reflected what hid inside her mind.

As the rain fell harder, she fought her tears back. It was in moments like this that Clémentine would unconsciously pick at her bottom lip until it bled. Her nails were scratching the skin off her lip, but she felt a large warm hand closing on her own, and moving down her side.

"That's a bad habit that you have. We'll have to work on that. Those lips shouldn't be bleeding unless I—"

"Unless you what?" Clémentine asked, but then felt a warm bubble forming upon her bottom lip. She looked into Vladislav's eyes and saw them turn from green to a deep red.

"Unless I want them to," Vladislav said with a voice that sounded hypnotized by what he witnessed.

Before she could lick the blood off her lip, she saw Vladislav move his hand toward her. He gently ran his thumb across her mouth. His tongue slowly came in contact with the drop, and as he took it in, he closed his mouth, and his eyes turned darker. She wished another bubble would come out but she felt nothing as her tongue licked the scratch at the same time Vladislav's thumb rubbed her lip again for a last faint drop. Her tongue softly rubbed against his skin and she wished he would've moved closer, but his hand slowly moved away, his eyes fixed on her mouth.

"What does my blood taste like?" Clémentine asked, trying to keep her mind from going to a sad place.

"It is very flavorsome. I have not tasted much blood like yours." His grin was now back, showing a little peek at his teeth she liked to believe were now fangs as she quickly came to know that those were retractable somehow.

It suddenly hit her head like a brick the memory of Vladislav in front of what seemed to be his bedroom mirror and the attack that was made on him by creatures she couldn't see or hear. She remembered the fangs not being present until he had a hard time controlling his anger and the black shadow appeared in the room. Only then did she see his fangs coming out.

"How was it?" His voice brought her back in the present, but she didn't know how to answer him. "My memory of Judith attaching me. You saw everything. What did it feel like?"

His voice showed curiosity and she knew he deserved an answer because that memory belonged to him and him only. Clémentine remembered the scene as if the memory was now her own and a part of her life.

"It's like it is now printed in my mind. I felt everything from the linen shirt on your back to the last scratch those creatures inflicted on you. I felt their poison penetrating your skin and leaving a scorching sensation. I smelled your flesh burning, and there was this tingling sensation growing inside your belly and the extremity of your arms down to your fingers. You control those dark misty shadows, don't you?"

"Yes, I do control the dark mist you saw. It's a part of me if you will. I don't know how it came into existence, but it is something that I can control and use to my advantage if needed."

His eyes lay upon Clémentine, wh who couldn't help but stare into the crimson of his irises that were slowly dissipating into the jade of his green eyes. "Is that all?" Vladislav asked with a detached voice that seemed to hide much more.

"I felt your desolation, your anger, and your guilt. I felt everything from your hunger to the pain you endured from each of those scratches. It took everything in me not to scream out loud from everything that I was going through with you."

Vladislav's hands were now pulling down Clémentine's hoodie, and she saw his discomfort caused by the fact that she actually shared his emotions. She turned around to face her window, and her right nails about to touch her lip, but she felt him moving her hand away. She thought he would let go, but instead, he closed his hand on hers. He held it the rest of the drive, letting her know that she was not alone.

"Don't think I'm uncomfortable around you. I was in your head more than once and read your mind. It is only fair that now you see a part of my life. Besides, I cannot think of another person I'd rather share my mind with." Vladislav's voice showed confidence and it reassured Clémentine that he didn't feel abused by her involuntarily intrusion in his mind.

"Nonetheless, I am sorry that it happened," Clémentine felt the need to say, as she couldn't erase the offended expression on the guards' faces.

It seemed like it has been an eternity since she felt the refreshing breeze of Vladislav inside her mind. Suddenly it felt as if Vladislav knew exactly what she was going through in her head. Clémentine easily deducted by the look on the twin guards' faces that they thought she wasn't worthy of the prince's blood and needed to be put back in her place.

"You will come to know that I do not share my blood with anybody. My blood, to me, is like my body; it is not to be spread around for everyone to enjoy. I am very selective with the ones I choose to pleasure, if that answers your question at all. I let you have me first, Clémentine. I wanted you to taste me, and that's all that should matter to you."

Vladislav's voice was so deep, and comforting that Clémentine finally found the strength to relax. His hand never moved away from hers, preventing her from picking at her bottom lip as she would have done if not for his touch. His thumb rubbed the back of her hand and they finally arrived at their destination.

"A hangar?"

"Yes, we're taking my plane. I don't wish to attract unwanted eyes on us if I'd fly."

Fly? His grip was now gone and he got out of the vehicle and came around to open her door. He helped her out and guided her toward the door where the plane waited for them.

CHAPTER 17
WELCOME HOME

When they arrived at their new location, Clémentine was quickly welcomed by two guards. They took her luggage and showed her to the room that she would inhabit for the time she would remain by Vladislav's side. They were staying in the Stowe Victorian house that belonged to one of Vladislav's old givers.

When Clémentine was taken away from Vladislav, she had a hard time letting go of his hand. She automatically hugged herself. *I don't know anybody here...I'm alone. Who are these people and why am I here?* Then she heard Vladislav's heartening voice: *"You're not alone Clémentine. I'm here. They are taking you away for now because I need to attend to some business that I'll tell you about later. I promise."*

Clémentine entered the guest suite and quickly took off her clothes to lie down in bed and try to rest, but her mind was going a hundred miles an hour. She moved the covers over her head and tried to focus on the moment Vladislav leaned closer to kiss her lip and suck the blood bubble that burst from her lip. She tried to understand why he didn't do the same in the car, but there was no point in trying to figure him out. Clémentine tried to then focus on the way he glared at her, but then it would quickly move to the wicked stare he gave Frederick when holding him against the stone wall. She felt his tender touch on her hand again, but then recalled his grip tightening around the guard's neck. He was capable of so much brutality. It scared her to think that maybe one day he would do those things to her. Would he?

Clémentine suddenly felt the need to know more about Vladislav. She focused on the memory she lived when she tasted his blood but had nothing to awaken her ability to enter his mind, remembering that all the times she did get inside his thoughts were either because he pulled her in or she could recall something specific. She had no need of his help to find him, but to get inside his mind; she either needed an invitation or more of his blood.

This house isn't his, I may touch the wall and see memories, but they don't belong to him. This isn't his home. It has no memories of him. I sense nothing about him.

Clémentine suddenly remembered missing a spot on her finger when she licked his noble blood, and because of the fright from the guards and also the pain that the memory inflicted on her, she didn't dare taste the last of Vladislav's blood. She tossed the covers away and opened the duffle bag, finding her jeans. She saw the red spot and hoped no one was looking when she licked the fabric as hard as she could. Her eyes closed, she hoped it would work, but felt nothing. After a few seconds of licking her jeans, she decided to put them back in the bag, thinking she had been acting like

an idiot.

She crawled back into bed and rested her head on the pillow with her arm underneath. Resting on her side, Clémentine stared at the window and watched the sun slowly making its way up in the sky.

"I'm sorry, my prince. I'm sorry." Frederick was blinded by a black piece of fabric. His hands were tied behind his back with a cord which seemed made out of silver, or at least was dipped in it.

"What did I say about Clémentine? Tell me!" Vladislav shouted with his deep voice so full of anger that Clémentine could feel his arms and hands tingling and his lower abdomen freezing, ready to command the dark ash-like mist of the room and bend it to his will.

"You claimed her as yours, and she was not to be touched." Frederick's voice was trembling, his skin lacerated, and his blood was splattering each time a leather whip covered in silver spikes brutally hit his flesh.

"Then why did you try mind spelling Clémentine? Are you challenging me?" Vladislav's voice got deeper, and she felt his fangs slowly coming out, leaving a sensation of sting behind.

"No! No, I wouldn't dare…I was just testing her ability. I thought she was a fraud and was taking advantage of your generosity."

"Quit your bullshit, Frederick! You belong to Matthias, and you're just a spy reporting every single movement I do. Your actions are worth impalement, but François won't allow it, and I, for one, respect his home and the way he rules his sector for the time the Celt is gone."

The anger rising in Vladislav's body became overwhelming, and the sensation of tingling metamorphosed into a mix of ice and haze as he walked toward the Scandinavian guard. Vladislav grabbed him by the throat, and he squeezed harder when forcing him to look into his eyes.

"I never thought he'd find out. I never thought he could mind read all vampires at will...I just...I just needed proof to bring back to Matthias that he found the last Gravedigger. If we had her, we could force her to do anything we want as long as Octavian's being tortured. She still loves him." Frederick thought to himself, unaware that his prince could read his thoughts. *"Octavian is still too strong to capture, and this Clémentine is also tough. Matthias will need to know about Vlad's feelings toward her."*

That's the moment Vladislav discharged his current. The mist thickened from the back of the room, swallowing every shadow in its path. The guard's blindfold slowly became wet as red streaks emerged from underneath, showing Clémentine how vampires cried. Vladislav's grip loosened as his beastly growl was heard loud and clear.

"My feelings towards her?" Vladislav's voice was so loud that she thought he would burst his vocal cords. "I'll have a report for him. Frederick is never going back. The treaty between us is over. I'll get my guard back, but you're not going anywhere."

Clémentine felt through his body the strange current that allowed Vladislav to turn all shadows into that cloudy volcanic mist. As it approached Frederick, Vladislav took off the guard's blindfold, only to see his eyes burning from the silver paper sewn to the fabric to blind him.

The vampire prince penetrated his mind once more to hear his thoughts. *"Please don't hurt me. Please, I'm sorry. Heaven help me, please help me!"* Vladislav stood up and grabbed him by the chain which was holding him in place, "My hero." He said aloud as he moved his chest inches from the fire in the hearth.

Clémentine could hear Vladislav's thoughts as he felt Frederick's screams weren't enough. *"Nobody disobeys my commands."* Then out loud he growled, "You raped Clémentine the second that you imposed your will on her. You failed because her abilities are way beyond any of us. However, your actions remain one of a traitor and a fucking low life bloodsucking rapist."

Frederick's cries were deep and hoarse. They came out from a throat that sounded irritated by all the terrifying shouts it produced. As the sound finally cracked, it left a chill coming down Clémentine's spine. For a moment, Vladislav held Frederick away from the fire, and then pushed him onto the ground and crouched by his side to make sure he would hear François' verdict.

"Your interrogation now being over, I find you are guilty of rape against Dr. Clémentine Roy, Gravedigger of Shamanic descent. The victim and the prince will give your punishment to you. You are now released until your punishment is performed," Francois leaned over and said to the accused with so much pity, Clémentine felt sorry for the guard. "Poor little fuck. I wouldn't want to be in your place right now. You chose the wrong vampire to fuck with."

Vladislav's disgust against Frederick was almost as intense as his anger. He stopped the guards from releasing Frederick as François tried to let him know that he had no right to hold him like this any longer. But the prince stated, "She's coming to me, and I want her to see him like this. She needs to know that I am to be feared." What troubled Clémentine was the question from François, "Why do you keep hurting yourself like this, my friend?"

Clémentine then heard herself knocking on the door, still living Vladislav's memory through his eyes. She saw the dark mist dissipating as the current in his arms and lower abdomen burned out within him. Once the doors opened, she saw herself talking to the guards, but heard Vladislav shouting at his bald twins' heads, "*Dute din cale!*"

Clémentine could feel that Vladislav's emotions were torn between excitement and guilt. She could hear his thoughts, and although she wished she could hear more, she felt just as much guilt at having raped him of the memory she chose to see.

"As much as I wish it were not necessary for you to see me as a dungeon master, I need you to fear me, Clémentine. I need you to see whom you are attracted to. I'm a monster."

That was the moment she saw herself covering her mouth before stepping back. *"I can't stand the look on your face, Clémentine...Clémentine, I'm so sorry. I wish I didn't have to put you through this. Why, why did you disobey me! Why do I even let you defy me?"* His emotions were again mixed, as there was anger transforming into shame, a feeling she wished he would never have to feel again in her presence.

There was a slight breeze that circled the scenery surrounding her, and it slowly faded away. Clémentine came back to her senses the moment Vladislav's hands closed on hers in the memory and a strong current built in his body. She felt a slight sting as his fangs pierced through his gums.

CHAPTER 18
LET'S PLAY WITH FIRE

"What are you doing, Clémentine?" she tenderly heard in her mind as her sleepy eyes opened, fixing on the white ceiling. She never thought Vladislav could know she was in his mind for a short while, but it seemed the vampire had many abilities other vampires lacked.

*Vlad, I mean, um...I was just, um...*Clémentine's eyes stared at the ceiling. Her breathing was coming in quick snatches and her hands closed on the white bedsheets.

"I require your company. I am done for the evening and dining alone seems rather uninteresting now that you're here with me." Vladislav's voice was so

trusting and kind that she thought maybe he was unaware of her presence in his head. After all, the stain on her jeans was a day old and maybe out of his mind's reach.

"Sure. I'm not really hungry but let me freshen up and I'll join you."

Almost an hour later, Clémentine was in Vladislav's company sitting at a maple wood table with a bowl of homemade butternut squash soup and a piece of bread. It was just like the vampire prince knew what her routine was when she found herself unable to eat. Clémentine took a bite and looked into the vampire's eyes staring at her with kindness as he talked a little about his meeting with his previous giver that he had released years ago. Clémentine learned that givers took oaths to be the vampire's food, such as never to reveal any secrets from their master, or belong to another more powerful vampire once they were released from their oaths. This kept them from becoming threats to their old masters.

Vladislav made sure that Clémentine understood that the term master was only used as a definition of a boss rather than an owner of beings. He mentioned that it was purely tradition as givers were free to leave as they pleased after they would be mindspelled into forgetting anything important they might have heard over their time spent with their boss. Vampires were paranoid creatures and Vladislav added that their paranoia had been proven necessary on more than

one occasion.

When her her soup was removed and she was done with her bowl of grapes, Clémentine pulled her loose burgundy wool cardigan closer to her skin as if she tried to tuck herself in and looked down, trying to hide her sense of guilt for what she did. The sleeves falling over her fingers, she wiped her nose before that one tear betrayed her, but it was too late, Vladislav had his hand over hers.

Clémentine felt Vladislav trying to make her look at him, but she resisted and freed her face from his other hand. She played a melody in her head, trying to keep him out of her thoughts, but she knew it was almost impossible to hide anything from him. Vladislav was a very special and very unique vampire. She knew because she had felt it from the two memories she had shared from his mind. While in Vladislav's head, she could relive his most intimate thoughts, and she now feared his uniqueness would one night betray him, and it would mean his end had come.

"Is there something you wish to tell me, Clémentine?" Vladislav said as he rubbed her back and it made her want to tell him everything that she had done. The memory of Frederick being tortured took over, and she said, "I've raped your mind Vladislav." Clémentine couldn't feel his hand rubbing in circles near the back of her neck anymore. She pulled the wool hoodie from the cardigan over her head, hiding her face just before she hugged herself again, afraid and terrified of what he would do to her next. Tears rolled down her cheeks and she had this horrible burning feeling in the back of her throat, trying to let out the cries she was holding back. She recalled what happened to Frederick and feared for the worst.

The moment Clémentine was about to give in to her fears, she felt his hands pulling down her hoodie. His fingers moved through her jet-black hair, playing with her curls. That brought her some comfort and she began to calm down.

"So I felt," Vladislav said with a comforting, but distant voice.

"I just want you to know before you do anything to me, that I am sorry. I shouldn't have done what I did. It was only when you accused Frederick of rape that I truly understood what I was doing to you. I just hope that you'll forgive me. I was too curious about you. I was attracted to you before I met you." Clémentine replied, unable to bring herself to look at him in the eyes and instead fixed on Vladislav's lower neck.

Clémentine again wiped her nose with the back of her wool sleeve from all the tears that were falling. She then picked at her bottom lip but Vladislav took her hand away and lifted her chin with his
other hand.

"You need to look at me now or you will look at me now…" Clémentine lifted her head, but her eyes wouldn't follow; "…look at me. The only thing that I will do to you is this." She felt the warmth of his skin closing on her as his lips pressed against her cheek close to her mouth. She moved her head down and felt him kiss her next to her ear, and then her eyes as they closed she felt his lips on her forehead.

"Vladislav." She said, moving her hands up against her face where his were resting. "I want to know why you are so kind to me. I did abuse you. Why am I being forgiven?"

"Clémentine, while you did see a memory of mine, your intentions were not malevolent. Frederick raped you because he wanted to bring you to Matthias, who would've tried to enslave you. Don't you ever compare yourself to such evil. Again, I've entered your mind way more often than you did mine and if someone needs to be forgiven, it is me, not you."

Clémentine closed her eyes as she let Vladislav caress her face, then softly rub her earlobe with his thumb and index before running his fingers through her hair. She enjoyed and cherished the feeling of his long, thick fingers playing with her locks of hair. It relaxed her entire body, and her mind began to unwind. But she also was curious about Frederick's judgment.

"I already told François that your opinion wouldn't be required." His voice, so cold and detached, reminded Clémentine why she feared him so much.

"Why is my opinion suddenly irrelevant to you?" She needed to know why Vladislav would only treat her as an equal when he would see fit. Was he that much of an archaic being?

"Would you rather I explain to you all the torture that you can choose from? Would you like me to show you the dungeon Frederick will be kept in and ask you for your top three favorite torments you'd like him to go through? Is that what you want, Clémentine?" Again, Vladislav's voice was so cold she thought she would catch a cold, and she decided to remain silent.

"That's what I thought," he retorted when his eyes crossed Clémentine's, who stayed speechless and found herself unable to fathom in her most nightmarish thoughts of what this dungeon might look like.

She understood that all Vladislav was hoping to accomplish from telling François her opinion wasn't required was protection. He knew Clémentine wouldn't be able to inflict any pain on Frederick and so he took it upon himself to live with his own decision of torment.

Clémentine should've been disgusted and offended by Vladislav's horrible way of resolving issues. But she had no right to judge his ruling, nor did she have the right to judge his world. Although she was a monster herself, she did not understand this other world he was a part of.

"You are very special, Clémentine. You are afraid of me and yet you keep coming back and disobeying my every order." Clémentine moved toward him, hoping to see him uncomfortable for once, but his nonchalant smile proved to be strong thus far from being submissive.

"When I am hired to give seminars about the legends and folklore of towns, sometimes I wish I would get this one call that would have me go to the place you lived. I want to sense if you are still trapped in there somewhere. Tell me, will you ever show me the real you? Will you ever tell me your true story or are you still trapped in your fortress up above your enemies?"

Clémentine saw Vladislav biting his lower lip, his cheeks reddening, and the way he looked away from her showed that she destabilized him somehow. It felt good for once to be on the other side of the flushing.

"You...you wish to know more about my life more than you already do?"

"Of course, I would do anything. It is no secret that I am intrigued by the real you. Now that I know you are here, standing before me, it takes everything in me not to bombard you with a thousand questions."

Clémentine's fingers moved through a lock of Vladislav's thick black hair that fell over his eye. She caressed the contour of his perfectly shaped cheekbone with her palm, and then she felt his hand upon hers.

"I'm just Vlad, you know. I'm only a fraction of the monster I used to be." His voice hid a little nervousness as it discreetly shook, and he tried to look away.

"Vlad?" Clémentine asked softly as her voice too camouflaged nervousness, standing so close to a strong and powerful vampire.

"Yes?"

"Who are you?"

Like a chapter that would unexpectedly end in a disappointed way, the vampire prince walked toward the boudoir on the other side of the dining room. As she followed him, he raised both his arms to stretch. Watching him, she remembered the feeling of the current growing in both his arms and lower abdomen. That vampire had so much power residing inside him, she wondered how he was able to keep it all locked up inside. Clémentine was curious as to why Vladislav moved away so unpredictably. She thought she was going to finally hold him in her arms.

The one historical being that had fascinated and fed her imagination for so long stood right before her. Yet, when he turned around, it was only to let her know his worries. As she lost herself in the bright crimson of his eyes, she heard his smoky voice enchanting her.

"I can't be so close to you Clémentine. I'm still a vampire. Despite my age, because I'm different, I require more blood than I should. Normally, the older a vampire gets, the less nourishment he requires. I, on the other hand, need to feed almost every week, and since you walked into my life, I need it even more to suppress my desires."

"You think you're the only one?" Clémentine asked, while pointing at her heart. "This thing you fed requires all the strength I have not to slash someone's throat open to satisfy my thirst."

Both their words fed their starving imaginations in no time. Clémentine wondered what desires a vampire could have, but then he reminded her of the fantasy he had shared with her. She remembered when Vladislav said that he would carefully choose the women he wished to pleasure, and she wondered if she would be one of them. He smiled and whispered, "I said I would taste you again. I will let you taste me, and let you feed from me. But, right now, you are not ready. I can smell you morphing, but drinking now would be a mistake."

The night was now at its peak and the vampire prince needed to feed. Clémentine could tell by Vladislav's eyes darkening by the second, and she saw him reach out for a flask left on the credenza adjacent to the fireplace. Vladislav picked up the flask but it seemed empty. He shook it but nothing seemed to move inside the container. Clémentine suspected that Vladislav needed his nourishment at once.

"If you'll excuse me for a short moment." Clémentine grabbed his hand to stop him from leaving the room. "No, Clémentine. Don't. Not this time." He said crossly.

The vampire prince left the formal boudoir and entered a small room. Clémentine wished she'd known what he was doing, although she had a good idea of what he needed. Was he calling one of his givers? *"Yes."* Vladislav replied inside her mind. Her thoughts were about what it felt like and if they enjoyed it at all. Her thoughts surprised her with the jealousy she felt of what the giver shared with Vladislav.

"I promise I will give myself to you, Clémentine, but as for them, I numb their mind and throat, so they don't feel a thing."

Clémentine thought about the reasons why the vampire prince would numb his givers, and his answer left her weak, with a pleasurable sensation going up her thighs to the back of her neck. Clémentine wished Vladislav wasn't as much of a tease, but then again, she enjoyed his arrogance. Although, at that moment, she craved him so much that it hurt every sensitive part of her body. She blushed slightly at the indecent imagery that took over her mind, and her thirst for blood was growing.

I wish you would just take me if you want to do so. I won't stop you. Clémentine wished she would have kept that thought to herself, as she felt her cheeks warming.

"The night I will give in to you, I promise I won't stop, not even if you beg me."

CHAPTER 19
ALWAYS A TORTURER

The next morning, Clémentine was back in her own bed. She remembered Vladislav telling her a story about his past. Later, she remembered him running his fingers through her hair until she fell asleep.

"One of his men must've carried me back here," she mused half out loud.

"No, he held you in his arms and brought you back here himself. Which is surprising, considering that all the years I've known him, he has never done that before. He must really care about you." A charming silvery voice replied.

She quickly sat up on the bed and looked toward the entrance, where she saw a tall man wearing a brown leather jacket with a pair of dark washed jeans and cowboy boots. When Clémentine took a good look at his face, kissed with a bronze tan, she realized he must've been in his mid-thirties. He had a very thick medium length hairstyle with long locks of espresso brown hair with a hint of black falling on both sides of his face. His eyes were a strange silver and black color mixed and looked quite ghostly. His elongated square jaw seemed somewhat familiar, and so did his overseas accent. She was acquainted with him; she felt it but somehow couldn't pinpoint the origin. His strong arms were crossed over his chest as he leaned on the doorframe. His thick masculine lips parted and he finally said his name.

"I'm Naten. We met. I'm here in replacement of Violette, who went along with Mika and Maxim. I will show you around, and later, Odette will probably want to meet you. She's the owner of the house, although the land and buildings belong to Vlad. Not to raise any suspicion, but he kindly asked Odette to own this place physically."

Clémentine agreed on the tour but asked the young man to leave her for a short moment so she could take a shower and put on some fresh clothes. Clémentine watched Naten turning around to leave and she noticed his large, broad shoulders. His physique could almost be reminiscent of Vladislav, but no one in Clémentine's mind could be as seducing as the Romanian prince. Naten seemed to be a few inches shorter but he still had quite a noble presence emanating from his posture and voice.

She slowly recalled Vlad's warm breath near her ear, his lips closing near her own, kissing her skin as an attempt to calm her mind. She knew Vladislav tried to make sure she wouldn't forget about him in bright daylight, and he did right. Merely the thought of him made her wish Vladislav would be by her side. But, he was sleeping the sunshine away, and he had left her alone in the company of a man whose presence somehow almost felt as overpowering as his own.

Clémentine wished she knew where Vlad rested for the day. She would've walked to his room, and lay down by his side in his...um, coffin? Did he sleep in a wood coffin, like in the movies? Did he own a bed like in many novels that she read? That thought somehow had her thinking about all the books and television shows she watched about vampires. As she stepped out of the shower, she tried to make sense of all the information she gathered on them over the years.

Once dressed, Clémentine joined Naten, who waited for her at the end of the corridor in what seemed to be a private living room. His smile was almost as charming as Vladislav's but lacked the confidence that came with his reputation. Naten moved his right hand behind her. With a subtle touch on the small of her back, he showed her the staircase at the end of the corridor to guide her toward the main entrance.

"It's such a nice day outside, I thought we'd do a tour of the garden," Naten said with such a bright smile.

"You're the guide," Clémentine said as she smiled and stepped outside.

Clémentine put on her faux short sheepskin silver-grey boots and wore a silver-grey wool toque before following Naten farther outside as she zipped up her black winter coat. Underneath, Clémentine wore a thick form-fitted burgundy and black striped sweater, over a pair of tight-fitting dark gray leggings. When she walked outside, she quickly reached for her wool gloves, finding the wind a little cold.

"I'm here to make sure you don't adventure alone in the mansion."

"Why is that?" Clémentine asked, wondering how much Naten knew about her.

"Vlad told me about your tendency to either disobey him or to sneak around."

"Well, I'm not that good with orders." Clémentine hugged herself, embarrassed about her intrusion in Vladislav's mind, wishing she could go back in time and stop herself from invading his privacy.

"It's okay, neither am I," Naten said with a smirk as he leaned toward her voluntarily bumping into her shoulder.

They walked through what must have been a very nice and impressive garden in the summer. However, in November, it was ready to endure a rough winter. That's the moment Naten confessed that he wanted her to see something Vladislav asked him to show her. Once they arrived at the end of the garden, there was a crafted iron gate covered in what seemed to be creeping plants. They were unable to see through the gate and the young man stopped, hesitating for a minute. Clémentine was confused as he grabbed both her hands.

Clémentine looked at his large hands entirely covering hers, and he slowly rubbed the top of the gloves. His head tilted forward, and he seemed to be trying to ask for forgiveness. His long dark espresso hair fell forward, and his full lips parted.

"I want you to know that what you're about to see, I am against it. I asked Vlad not to do this to you, but he said it was a necessity. I opposed but he insisted. No, rather he ordered me to bring you here." Anxious and nervous, Clémentine asked what it was, but Naten wanted to be sure she understood. "Don't get me wrong. I am all for the punishment inflicted on that filthy excuse of a creature. I would've done worse, to be honest, but I am against you witnessing it."

Naten turned toward the gate, ordering Clémentine to stay behind him. She tried to peak over his shoulder, but even on the tip of her toes, Naten was tall enough that she couldn't see anything that lay ahead. Clémentine guessed Naten was about six feet in height, just a few inches shorter than Vladislav. Naten held her hand and opened the gate. They walked by what seemed to be either an old guesthouse or what would've been the home of the caretakers back when the house was built.

They walked past the building and entered on the side toward the back, where there was a stone entrance shaped like an arch. An old heavy wooden door rested in the stones, and Clémentine knew what would be there when Naten opened it. She didn't want to see it. She squeezed his hand so hard she thought he would've withdrawn it, but instead, he turned around and looked straight into her eyes.

"I have to show it to you, but you don't have to look if you don't want to."

"What were his words? Please tell me," Clémentine asked as she saw Naten looking away not to cross her gaze any further.

"He said I had to make sure you would see him, but he doesn't need to know you didn't look." His hands rested on both her cheeks, but Clémentine knew there was no way around Vladislav's orders.

"He will know, and somehow, I know you know this better than I do."

Naten held her hands and said he would stay with her and never leave her side. Although his words were supposed to bring comfort, it somehow made her wish he stayed quiet. At that very moment, she thought about all the horrifying scenes from horror movies she had watched. She enjoyed a good scare, as long as it was entertainment and neither humans nor animals were hurt in the process.

When Naten reached for the doorknob where a heavy metal lock was hanging, Clémentine stepped behind Naten and grabbed the end of his coat. She heard him unlocking the padlock, and the heavy chain fell to the ground. As he slowly opened the heavy wooden door, she could tell it was very tight in the frame since he had a hard time pulling it towards him. Once the door opened, there was no sound. The smell of burnt flesh and iron spread out with the cold wind of fall, but nothing more.

Clémentine stood still behind Naten, and now both her hands were holding on to his jacket. She felt his right hand on the side of her thigh, warning her that he would turn around. "Keep your eyes closed as I turn around." He was now facing her, but her vision was blurry by all the moisture covering them. Clémentine begged him not to force her, but the expression on his face told her everything. As her tears fell, the guilt in his eyes showed.

"I'm sorry," Naten whispered as he moved her before him and held her close against his chest, hugging her tightly against him.

"Frederick!" She yelled when seeing the heavy wood stick coming out of his chest. Clémentine tried to move away from Naten.

"Clémentine, stop! You can't touch him!" Naten shouted as he held her in place.

"Take him out of there!" She ordered as she turned around, fighting his every attempt at holding her in place.

"We can't! We'll only make it worse for him!"

Clémentine turned around, and now that the anger had dissipated, the horrifying view sank in. She stared at Frederick, who was held above ground by the wooden stick impaling him. He was obviously burned in many places on his naked body. His clothes turned to ashes on the ground where his blood had been dripping for hours. His head was leaning down and he was unable to move or he would have to endure the pain. He never moved to look at Clémentine who wished he wouldn't because she felt responsible for his suffering.

Blood was dripping off Frederick's mouth which was partially open in a resting way onto his chest, only to fall down the wooden beam. Bruises were covering his wounded flesh and both his arms were resting on both sides of his body. He seemed to not be strong enough to make the effort or simply the idea of moving frightened her. She couldn't tell. The only image she had was of him in excruciating pain and it was her fault.

"This is entirely my fault, Frederick. I'm so sorry. I wish I had never met your torturer." Clémentine whispered as she let herself fall onto the cold dirt where dried dark leaves were covering the ground. Both her hands were on the frozen dirt and she felt her tears rolling down her cheeks. Naten, who roughly turned her around to face Frederick, quickly helped her up. His frown and his tenor voice were new to her but what he said shocked her even more.

"You feel sorry for that piece of shit? He raped your mind and was ready to abduct and sell you as a slave to Matthias. Do you have no self-respect?"

Clémentine stepped back from Naten's grip and slapped him. The young man moved away, and as he violently opened the door wider, he shouted, "You're lucky Vlad respected Clémentine's kind heart and only impaled you here. If it would've been me choosing your fate, you'd be thrown in a coffin alive and wrapped up in silvered bandages for as long as you'd live."

Clémentine saw Naten get in the exterior dungeon cell and barely heard him whisper. "You get close to her again and I'll make sure to turn your life into a nightmare. I am Vlad's best friend and he taught me everything he knows. Believe me when I say that I possess the knowledge of how to make you wish you were never born." Then she heard the most dreadful scream she had ever heard. It came from such a deep place in Frederick's body that his voice gave in and cries were heard. It went through her body and left her veins   cold.

CHAPTER 20
BEWARE THE PAST

Naten stepped out, shut the door as forcefully as he could, and locked it behind him in front of Clémentine who remained outside aware that a shed attached to the mansion was in fact a dungeon cell. Clémentine watched him walk down the little cement step and let him grab her by her upper arm to walk back to the gate. As they walked past the building, just before the arched iron gate covered in creeping plants, she forced him to stop by not following his steps any longer.

"Come on. We have to go back to the house." Naten said as he grabbed Clémentine's hand, but she withdrew it at once to make him pay attention to her.

"I'm sorry I hurt you, Naten. It won't happen again." Her guilt for having slapped the one person who cared about her in this madness that seemed to have become her life needed to be washed away with Naten's forgiveness.

"It's...it's fine. I might have deserved it. No, I mean, I did deserve it. I just couldn't understand why you felt pity for a vampire who tried to extract information out of your mind then sell you like a piece of meat to his master. The only difference between a vampire rapist and a human rapist is that they take over your mind and adjust your thoughts to their liking. However, the essence of the gesture stays the same. Frederick is not a kind vampire; believe me. He was an abuser and sociopathic killer when human. There's no moral compass with him."

Naten stood before her, both his hands in his front jeans' pockets. His caramel brown faux leather jacket was open, showing his buttoned-down beige shirt that allowed Clémentine to see a gold chain around his neck. She wondered if it was only a chain or if there was a pendant attached to it. Then her attention quickly turned to something else. Clémentine found herself still under the impact of what Frederick would've done to her, so she tried to think about something else. Focusing on Naten's clothes seemed to be a good start until her imagination started running wild. She was torn between Frederick being tortured and his fangs stuck in her throat. It seemed that nothing could calm her mind.

"I...I guess I didn't realize what he would've done to me," Clémentine said as she hugged herself.

"He would've ravaged you. He's an animal and not the good kind. I'm sorry if I'm out of line here, but not all vampires are the Romanesque kind. In fact, only a few handfuls are." Naten said with much comfort in a soft voice as he took Clémentine's face in his palms to make her understand how much of a monster
Frederick was.

"I guess Vlad isn't one of those." Clémentine smiled uncomfortably as she looked away.

"Why would you say that?" Naten asked, trying to understand her train of thoughts.

Clémentine knew who Vladislav was to Naten, his best friend and oldest one. But she chose to ignore it for the time being as she was now frightened to go back to the manor. She stared at Naten, and she could easily see the resemblance, and his charm was undeniable

"If he was a Romanesque kind of vampire, I would have never seen that terror back there."

Naten frowned again, his soft looking and rosebud lips were now tight, and as they opened, she could tell he was uncomfortable. Did he fear Vladislav as well? As they stood talking, another imposing man walked and Naten introduced him. "Damian

Blackwood, Vlad's adopted son." Damian said with a strong voice while pointing with his index finger toward the dungeon Frederick was kept in, "He wanted you to see to what end he would go to protect you. Believe it or not, it's actually a loving gesture on his part. This had nothing to do with you fearing him. He has feelings for you, which I've not seen him express or feel in over two centuries. You should just be thankful for his attention."

Naten, without physically touching Clémentine, moved his arm behind her back, and as she moved toward him, she could feel Damian's eyes staring at her. It was as if he was testing her every move. Something was wrong. She could feel it. In her thoughts, she began to wonder if Damian hid something darker than his father.

"Don't you touch her like that, you scumbag! You know she belongs to my father!"

"I did not touch her. Besides, I can do whatever I want, Damian. You know it."

Clémentine, eyes wide open, about to jump down Damian's throat, but she felt Naten's arms holding her away from Damian. He bent down and whispered, "Give me a sec. He's like a nephew to me. I suspect something's wrong with him." Clémentine nodded as he addressed Damian with a firm voice, "Belittle her again, Damian, and I swear I'll have you banished from my sector and claim Clémentine as mine. Your father would have nothing to say as your kind answers to me." Again, about to lose her temper, she heard Naten say, "Calm down. I'm helping you here."

Clémentine looked at Damian with a sour look. He had an even more condescending look on his face, harder than what she had seen from Vlad. He stepped away from Naten and reminded him that he had seen his father impale people for less than what he was doing with Clémentine. Although morbid, it was a somewhat comforting thought.

"Don't you have a wife to take care of, Damian? Weren't you here just to show off Coralie and fuck around?" Clémentine looked up, snuggled in Naten's arms, who kept his eyes fixed on Damian. It seemed that he was quite sure Vladislav would have them impaled if they didn't stop fornicating behind his back. Clémentine was about to say she only met Naten that day, but he stopped her, "If you say anything to Vlad, you know what I can do to both of you. Don't you ever think because you're a Tepes that I would not end
you both."

Clémentine heard a cry from a dog and automatically looked around. When she turned back, Damian had vanished. Naten said, "It's okay, it's all over now." Clémentine looked up at Naten and asked him what type of monster he was. He chuckled as he pondered her question. "I'm...I'm something other than a vampire, and way older than you might think."

Clémentine wondered about many things concerning Naten, but nonetheless, followed him back toward the mansion. The chilling wind of the coming winter was now present. As the day slowly faded away, she wondered when she would see Vladislav again. But she was also curious as to how long his son was staying around.

"Um…how long will Frederick stay there?" Clémentine asked Naten, uneasy as she crossed her arms below her chest trying to stay warm.

"He will be there until our departure, and then Vlad will decide if his punishment will end or if he will be impaled again once we set foot in his sector. Also, before you say anything, I didn't oppose you seeing him as much as I didn't agree, because I know that times have changed. What Vlad considers loving and thoughtful can be frightening for others. Remember, he was not called Vlad the Impaler for his love of knitting."

Clémentine continued to follow Naten to the house, and they strolled slowly through the withered garden. "I was talking about Damian mostly, but it's disturbing to know that Frederick will stay there a while." Naten tried to apologize, but he was still quick to mention that all Vlad wanted was the best for her, and so did he.

"Why does he care so much?" Clémentine asked, wanting to throw out several more questions.

"You really want me to talk about him, don't you?" Naten said with a chuckle as he looked down to face her.

"Yes. I want to know because you know him better than anyone else, other than his closest people." Clémentine replied, hoping it would be enough for him to spill everything.

"In all the years I have been by his side, I have never seen Vlad care for another being the way he cares for you. I've never even seen him date anyone. In his mind, what he asked me to do today is a gift and a sort of declaration of his affection for you."

Clémentine couldn't tell if she was scared or flattered. She choked on her saliva, and decided to take a moment to deliberate. There were thousands of questions jumbled in her mind. She wanted to know more about the man Vladislav used to be and the vampire that he had become.

"A moment ago, I wanted to leave and ask you to call me a cab, but—" Clémentine heard Naten cutting her short by saying, "Please, don't do that. Give Vlad a chance to explain himself. I told you, this was supposed to be—" A third voice suddenly cut him off, "It's okay, Naten. I'll take it from here."

Clémentine looked at the tall man stepping away. The lady bowed to him and he responded with a short one of his own. "I will see you either later today or tomorrow. Contact me if anything is not to your liking Mlle. Roy."

An older lady was now standing beside Clémentine. She immediately knew it was Odette, just by the way she appeared and acted around Naten. There was a unique coldness in her posture, and she somehow left the impression that she ran the place. She probably did. However, the only thing Clémentine knew was that Odette was Vladislav's giver. What Clémentine didn't know was that Odette was his prime giver. She was, therefore, his only source of blood for a very long time, until he let a younger lady come in.

"I could've been Vlad's sole source of sustenance, but I forgot what my place was and he went after another source of nourishment for a time." Odette's voice seemed to show guilt and her eyes were full of shame. She really cared for Vladislav and it was deeply felt in her every word. "I fell for him. I shouldn't have because he warned me that he would never be able to love again. He said that emotion left him a long time ago and he didn't wish to live with it again."

Clémentine was now filled with confusion. Naten told her that he never saw Vladislav care for another woman in such a way for all the years that they had been together. She might not have known how brotherly their friendship was or how close they were.

All Clémentine knew was that Vladislav was incapable of love and it left her wondering if he was worth all the fantasies she had. Would they ever share anything real in the end?

Clémentine listened to Odette talking about the memories of Vladislav that they had shared together. Her eyes were lost in space. Odette barely ever looked into Clémentine's eyes. It made her feel somewhat superficial in the scenery of the garden. She thought maybe Odette saw her as nothing but an obstacle in her way to reclaim what once was her prince or as she wanted to see Vladislav.

"He used to come to me every time he needed someone to listen to him. He would step into my room and sit by the window. Sometimes he would stay silent. But other times, he would ask me to come sit at his feet and he would play with my hair. He would stay for hours at a time with me."

Clémentine wondered if when he would require her nourishment, how he would feed off her. What she said next, explained what a prime giver had the privilege to share. It somehow awakened a little jealousy in Clémentine, who thought she would never feel such feelings toward someone she barely knew. However, she had to remind herself that she was dangerously attracted to him.

"I remember every time he fed off me. He would make me look into his eyes and I would fall asleep. When he was finished, I would awaken in my bed. He wouldn't leave right away. Like a true gentleman, he stayed with me for a while before leaving. I always knew he would come back to me a week or two later."

Clémentine could almost feel her love for Vladislav. It was very obvious. Odette's feelings for the vampire prince were true, strong, and very possessive. Odette had loved him for a very long time. Her feelings had never changed and most likely never would. Clémentine suddenly felt very uncomfortable in her presence and with good reason. The woman's platinum blond hair was flowing in the cold wind and the locks were wrapping around the neck that had belonged to Vladislav for a very long time. Her fear was that it was still true and the connection remained.

Odette's grey eyes were fixed on hers for the first time and it made Clémentine want to walk away. The sun was slowly falling from the sky and she wished Naten would come back. She wanted to be with Vladislav

"Vlad will now nourish himself off of you. You will fall for him as I did but remember that he will never love you. Although he never confessed it, I know that he loves me and that he will always come back to me.

"I have no intention to become his nourishment. I also have no intention to stay with him longer than I have to." Clémentine wished she would have sounded more convincing but her voice betrayed her.

"How do you expect me to believe you? You are still here. If he didn't mean anything to you, you wouldn't have come to Vermont. You could have left with your friend."

"The Belvoir Coven needs Vlad to represent us when we present ourselves to the world. I'm the last of my kind, and he saved me. I thought I might require his protection a little while longer. To be frank, after what I've seen and heard today, I believe he is not the help we need. Now, if you will excuse me. I have a cab to call."

Clémentine left Odette in the middle of the frozen garden and walked straight to the doors of the vast Victorian home. Deep down she almost wished it was hers. The mansion was three stories high, and constructed of burgundy painted wood. A large porch skirted the entire building, giving the sense of security and warmth.

From the front, the entrance was accessible by six wooden stairs. A tall double wooden door rested between two tall oval windows. The first floor had four French windows, while on the second; a large and tall tower was built on the right, with many smaller French windows embellished around the level. The third floor had a balcony in its center, where Clémentine guessed the master suite was situated. The shingle roofing was of dark gray, and three brick chimneys were elevated on both ends, with one just a little off-centered on the right.

The Victorian home was imposing and stood proud in the middle of a green landscape, surrounded by mature trees. Its stature was enchanting. Clémentine loved it but sadly, after her conversation with Odette, she felt hurt, helpless and like an imbecile. No authentic Victorian wallpaper, furniture, or decoration would be able to erase the sentiment of shame she felt to have fallen for Vladislav's vision of euphoria. She somehow thought maybe it had been his mind spell that lured her into believing that she was attracted to him. It was easier to think that then accept the fact that she had fallen for the vampire.

She marched down the corridor to the suite that was assigned to her. She stopped to admire the old Victorian painting hung above a decorative table. She recognized Vladislav, but also the younger man standing by his side. Damian had his left hand on top of Vladislav's shoulder as he sat in a rococo style chair in the colors of dark oak and forest green velvet.

Everything around her was so incredibly authentic to the time it was acquired, it almost felt like a perfect setting for a romance novel. Odette's words were revived in her mind and she heard that grating voice, saturated with bitterness, *Vlad will never love you. He will always come back to me.* Clémentine should've known better than to dream about a relationship with a vampire prince; the vampire prince of Romania to top it off. She opened the door to her suite, walked to the bathroom attached to it, and looked at herself in the oval mirror framed on the wall. Her eyes were red, her skin was pale, and she needed to rest. She didn't want to think about all that she had been through that day.

It then dawned on her that she hadn't eaten much since her arrival in Vermont. She turned on the facets of the ceramic shower, wishing it would heat up faster. She felt the need to wash Odette's voice away and forget everything she saw and heard that day.

As Clémentine let the water fall down her head and body, she wondered why Vladislav has not asked for her presence at the dinner table yet. As she glanced at the clock on the wall, she realized it was early for vampires. Vladislav was up, she knew that much, but he must have been hard at work on some of his vampire duties.

It's better that way. I don't think I want to see him right now. Who am I kidding? I need to see him and ask him what this is all about. I want to know why he's acting as if he was single when he still has feelings for his ex-prime giver. I need answers. I can't have my heart broken all over again. I just can't.

With her left-hand, Clémentine decided to add more of the hot water, placing herself right below the jet to hear nothing but the water covering her ears. She tried to relax, but suddenly the vision of Frederick with a bloody stick coming out of his chest surfaced, and she could smell the burned flesh in the air. She opened her eyes in horror, but remembered what Naten had said. *"It was a demonstration of his affection for you."* Then it was quickly replaced with, *"He is incapable of love."*

Clémentine got out of the shower and wrapped a white towel around her body. She applied some vanilla body lotion to her skin and put on moss green underwear and a lace bra. She tied her wet hair up into a bun on top of her head to help her natural curls look better once dry. It didn't take long after that for Clémentine to feel Vladislav entering her mind. It was as smooth as a knife cutting through warm butter.

"Please Clémentine, don't leave me."

How did he know she was about to put her belongings in her gym bag and call a cab? Of course, he must have read her mind. Clémentine closed her eyes.

"I am so sorry Vladislav, this is just too much. This is not just fear anymore. You terrify me."

"Please, I have asked you to call me Vlad. I want you to stay. You have agreed to my protection and also to help me. Won't you stand by your word?"

She could almost hear him coming up from wherever he was. She put on her grey jogging pants, and was about to grab her light pink tank top when everything shifted. As she turned to head to the door, everything went black and she fell to her knees, slowing her motion to the floor. Then her world turned   black.

CHAPTER 21
MY ÎNGER

Clémentine's head felt like it was being hit with a hammer and needles were trying to scratch her brain. She barely opened her eyes, but nothing was staying in focus. She felt one strong arm wrapped around her chest while her body was resting against a man's torso. She looked up and recognized the wild black hair down his neck, and although she knew who he was, she could barely make out his face.

"Vlad?" It was so hard to talk. Clémentine feared she would be unable to speak any further.

"I'll speak aloud, you talk to me in my mind, my *înger*."

Clémentine felt comfortable against his chest. She could smell his mossy woodland cologne and she felt his fingers playing with her hair as if he was trying to keep her calm and relaxed. Her eyes closed again. The way Vladislav made her feel so secure and cared for brought in her a sentiment of serenity, but the moment she felt Vladislav's lips pressed against her forehead, she remembered all the things Odette told her. It brought tears to her eyes, and when she opened them to look up into his by moving her head further back, the tears rolled down her face.

"Why are you crying, my *inger*?" Vladislav's voice was so low, almost like a whisper. She felt his hand caressing her head, but then it stopped as he kissed her eyes and repeated the word *inger*.

"What does that mean?" Clémentine found the strength to say aloud.

"It means angel, because of the joy you bring me." Then she felt his hand moving a lock of her hair away before he said. "I'm sorry for what I've done to you. I thought showing you to what end I would go for you would make you realize I care about you. I guess you will have to show me how you wish me to show you my affection."

Clémentine reached for Vladislav's hair, which was loose on one side of his head to teach him a simpler way to share his affection. She realized he must've taken another shower after his "business," when her incident happened because his hair felt half dry and was curlier than usual. Most of all, they were loose like a fountain of a night sky; each bead of water sparkling like stars in the twilight. She wished she could've seen him more clearly and admired his wild and raw beauty.

Clémentine was so used to seeing Vladislav more formal, his hair placed and brushed back, but now it was loose. She could tell he only wore a tank top, because she felt his skin against her own and his legs were placed on both sides of her body. He was himself, nothing more and nothing less. Vladislav was not trying to inspire fear in anyone, or trying to impress his house. Clémentine tried to hold herself back but what Vladislav had shown at that moment was pure and she couldn't resist.

She closed her hand on a thick lock of his dark hair and was about to pull his head forward. She could now see his mouth softly opened and about to touch her lips. She felt it, his upper lip against her own, and the warmth of his breath. She even felt his arms strongly tightening around her waist. A burst of desire overtook her entire body. A low growl emerged from his throat and she could feel him swollen against her. The sound of footsteps entering the room was followed by a well-practiced worried voice.

"Oh no! Is she okay?" Odette asked overacting her concern.

"She will be soon," Vlad answered, tightly holding Clémentine against him, refusing to move his head.

Clémentine wondered how Vladislav would be able to help her when she couldn't even remember what happened. All she recalled was her desire to leave the mansion and call a cab to bring her to the Burlington Airport so that she could go home. She remembered hearing Vladislav's voice, and the rest was blank. What happened was nothing but a blur in her memory.

"You fainted. It was a good thing I was in your mind when it happened, or else I wouldn't have felt your thoughts going from grey to black. I ran down here as fast as I could and saw you lying on the floor. I took you in my arms and that's when you opened your eyes. You scared me, my little *inger*." Vladislav whispered in Clémentine's ear with the most tender voice she had ever heard.

To Clémentine, it almost felt like Vladislav wanted to hug her tighter, wrap his arms stronger around her body and kiss her, but he controlled himself not to. She felt his lips against her forehead, but there was no kiss. At that moment, Clémentine moved her eyes toward the entrance of her bedroom and could make out the silhouette of Odette, Damian, and Naten, and there were a few other people she had not
seen previously.

Tell me, would you have kissed me longer if it weren't for them?

"Yes, and I would do it now if it meant that you would stay and not threaten to leave me."

Do it.

"Yes. Anything you want."

His lips locked on hers, and his movement, although firm, stayed gentle. As his mouth slightly opened, she felt his tongue slip between her teeth and came in contact with her own. He held her tighter, and as their kiss changed from slow to more robust, he stopped. His lips still against her own, he whispered, "I must stop." He said as he moved behind her, his legs apart on each side of her body to hold her from behind against him for what would be next to come.

"Yes, I know." She answered aloud.

The kiss showed those in her room that he had great affection for her, simply because she had asked for a kiss he did. But then the words from Odette surfaced, and the nightmarish scene of Frederick in the solitary room in the outside shed-dungeon took over. It suddenly got mixed with the present moment where being lost in Vladislav's arms felt like the most wonderful feeling she had ever experienced before. She heard Vladislav clearing his throat to speak. Clémentine was curious as to what he would say, but his tone shocked her. It was even softer and gentler, somewhat a little different from what she had heard before.

"Clémentine, I have to know if you trust me. I have saved you before and I want you to know that I would do it all over again. But do you trust me?"

"Yes," Clémentine said, nodding, blaming her hastiness for answering on the horrible headache that she was experiencing. Vlad the Impaler was the one the Belvoir Coven needed despite her emotions, her hesitation, or jealousy from a memory. Vladislav had shown her nothing but kindness, sometimes in an arrogant way, but always with respect.

"My *inger*." Vladislav replied before he said, "Your thirst might grow, but I'm yours. All my blood belongs to you."

Clémentine heard loud gasps and obfuscated whispers. Her vision might have been blurred, but her hearing was still as sharp as a wolf. She could hear them, offended and shocked by what Vladislav just said. Then she heard a fruity voice traveling forward and it was one that she had not heard before. The mysterious voice was asking for Vladislav to let him do it for him, whatever it was, because Clémentine was unaware of what Vladislav's blood being given to her meant. However, she knew that she needed it. He already claimed her as his anyways, whatever that entailed.

"Don't touch her!" Vladislav growled at everyone present. Clémentine felt his arms squeezing tighter, almost caving in her ribcage before he continued, "My blood is mine to give. I give it to which I believe is deserving. Besides, I don't recall asking for any of your opinions."

Clémentine craved his blood. She had been fighting the desire to kill someone ever since she fell to her knees sick. She could barely think about the word without her insides moving to the thought of the sanguine liquid. Vladislav kept her in place with his supernatural strength. With her overly sensitive hearing, Clémentine heard a porcelain sound digging into something soft, but with a stiff resistance, and then heard a tear and unexpectedly something warm and wet was placed against her mouth. She couldn't resist and her mouth opened.

Her hunger won over her fear of seeing more from Vladislav's past. Her Gravedigger gift would soon take over and she would find out more about him. His memories, each more brutal than the next, would leave her either in terror or wishing she had done what he did herself. Yes, Clémentine had demons of her own. She was scared. His blood might have meant something more than feeding her when she needed it the most.

There were loud murmurs in the room. They were calling her names, as if drinking Vladislav's blood was an offense. She heard one loud masculine voice calling her a cunt for wanting to drink all of his blood. She suddenly wished she had left. She thought about getting up and running away that instant, but her body felt heavy. Every move she made had her so dizzy that she was unable to move. She stayed where she was and kept drinking.

Clémentine was no slut. She was not easy, and, in her mind, drinking the blood of Vlad meant she kept his wishes true, as she was his. Yet, her desire to vanish overtook her mind. A soft breeze enveloped her fear, sadness, and anger like a caress, and she heard Vladislav's voice fueled with anger shouting in Naten's direction, "Get them all out and take care of that *pulă*."

The door might have closed, but Clémentine could hear footsteps in the corridor walking back toward the bedroom. Odette begged Vladislav to let her stay by calling him, "My Vlad." Clémentine suddenly felt Vladislav's body crisping, his muscles were tensed, and she wondered if it meant he did have feelings for her. But when she felt his lower abdomen burning, almost turning to fire against the small of her back, she thought maybe nothing was left of the feelings he had once felt for her.

"You are testing my patience and pity for you. I have asked you many times never to say those words. I am not yours. Say that again, and I'll have your tongue cut off quicklife."

Clémentine knew that the term quicklife was meant as a great insult toward breathers, i.e., humans aware of vampires. Vladislav added, through her mind, that in the vampire world, quicklife was considered a swear word when referring to either a human or any other mortal creature. All that had Clémentine wonder about the relationship he truly had with Odette. She felt her body drowning in a cold sweat, followed by a sensation of being set on fire. Her vision turned to black and she only had the strength to mumble, "Vlad...Vlad, I need you."

"*Înger!*" Vlad replied as Clémentine dug her fingers into his arms to get his attention.

Clémentine felt her body being pulled up higher against Vladislav's chest and then she heard his flesh tearing apart once again. She felt him moving her, so her head would fall backward, and his other arm was now held against her mouth. She heard his voice like a disembodied echo.

As she was about to lose consciousness, she opened her mouth and the warm, salty liquid fell in. It almost choked her until she finally found the strength to swallow. Once she felt it going down into her body, there was a sensation of freshness and tingling. All of her pain was gone and she felt stronger than she ever had before. The recovery was almost instant and so she grabbed his arm with both her hands, holding it in place as she dug her tongue deeper into Vladislav's wound. As she drank, she heard him softly growl, and it would have almost been mistaken as a beast if not knowing he was a vampire.

The moment Clémentine opened her eyes, she realized her vision was clearer than it had ever been. She was not about ready to let his arm go, but she felt it immobile and offered no resistance to her grip. Clémentine felt Vladislav leaning back against the foot of the bed; he spread his legs wider on both sides of her body to leave her more space, and she felt his other arm pulling her closer to him. Her back now rested against his chest again, but never did she stop licking his blood. Slowly the wound began to close under her tongue.

"I want more," Clémentine whispered as she let go of his arm and turned around to face him.

"I know you do. You are a very hungry, little *inger*." Vladislav replied with a small chuckle and a smirk.

Clémentine felt Vladislav's hand caressing her head but all of her attention was on his arm. The wound disappeared, and she looked for a drop of his blood, but none was left. She had licked him clean.

"Look at me." Vladislav's voice was deep.

Clémentine turned again to face him. His eyes were on her lips. She saw him closing in, right next to the side of her jaw. Standing so close to her, his body touching her own so she would lie down. Using his vampire speed, they were now in the middle of the bed. His tongue snaked out and licked the blood that dripped off her mouth as he cleaned her face.

"You want more?" Vladislav asked with a loud breath.

Clémentine nodded but stayed silent as she fixed on his mouth. She saw one of his fangs scratching his tongue as he moved it along sideways to cut it open. She opened her mouth to let his tongue in. Clémentine felt his lips against her own again, his tongue against hers, and she would give in to him. Suddenly she heard a gasp. Vladislav's fangs retracted, and his mouth closed.

Both Vladislav's hands were on each side of Clémentine's face, and he made her look into his eyes, almost as if he was asking to be excused. She could tell by the crimson of his eyes that something was wrong. Clémentine rolled on her side to let Vladislav get on his knees to get up, and she grabbed his hand. Her wish was that he would stay because she feared if he left, what they had at that moment would be taken away. She tried to beg him with her eyes but he crouched by her side, and giving her a quick kiss on her head, he began to get up. She slowly let go of him.

When Clémentine heard the door close, she wondered how long it would take for Vladislav to heal his tongue. It took about two minutes for his arm to heal, but she remembered her tongue moving in preventing it from closing. She compared it to the time he took the pocketknife to cut his palm and it was almost instantly gone. Maybe a few seconds, she guessed. As she sat there, she heard his voice growling on the other side of the door.

Her suite was in the shape of a T, and the entrance door was the foot of the shape. Her bedroom and master bathroom were on the right. At the same time, a vast living room was on the other side. Both spaces were divided with large mural glass French window doors that obviously had been renovated, as it was not something very common to the Victorian era.

Where Clémentine stayed seated, he could see a part of the corridor. However, she was mostly facing the living room. It suddenly came to Clémentine's mind that when she was packing her things away, she only wore her bra; did everyone see her in it? She quickly looked at herself and realized she wore a large white vee neck sweater. She gave a sigh of relief. Then she thought about Vladislav in a tight tank top, showing his muscular arms and abdominals. She wanted to touch him again and feel his skin against hers.

CHAPTER 22
DESCENT TO MADNESS

A bloody memory...

"...Vlad, I love you, and you cannot tell me that after all this time, you don't love me."

Clémentine stood in a large bedroom, but her attention was on the walls. They were covered in old aged baroque fantasy wallpaper with intricate swirls and feathers with flowers. The large bed on the right had sheets that were in colors of gold and gray. The large guillotine windows on both sides of it were open to let in a cooling breeze and the furniture all around was antique pale beige from the same time period as the wallpaper. Everything was in mint condition.

When Vladislav's attention turned back to the woman who had been clearly talking for a while, although disinterested in her feelings, his eye landed on Odette. The woman must have been about twenty years younger, surrounded by a decoration that was much different than the mansion in Stowe. However, the colors and the style itself seemed to be of the eighteen hundreds.

"More than once have I warned you about this, Mrs. Lefebvre. The love that you have for me is not something that I feel."

Vladislav's words were true because Clémentine could feel his sincerity and his every emotion. While in his memories, nothing could be hidden from her, and she felt relieved despite questioning the emotions he had for her. Instead she chose to focus on the memory.

"Then why is it that you always come to me?" Odette's voice cracked as her eyes filled with tears and started overflowing onto her reddened cheeks.

Vladislav looked upon her face, and he felt compelled to tell her the truth, despite her feelings. It hurt him to know he would come to let her understand that what she thought happened between them on his part might have been nothing but pity.

"When I found you, you were a young lady wandering the streets alone. I could smell your virginity a mile away, and I knew it would attract others like me. I took you in before you could be attacked. What I did, I did for me, but also for you as I knew I could give you all that you wished for...money, luxury, a castle, and save you from a fraternity of merciless vampires that wasn't under my jurisdiction coming your way."

Vladislav's memory of Odette was nothing but true. If it had not been of Vladislav, Odette would've been ravaged and all her blood drained. He found her, took her to his home, and gave her everything that she had ever dreamed of, but it wasn't enough.

"You expect me to believe that was it?" Odette's eyes watered up. Her brows lowered as her ringing voice got louder in anger.

"Yes, because it is true. I took you in, I made you my prime giver, and gave you everything that a prime should get. You had your own quarters, you had some privileges that only the prime giver of a prince should have, and I respected your status." Vladislav's voice sounded desperate for Odette to believe his words.

Although Clémentine could feel how real his words were, sadly, Odette seemed to be lost in a mirage and refused to accept the reality of her surroundings. There was something Vladislav hid and was out of Clémentine's reach. She might have felt tempted to grab it because she could have, but refusing to be a violator again, she let the memory play through untainted.

"My dear, you come to me and sit in my bedroom for hours!" Odette's hands reached for Vladislav's face, but his grip tightened around her wrists as he gently moved her away from him.

"I once did when I was told you were feeling rejected by me. Have you forgotten how many times I had to remind you that you were my giver and not my lover? I have warned you a hundred times over not to confuse my connection to you with love." Vladislav tried to sound clearer, but he could tell Odette only heard what she wished to hear.

"It is now clear to me that nourishing myself from you only and my gift of a long life to you might have you confusing privileges with love. Our blood might have touched once, but it has been a mistake that I promised not to make again. You are a prime giver to me and have never been anything more and never will be."

It was with sadness that Vladislav said those words, and although he meant each of them, it had not been any less painful for him to speak aloud when he witnessed Odette's eyes overflowing with tears.

"I refuse to believe this, Vlad!" Odette's eyes were half-closed as her body leaned forward as if she would fall to pieces with another word, so the prince held her up in a very distant way.

"I respect you as my prime giver Mrs. Lefebvre, respect me as the prince." Vladislav's tone of voice was icy. It was obvious that he tried his best to make his prime giver understand her place and not to overstep her boundaries.

Clémentine could feel Vladislav's annoyance; he had tried to make Odette understand her place in his life more than once. Somehow the Romanian prince was attached to her, but if it wasn't because of love, what could it have been?

"Forgive me, but this doesn't change the fact that I refuse to believe I mean nothing to you." Odette's head tilted forward and her eyes fixed on the wooden floor.

"I am sorry, but another offense, and I will be forced to punish you. I am not yours and don't ever call me as such before anyone again. Present yourself as my lover one more time and it will be the end of our agreement." Vladislav coldly said as he was about to walk out her door to leave Odette alone with her sadness.

Vladislav closed the door and walked away from her quarters. He stopped Damian, who seemed to be on his way to an official event, wearing a very formal suit. Vladislav showed him something and the young man automatically followed the Romanian prince to his quarters on the third floor of what seemed to be a very vast mansion.

There was a grey mist taking over Clémentine's mind almost to let her know the memory was shifting to another time. She saw the two front doors of the mansion she was in from the previous memory opening widely. The sun was almost gone as she looked into the distance and saw traces of pink, lavender, and burned yellow in the sky. A black luxurious elongated vehicle stopped in front of the stairs leading to the manor, and a chauffeur walked around the vehicle to open the door for the woman standing beside Vladislav.

"Au revoir Madame Lefebvre et bon voyage," Vladislav said in Odette's maternal language. He was hoping it would somehow make her feel better, but the tears in her eyes showed isolation and a sentiment of being rejected.

"You promised me this wouldn't be the last time we would see each other." Odette's detachment was well-practiced, but there was nothing she could do to hide from Vladislav. He had tasted her way too many times and could see through her act easily.

"You know me to always keep my promises but you need time away from me. This is not a punishment. It is for your own good." Vladislav knew what she would say next, and it hurt him to have to tell the truth.

"I am to be replaced, am I not?"

"It has already been taken care of," Vladislav answered as he nodded.

Vladislav helped Odette in and kissed her forehead before she would leave his home and be on her way to Vermont, where she would move into the new home he had bought for her. It would soon be under her name for his convenience, should he ever need to go to North America. The goodbyes were heartfelt and painful for both of them, more than he ever thought it would be. As he kissed Odette a second time on her head, he heard her whisper.

"I'll never forget the night you made love to me."

"Nor will I," Vladislav answered. It was the truth, but the emotions he felt were very hard to describe.

The window closed and the vehicle left the entrance and passed the gates down the path that led to his home. Vladislav stepped back slowly and as he was about to turn around to walk back toward the door, he saw Damian coming toward him with his new giver.

The woman would be his new prime probably for the next forty years. This time Vladislav would be very careful not to hurt her, or at least he promised himself as much. "Miss," Vladislav said as he stared at her, unaware of her name and barely interested to know.

"I am the prince you'll be serving. You may refer to me as such." She raised her brows and showed disinterest in the prince as well, "Hello, my name's Bianca."

Clémentine felt Vladislav's emptiness and his cold detachment to the new giver. She wondered if Odette caused it all. Maybe he did have feelings for her but never wanted to acknowledge them. As the memory faded away, she realized that she would never know the answer. That is, unless Vladislav himself would agree to reveal what he had been hiding for all these   years.

CHAPTER 23
PAIN OR NOTHING AT ALL

The moment the memory finally dissipated, Clémentine wished it had been anything else. She heard Vladislav rushing in, as if he knew exactly which memory she had witnessed. He always seemed to know what she had seen. Her eyes were covered in tears as she realized that everything Odette had said was true regarding his ability to love, and it left her heart breaking. The worst part was, it left her feeling ashamed and humiliated to have even considered sharing her bed with him.

Clémentine got up from the cold floor where Vladislav had left her and grabbed her duffel bag, ignoring his presence in the corridor next the glass door. She was irritated with herself for letting Vladislav possess her mind so easily. She felt the need to walk away and never return even though she knew that what Vladislav felt for Odette were all emotions related to pity.

The problem was not his relationship with Odette, but the humiliation that she felt. Odette had warned her he would never be able to love. Yet moments earlier, she was ready to disregard it all based on the fact that she felt secure in his arms and the way he cared for her felt real. The memories awakened in her cut her open like a knife. Love was something that would forever be out of reach for both of them.

Maybe Vladislav wanted to lure Clémentine into becoming his new prime giver so that she would become his nourishment willingly. Perhaps he only thought about having his way with her and then throwing her out once he was done because, for all she knew, her need for his protection might have been a lie. Vampires are not to be trusted; that's what she read in novels and heard in shows.

Clémentine took her duffel bag and walked out of the T shaped suite she used. As she turned to her right to meet with the main staircase, she heard Vladislav's saddened husky voice cutting through the coldest silence she had ever been a part of in her entire life.

"Leave the bedroom I gave you, it's fine. I'll give you a bigger and more pleasing one. Walk out the door of my home and I'm gone forever." Vladislav's voice cracked, Clémentine heard it.

"I deserve more than this, Vlad." Clémentine passionately said as she stopped in her march toward the stairs. Vladislav walked up to Clémentine and she could feel his power surrounding her entire body. His hands both rested on her shoulders and his voice sounded so pained and hurt she felt as if a knife pierced through her belly and a fireball built up behind her throat.

"More than what? I have given you everything that I am. I have shown you how much I…please, my little *inger,* give me a chance. This isn't easy for me." Vladislav's words were choked by the pain in his voice and how low he spoke into her ear.

"I deserve to be loved, not just cared about. I had a life before you came into mine. Now that you claimed me as yours, I don't know if I'll ever feel loved again. I might turn mad as she did. I don't want that to happen to me. Yes, I am attracted to you. We kissed. So what? If I'm yours, you might find somebody else to love. Will I then be tossed aside like she was?" Clémentine managed to say with a burning sensation building up in the back of her throat.

Vladislav's eyes rounded, like a hammer had hit his head, and he stepped away out of balance without a word. With astonishment on his face, for once, he seemed to be without words. As the Romanian prince looked back at Clémentine, she noticed a thin red line underneath his irises, At least it proved to her that she somehow meant something to him.

"Clémentine, my *inger*, you have to understand that you're the first woman I have shared myself with or even let disobey me in over five hundred years. I have let you stop me, grab onto my clothing, and talk back to me. Never have I ever let anyone do this in public with me. Love was not something I thought I'd ever feel again because I never felt it since…since then." Vladislav's voice tried to hide his mortal past, but Clémentine had read all about it, she knew about her.

"I'm not like you, Vlad. I don't have an eternity to spare with only the hope that one night you will come to me and say you love me. That is if we fall in love with one another. What if we don't, and I'm stuck like her?"

"I won't rob you of love, Clémentine. If you ever find that I'm not good enough for you, I'll let you go. I promise." Vladislav said as he smiled with considerable pain, wiping his eyes with the back of his index finger.

Then both of them heard someone coming their way, so Vladislav moved back into Clémentine's bedroom. She figured he wanted to hide, so as not to appear vulnerable. She saw his strong back as he faced the other side of the corridor, his hair drying wild against the back of his neck. Clémentine knew

Vladislav had not shown any weakness to his men, his family, or anyone else in a very long time. Perhaps it had even been too long since he allowed himself to show anything. Somehow it pained her to see him brittle because of her. Nevertheless, she had to take care of her own heart first.

"If you decide to step back in, I promise to give you all that you had ever dreamed of and more. I will show you how much I care for you, this I promise. But, if you leave because you think I will never be able to love you, despite my confession, I'll understand. I won't hold you to your word, but don't ever come back, because all you'll find is a closed door and a threat to leave my land. I still have to act as Vlad the Impaler to protect my people...and you, from me." His voice cracked in between each sentence. "Because like you, I do have a heart and I do not wish for someone to break it again."

Clémentine never hesitated. She walked back to the room as fast as she could and into Vladislav's arms. As soon as he heard her steps, he turned around to pick her up. Her legs wrapped around his waist and he brought her to the bed where he gently laid her on the edge of the mattress.

Vladislav sat beside her, but she stood back up, and he spread his legs apart so she could stand in between. Clémentine's body was so close to his that she could feel his warmth mixed with fire. She lost herself in his emerald eyes, a thin red line still present, reminding her of the pain she might have put him through threatening him to leave for the second time in one night.

Clémentine leaned in to kiss his sadness away. Her lips came in contact with his eyes and she felt Vladislav opening up to her. His arms moved around her body, his hands then moved down, stopping at the small of her back. After a short hesitation, both hands moved to the sides of her hips. She found herself wishing she was wearing something other than a pair of grey jogging pants.

"It doesn't matter to me what you are wearing. You're beautiful regardless," Vladislav's whisper sounded like a whir.

"You're a good liar," Clémentine answered with a smile wishing he were shirtless.

When Clémentine backed away from Vladislav, she licked her lips to grasp any blood left from his eyes. When she looked down into his eyes, she noticed the pain still present in his mind. As she glanced at his mouth, which was partially opened, she couldn't look away from his enticing curved lips. As she stared, she gasped when seeing his fangs piercing through. Her eyes moved up and saw the bright emerald green dissipate into a swirl of crimson.

All of Clémentine's fantasies suddenly competed in her mind, as a sudden rush of heat possessed her body from her lower abdomen to her loins. She craved Vladislav and her inner thighs burned from the desire of letting him in. When Clémentine saw the cocky smile on Vladislav's face, she knew he had read her mind. While his guilt was gone, she was not sure how far she was ready to go yet.

Both of Vladislav's hands were now on Clémentine's waist and in a vampire second, she was lying on her back. Vladislav was moving in closer with his fangs showing through, and his grin now pressed against her skin. It was there he stopped. He lifted his head away from her cheek.

"I'll only go as far as you want me to, Clémentine. I would never force you to do anything you wouldn't be comfortable with but I promise you it is as pleasurable as you've imagined." Vladislav said with an overconfident grin.

Clémentine then felt him deep in her thoughts. He was not trying to access her memories but reading her emotions. She felt that he was confused and troubled. Clémentine saw him move his head from the side of her neck to face her. His body now rested upon hers and his hand caressed her face. The moment his kiss touched her cheek, she pressed her face against him. She didn't want him to stop but she did need an explanation about the guilt he felt.

"The reason I entered your mind is because if I want us to share an intimate bite, I need you to feel what I feel. That way you go through the pain a mortal wound would inflict on you. I need to guide you into my mind and make you share what I feel as I bite you."

"It might sound strange, but I know because I shared your memories, and some of your vampire instincts were revealed to me. I understand the procedure. If you don't share your mind with me, I'll feel the bite and the burn. I know."

Clémentine knew all about a vampire's bite because of all that she had shared with Vladislav through his memories. Vampire instincts seemed to be very hard to suppress. She even was aware that once a vampire was aroused, there was not much that could quell their desire to bite over and over, as it is part of their nature. It reassured her to know Vladislav was so tender and kind, but what about his guilt?

"Then why are you suddenly distant with me? Is it because you wish for me to feel love before we go any further?" Vladislav's confusion was apparent on his face as one of his brows lowered, and his head tilted to the side.

"No, not at all."

Clémentine shook her head and caressed Vladislav's face with her hand. She wished she hadn't seen the memories of Odette. She desired even more not to have heard her words from earlier that day. Clémentine's eyes fixed on Vladislav, hoping he would say or do something that would only prove to her that there was hope for them and it would not only be all about their attraction to one another. She thought about his prime giver's words earlier that day and she was so scared to have her heart broken again. But she remembered Vladislav's words from earlier. *"Because like you, I do have a heart, and I do not wish for someone to break it again."*

Clémentine felt his kiss on her palm. He was holding her hand with so much care. She thought he would've said something to make her feel his affection for her but suddenly his eyes looked up and they were of a different type of red. The guilt he had been feeling had been replaced by fury. Clémentine tried to move away, but his strength was too great. She was stuck beneath him, unable to free herself from his grip. When Clémentine turned her head to the side, she noticed that the room was drowned in a thick white mist. At the same time, Vladislav's temperature was lowering, almost to the point of icing her abdomen. His lips were pressed tightly together, and she began to fear for her life.

"Vlad, you're scaring me," Clémentine said, her eyes terrified, as they opened wider when she realized he would not move. "Vlad, please! You said you would never hurt me."

There was no response from Vladislav. Clémentine thought maybe he despised being refused and wished to possess her regardless of her feelings. Clémentine felt powerless and weak, unable to move. She thought perhaps the only way left was for her to use her mind. She shared his emotions. She knew him deeper than most and refused to believe he was just an ancient vampire about to take advantage of her. Vladislav was more than that.

Vlad, please, you said I was your little igner because I brought you so much joy. Remembering those words made me stay. Nothing else would have made me stay other you calling me your angel.

The mist might not have gone away, but Vladislav's grip loosened and the red in his eyes moved from bright to dark. Something was happening. She was getting to him.

"Say that I'm your *igner* again, please…baby."

Vladislav's eyes slowly rounded as he ran his fingers through her hair. Clémentine heard him say sorry a hundred times over and his arms slid beneath her to hug her tight.

"Baby? I have never let anyone call me that before." Vladislav whispered in her ear.

It only took a second for Clémentine to remember that Odette had been threatened with punishment because she called Vladislav hers. She wondered about all the atrocities she could be put through having given him a pet name with the sole purpose to show him that he meant something to her and that she cared for him.

"You can call me anything you wish, Clémentine. I have asked you to call me Vlad, haven't I?" Vladislav made it sound as if it was a privilege. "It is. If you pay attention, you'll see that everyone around here except you, Naten, or my son have the right to call me Vlad. One thing I would prefer is that you not call me baby in front of my people...for now." Vladislav added with a smile.

"You loved her," Clémentine said as if it was a sudden realization.

CHAPTER 24
PSYCHOPATHIC GUILT

Vladislav moved from Clémentine as he still lay upon her, but once on his back, she felt his fingers quickly reaching for a lock of her hair. His head was resting on its side and he was looking at her hair. Clémentine wondered where this habit of his started and if it brought him the calmness he seemed to be looking for. When his eyes met hers, she listened to him, finally opening up and answering one of her most important questions.

"I did not love her. What she had mistaken as love was pity and guilt." Vladislav answered with much detachment.

"You two did sleep together. You said you would never forget it." Clémentine added almost jealousy to the memory.

"I did," Vladislav answered after he cleared his throat. He looked Clémentine straight in the eyes, and told her everything; "Mrs. Lefebvre was a virgin when I took her in. She agreed to be my prime giver in exchange for all the privileges that it would bring her. She also agreed to be mine entirely. She willingly accepted those conditions and understood every word as I explained it to her."

Clémentine was now on her side, facing Vladislav as he also turned on his side to face her. She felt his hand moving forward to reach hers. His other hand was still lost in her hair as he kept going with his memory of Odette.

"One night, it was brought up to me that Mrs. Lefebvre had secluded herself and declined to eat. When I went to see her, worried about her well-being, she confessed to me that she refused to be a virgin forever, so she begged me to release her."

"What did you do?" Clémentine asked, wanting to know the rest of the story.

"I asked if that was truly what she wanted because I would do so. I never forcefully kept givers against their will. My givers were always free to go as they pleased. Mrs. Lefebvre said that she wished to go because she felt rejected, uncared for, and undesired."

"Was it true?"

"Yes."

Vladislav's answer sounded filled with regret. If those feelings were non-existent, he was only sharing the truth with Clémentine. She realized that it had led to the biggest mistake of his life.

"Because of my guilt that she was feeling those horrible emotions, I decided to spend a little more time with her if that was all it took to make her happy. I would come by her chambers a few times a week and have small talks. I would have her nourishment directly from her wrist, instead of my flask. Although I noticed a change in her eyes, I never thought it was serious. Instead of looking at me as her boss, the spark in her eyes should have warned me of her attachment."

Clémentine noticed Vladislav swallowing harder before he continued with the story. She feared they were approaching the night that he had spent with her.

"One night, I sat in her rocking chair by the window, I asked her to come to me so I could quench my thirst. As I was drinking, I felt her fingers running through my hair. I looked up and saw her biting on her lower lip. I should've walked out but I knew what I did to her. The guilt I felt was enough to allow myself to give her one night. That's the least I could do, I thought. But she's been holding on to that one night for forty-two years."

"Wait, you slept with her one night? That's all she ever had?"

Clémentine wondered if it was because Odette was a virgin that Vladislav wanted to keep her to himself. She heard Vladislav through her mind, at first shouting to get her attention, then his voice lowered to his normal tone.

"The same rule goes for a man. I'm just not attracted to them that way!" His voice lowered. "Mrs. Lefebvre was always welcome to have relations with other mortal men in my house, just not another vampire because of the mind spell factor. It would be too dangerous for me to have secrets revealed to enemies and it is part of their oaths when they accept to   be our nourishment."

"Oh, I guess I overreacted a little." Clémentine expressed, feeling her cheeks warming up as she looked down.

"It's okay. You couldn't have known." Vladislav answered, moving his hand under her chin to make her look into his emerald green eyes while he went on.

"Remember when I said I need to guide your mind into mine when I bite you?" Vladislav asked, and Clémentine nodded. "Well, when I have an intimate relationship with a mortal, I do it almost instantly to make sure I don't hurt them. However, when doing such a thing, you share a very secret part of yourself. You add to that the emotions that you go through while being orgasmic and it can be very overwhelming.

I guess what I am trying to say is that when I bit her, I accidentally scratched my lip. A few drops of my blood came in contact with hers."

"What does that do?"

"It creates a connection. The more you share, the stronger the connection is. Somehow she felt it and confused it with love."

There was something Vladislav was not telling Clémentine and she knew he wanted to say it. He refused to say it aloud. She moved closer, her hand holding his face in place, and she saw his brows lowering and a grin widened in the corner of his mouth. It was almost as if he was daring her to fish the information from his mind. Vladislav was lying on his back and both his hands were moving up and down her back.

"Do it. It's okay." Vladislav said.

Clémentine went in easily, having shared Vladislav's memories enough times now to copycat his moves when he would enter her mind. It was, after all, part of his vampire instincts and she now shared his knowledge. It seemed very comfortable for her now to move through his thoughts. Clémentine focused on what she wished to know and suspected he kept it from her. Once she found it, she gasped, and when she was back in the present moment, she had one of her hands over her mouth. She looked at Vlad and asked with a confused look in her eyes.

"She thought that you were giving yourself to her, that's why she was confused."

"There are three reasons why a vampire would give his blood to another being. One is to heal the being. Two is to mark their territory, and three, to belong to that one being. If a vampire mixes his blood with another being, it means that there is a union between the two that could never be broken."

"If there are three reasons, why would she think you were hers?"

"Because of the oath she took. I had already marked my territory, and she did not need to be healed."

Following Vladislav and Odette's night, she would've been in need of being healed because of the wound left on her neck. However, Vladislav brought a crystal flask of another vampire's blood to close Odette's wound. He did not want to use his own and aggravate her thoughts about him and feed her imagination. It was a mistake. Clémentine asked how Odette was aware of his blood falling into hers.

"I wished not to keep that secret, so I told her," Vlad confessed.

"Why did you do that? She wouldn't have known."

"Odette knows my mouth by heart. When I bite, I leave no drops behind. When I moved my head away from her neck, I felt a sting on my bottom lip and she saw the cut. From that moment on, she knew

my blood had mixed with hers." Vladislav said with much guilt in his voice, regretting his unfocused mind at
the time.

Clémentine tried to make him feel better. She let him know that in the heat of the moment it's easy to lose track of what's going on inside one's mind. He reminded her that his moment of inattention cost him Odette's sanity.

"The smile on her face was so pure and filled with happiness. I had to let her know after our most intimate moment that she meant nothing to me. I couldn't bring myself to do it. I was her first and I was about to break her heart. I simply said that it was a mistake and it was unfortunate that it occurred, but she didn't listen." Vladislav said with a modulated voice.

Clémentine held his hand close to her heart but lifted it to her face and kissed his palm. Somehow, she knew he needed to tell the story to someone to lift a load off of his shoulders. He admitted that no one knew about what happened that night. Clémentine found it very hard to believe, thinking that Odette would've bragged about sleeping with Vladislav because she would too.

"No. I made her promise me under the punishment of impalement never to reveal to anyone about the night we shared." Vladislav's eyes turned red and his voice grave and stentorian.

Suddenly Clémentine felt very uncomfortable and breathed a little loudly. She was about to promise that she would never reveal to anyone under any circumstances, even under torture, if they would ever spend one night together. Vladislav's strong abs contracted as he lifted himself halfway up with a smile.

"You can brag to anyone you want my little *inger*."

"I don't understand why I would have the right to."

"Isn't it obvious?" Vladislav said as he leaned in to kiss her near her ear.

Vladislav's guilt was explained by the way he treated Odette and then through a mistake he made while trying to fix his behavior. Clémentine then asked if he truly never felt love with anyone else than the one he knew in bright daylight. Vladislav shook his head as a sign of negation. He confessed that he never wished to be attached to anyone else, in fear of losing that loved one again. But he then corrected his words, with a low and almost shy voice; "Although I fear that one night it might all change."

CHAPTER 25
KNOW YOUR ENEMIES

Clémentine admired his courage to say those words but knew with the story he shared that he might never drop his guard and truly let Clémentine in to love her. His wish was to show Clémentine affection and hoped that it would be enough to keep Clémentine by his side. But she would have to decide sooner or later if his affection would satisfy her desire to be loved.

"As a prime giver, Mrs. Lefebvre was my employee. By calling me hers in front of my people or other givers was not only inappropriate but also false and unprofessional. It showed disrespect to me. I asked my most trusted guards to ask their givers to warn her about not using those terms but it made no difference."

"Have you tried talking to her again?"

"I did, numerous times, but she wouldn't listen. As the years went by, she became more and more delusional about a secret love story happening between us. Before it got out of hand, I moved her to

Vermont and bought her this place. I promised her I would visit. Fifteen years later, here we are."

Vladislav paused before he ended the story and Clémentine wondered if there were any other details he hadn't shared with her. She knew deep down that Vladislav had opened up to her. By the look in his eyes, she knew he wouldn't hide anything from her.

"When Mrs. Lefebvre agreed to move to Vermont, I asked if there was anything she wished for. Her only request was for a vial of my blood. I reminded her that what happened was an accident. Her reasoning was that if she would be wounded there would be no vampires around to heal her."

"You agreed?"

"I agreed. But what I gave her was the blood of the duke of North America. She didn't need to know it wasn't mine. I didn't want to inflict any more pain on her. I lied to her and gave her Dragomir's blood. She hugged me tighter than she had before and thanked me a thousand times. It was just one more thing that piled onto my guilt."

Vladislav was now again on his back and Clémentine was sitting by his side. His hand was playing with her fingers, almost like a massage. She was on the verge of falling asleep but she needed to know more about him. Now that she knew that all the years that Odette spent by Vladislav's side had brought her to the point of delusion, she somehow feared the same would happen to her.

There was a soft and cool breeze enveloping Clémentine's every thought. It was as if it was trying to put her worries to sleep and prevent her from overthinking everything. She heard his grave and smoky voice humming an old melody that she thought dated from his days in the sun. He sang no words but the humming was enough to make her smile and admire his vocal talent. That was something else he admitted that he wanted to keep secret.

"I want you to know that I have learned from my mistake with Mrs. Lefebvre. I never had a prime giver after her."

"Then what about this Bianca?" Clémentine asked, remembering his memories as vividly as if they were her own.

"Bianca? Oh, yes, she is Connor's wife now, one of my guards." Vladislav answered after rubbing his eyes, trying to remember the name.

Clémentine didn't understand. By sharing Vladislav's memory, she knew the Romanian prince had his givers that only he could feed from. She shared his knowledge and now they were her own. She mentioned it to Vladislav, who then pulled Clémentine
towards him.

"Naten fills up my flask."

Clémentine quickly moved away, disgusted by what she had just heard. Naten was Vladislav's best friend and food. He was a sort of monster too. Wasn't that some sort of anthropophagy or sadistic BDSM on some level? She felt horrible for Naten who had no choice but to be his own best friend's nourishment. But then, what about Vladislav mentioning earlier that he would only have female givers? "Wait. First of all, Naten isn't my source of nourishment. I could never do that to him, he's my best friend. Besides, even if I tried, I don't think I could."

Vladislav's brows lowered, his eyes looked up into Clémentine's. He lifted himself up on his elbows to try to get Clémentine's attention, which wished for nothing more than an explanation.

"When Mrs. Lefebvre left, I needed givers but told Naten I wouldn't have a prime one anymore because of what happened. Naten helped me find a few givers. Since then, he has been my messenger. He gets my nourishment and brings it back to me. I don't even know who they are or what they look like. Satisfied?"

Clémentine nodded. She could now breathe and it made sense. After all, she had been by Naten's side in the bright daylight.

"Second of all, Naten isn't a vampire. He's a monster, but nothing like you could ever imagine."

"He said he was old. What is he?" Clémentine asked, wildly intrigued.

"That would be for him to tell you, but let's just say, that regardless of us not sharing the same blood, he means nothing less to me. He is my best friend and one I consider a brother. There was a night where I had to leave the boudoir when you stood by my side." She remembered Vlad walking back in with that one drop of blood on his lip. "Despite my disgust, I sometimes have no choice, but to rely on the option to have one of my givers fill up my flask. Naten is just the messenger. Other times, it's even more degrading. Naten brings me the giver, and I mind spell them into a happy state of mind. Then I take what I need and send   them   on their way."

"Moreover, it was my first-time meeting one of my givers and I ended up face to face with a man. Naten thought I might prefer it that way, no attachment, as those men were entirely attracted to women. Problem solved apparently." Vladislav said, a little embarrassed that his best friend kept it a secret from him but it made Clémentine chuckle when he explained, "Feeling the flesh tearing apart, the blood going in is very arousing for a vampire, regardless of your sexual preferences. That is one more reason I never wanted a man to be my prime giver. That night, I asked my male giver to look in the opposite direction while he gave me his arm and I drank off his wrist."

Vladislav heard Clémentine chuckle a little more. She noticed his cheeks reddening, and she could tell he tried to erase that moment off his mind.

"You could've mind spelled Odette from preventing her broken heart." Clémentine said. "If mind spelling is as strong as you say it is, you could've spared her the delusions of you and her carrying a forbidden love story or what not."

"A mind spell is powerful. Powerful enough, that it can damage a human brain in long-term use. I only practice a mind spell if I am obligated to do so and when there are no other options for me to rely on. It creates false impressions and memories. It violates your thoughts, as it reshapes your very essence. A mind spell is for a predator to use on its prey, to lure it into trusting the very one that will devour it." Vladislav explained with a grave voice.

"Moreover, tell me, Clémentine, who am I to deprive Odette of her first and only night with a male? Despite the fact that she is delusional, I know for certain that she cherishes that memory. Besides, she has suffered enough. A mind spell is something that sometimes I wish vampires wouldn't have in their possession. We use it more often than we ever should, and I for one, despise it."

That night, in the light of a dying flame in the hearth, Clémentine saw Vladislav differently. He showed much more compassion toward humans than she would have thought. He even despised one of the most powerful advantages vampires had, a gift that permitted them to alter the memories of those who thought they were only myths. Of course, Vladislav explained that it permitted the Vampire Empire to stay a secret among breathers. It also gave them the opportunity to take advantage of them and use them throughout history to provide them with everything they had ever dreamed of—power, money, and blood.

"Vampires are distrustful creatures who bathe in the blood of those they bite."

Like you once did in sunlight…only you drank out of them while they were still breathing. You were a vampire walking in bright daylight.

Afraid of how Vladislav would react to her last statement, Clémentine barely found the strength to look into his eye after realizing that while she was thinking, he could hear her thoughts. The one who had inspired generations of horror movies, novels, and music.

"That was a long time ago. Years of torture change one's perception of pain. Besides, it is wrong to think I drank the blood in front of their agonizing eyes. I have never done that myself."

His voice sounded afraid of a memory. Clémentine knew at that moment that not everything about Vladislav had been written in books. There was a strong chance that much of the information had been embellished. She reached for his hand but he withdrew it. She asked why but his words cut through her like a knife.

"You are afraid of me and I do not wish to feed your fears anymore. Not too long ago I wanted you to be afraid so that it would keep you away from me. I did it to protect myself from you. But now, now I wish for you to come to me when you are ready. Just know, Clémentine, that I am not a psychopath. I never was."

Clémentine slowly approached Vladislav and took his hand. He tried to move away but she held on. She saw in his eyes a specular light, brighter than it should've been because a filter of pink slowly covered it. The color reminded her that Vladislav wasn't emotionless to things that she would say or think. He was capable of feeling pain, guilt, shame and fear, probably even deeper than breathers.

"What I feel for you is something that I haven't felt in, well, over five hundred years and it scares me. All I ask of you, Clémentine, is to be patient with me. Will you?"

Her eyes suddenly covered in tears and she leaned in closer to him. The moment her forehead touched Vladislav's chin, she murmured, "I will."

Clémentine lay in Vladislav's arms, her head resting on his chest. She felt his fingers running up and down her neck and it somehow made her feel very special. It was in her mind that Vladislav asked Clémentine if they could stop talking about his past with his givers. He also mentioned her possessive nature. Vladislav, of course, told her that he could feel deep within her thoughts her wish that he had not become close to Odette.

"I won't lie. I am a little jealous and possessive of the man I agree to be intimate with. What is bothering me, though, is not that you agreed to spend a night with her, but that you wished not to have any other prime givers. I feel like that's what you want me to be."

Clémentine felt Vlad move underneath her and, as she sat up, she looked at him moving on his side. He touched her face, and with the saddest look she had ever seen, he said, "I will never have you as my prime giver. I have already told you that." Clémentine wondered if she wasn't good enough or maybe it was something else. Vladislav roamed about in her mind to answer, *"You mean much more to me. I will not have you be my source of nourishment, nor will you forever be my guest and personal mind reader. I will want more."*

Clémentine lifted her eyes to see a dark mist surrounding the room again. She moved her body and noticed it coming closer. When she looked back into Vladislav's eyes, she saw the bright red color covering his irises. Something was happening to him.

"You are scaring me again," Clémentine tried to escape him, but it only took the prince one second to keep her in place.

"Don't be, that's just a part of me you will get accustomed to. I told you my eyes turn red in three circumstances. Two out of three are happening. As for the mist, you know I control it, Clémentine. You felt it coming from me when you shared my memories. It is an extension of myself," Vladislav said with a sensual voice that Clémentine found hard to resist.

Clémentine remembered how scared she felt when his eyes had turned bright red and he barely responded to her pleas. She had to know what happened so that she would never cause it again or she would have to leave for her own good. She watched him get on his knees and, moving his arms forward to lead her into them, he gently kissed her near her lips and then moved his mouth next to her ear breathing slowly. Clémentine was having a hard time articulating her next question.

"Your eyes and the mist, the same thing happened earlier, but you were angry. I would like to know why."

"I was angry with her, not you. I knew she tried to scare you, and it hurt me because I—"

Clémentine wanted him to say it because she knew what he meant to say all along. It excited her more than he could have ever known. She caressed his hair and closed her hand on it, almost forcing him to say it aloud. "I want you. I want you so much that it hurts me and no one has ever hurt me this deep before."

His eyes were on hers and she stared at his crimson irises as they rolled back when she tightened her grip on the back of his head. She pulled him toward her, their mouths so close, and said in a whisper, "Tell me why you want me." Vladislav's smirk made her shyly smile as he answered, "You are the most beautiful woman I have ever seen. I know it sounds shallow, but everything about you fascinates me. I want you and I will possess you." Clémentine rubbed her forehead against his only to reply, "Keep talking like that and I might let you."

CHAPTER 26
A KICK IN THE HEAD

The morning that followed, Clémentine woke up in Vladislav's white shirt. She wished she would've been naked but with all the drama that happened the night before, nothing else took place after she was entirely seduced by Vladislav's possessiveness toward her.

The night before...

As their foreheads touched, Vladislav's fangs quickly appeared. Clémentine noticed how fast he looked into her eyes, as if he wanted to know how scared she was. Clémentine only found the strength to whisper that she wanted him to be real and not hide anymore. In a vampire second, Vladislav picked her up and had her sit on his lap facing him. Her legs wrapped around his waist and her arms were around his neck. She felt his fangs rubbing against her neck and she realized that they had never truly kissed.

"Maybe let's start with the beginning," Vladislav whispered.

Clémentine felt him moving his head from her neck to her chin. His lips were pressing against her skin and she moved her head down slowly. Finally, Clémentine could feel his lips against her own. She felt Vladislav pressing a little harder, his hand behind her head; he pulled her closer to him. She then felt the tip of his tongue teasing her and, as she parted her lips to let him in, she heard a growl and his tongue swirled with hers as she felt his lips moving.

"I want you." Vladislav softly shared through her mind.

Vladislav's fangs touched her bottom lip. He retracted them almost instantly and Clémentine found it hard to open her eyes, as she was lost in a fantasy. The moment she felt him stop, she ordered him not to. Clémentine knew Vladislav was afraid to hurt her but she reminded him that she wasn't as brittle as she might have looked. His arms holding her tight, he gently laid her on her back and his body rested on top of hers. She wrapped her legs around his waist, hoping it would prevent him from attempting to escape.

"I'm not going anywhere, even if you would beg me to. I want you." Vladislav said with a smile.

Clémentine felt his power. Small little black veins showed through his skin on his forearms and lower abdomen. He stood up on his knees to take his tank top off, only to throw it on to the ground. She saw the white fog surrounding the bed, and in a vampire second, the prince was gone.

"Vladislav?" Clémentine said loudly, as she lifted herself up on her elbows to try to see through the mist.

"Yes."

The prince reappeared before her at the end of the bed but now she could see a warm faint light in the corner of the room, glimmering through the smoke. Vladislav admitted feeling her skin turned cold and he wanted to warm up the room. He fed the fire in the hearth to make sure she would be comfortable. Clémentine could feel the foggy ice but he admitted that although cold, the fire would eventually warm the room and provide a light as he wished to see her in his arms all night.

"First, please say my name again." Vladislav said with a very shy voice, almost embarrassed.

"My Vladislav," Clémentine whispered, hoping he would enjoy it, although there was always a doubt in her mind that he never would.

"I do like it, say it again…Say that I am yours."

Clémentine repeated it as often as he wished, and once she saw him taking his fangs out, his bottom lip curved in and his right fang scratched it. Hypnotized by his blood, knowing all the knowledge it contained that she could possess, the powers it transmitted, and the overwhelming burst of energy it provided, she wished to have it. Vladislav knew.

"You want it?" Vladislav asked with a very seducing voice.

"Yes."

"Come and get it."

Clémentine moved forward licking her lips in delight. On all fours, she was about to crawl to him on the bed to lick his scratch clean, but Vladislav's eyes brightened, and his brows lowered as he frowned. He angrily gazed at Clémentine and shouted with his grave voice, "Come any closer and you're dead."

Clémentine stopped in confusion, immobilized by terror. She saw Vladislav rolling his eyes and murmured as he moved forward to touch her face. "Not you, my little *inger.*"

Vladislav's right hand was behind Clémentine's head and she felt him pulling her toward him. As their foreheads touched, she saw him scratch his bottom lip a second time. He gently pressed his lips against hers, and kissed her with so much hunger she almost thought he took her heart. He murmured softly, "Enjoy my *inger.*"

The Romanian prince kissed her, leading his bottom lip into her mouth so Clémentine could suck his blood into her own. It would be his way to stay with her a little longer. When he left the bed, the mist stayed around her like a blanket. She heard his voice inside her head, asking for her to continue without him, but she answered that what she wanted the most was him, and nothing else seemed to be enough anymore, not even her own touch.

Clémentine licked her lips, absorbing every single drop belonging to Vladislav. Now that she knew all the pleasure it could give her, the strength, and energy, she found herself craving more each time. The down side was that somehow she would see a memory belonging to him. As long as he would be the one willingly giving it to her, she would not feel the guilt she once did.

Clémentine waited to be transported in another time and place that she wouldn't know, sharing another of Vladislav's memories. She would also gain some of his knowledge. That allowed her to use her own mind reading abilities to the fullest, both instincts being exactly the same from mortal to vampire, but nothing happened. Not even her extra sensorial senses ignited. Clémentine wondered why the sudden vision of Vladislav grabbing his tank top to pull it off took over her mind, and the vision of his strong very masculine chest with a light layer of dark hair   nearly compelled her.

Her frustrations cut her imagination short and she realized they had been interrupted twice now. She wished Vladislav would do something about it. With many thoughts running through her mind, she reached out for his tank top. She noticed the mist was staying in the room and there was an aroma of frosted ice that wasn't coming from the windows. Once she brought his tank top to her face to inhale his scent, she lay down under the covers and closed her eyes.

Deep in her thoughts, she heard Vladislav's voice like an echo. He sounded almost as frustrated as she was and he mentioned that he would make sure next time no one would interrupt them. Clémentine smiled and said that she wished he would come back and kiss her neck with his fangs. Then her legs would be wrapped around his waist and she would lead him in. With those words, she heard a growl.

"I will do all that you wish me to do. Believe me inger, the one who interrupted us twice will not be doing it again." Vladislav said with an icy voice and added, *"She will be indisposed for a while."*

Clémentine knew Vladislav's vampire crew were all men. From that, she easily deduced that it was one of the helpers or givers that were the source of their continual interruptions. She wondered if it was

Odette but Vladislav was now gone from her mind. As she curled up in bed under the covers, she hugged his tank top and thought about him. Falling asleep was now next to impossible. She laid her eyes on the log cracking in the hearth and wished Vladislav would come   back to her.

I hate it when you're not around, when I can't feel you in any way. Your warmth is going away and now it feels like you're entirely gone. I guess you were right when you said that if you left my mind, I would find myself begging you to come back.

Not long after her thoughts, Clémentine noticed the mist around her thickening and surrounding the bed. It provided her with comfort, and when it approached her body, she was about to reach out for it. She had a slight fear that it might hurt her in some way. She simply stared at it, hoping that its   master   would   follow   it.

CHAPTER 27
THE PHARAOH KING

The morning that followed, Clémentine realized that the mist was all that she remembered from the night before. She wished again that Vladislav would've stayed and that they would have both been naked in bed. The smell of coffee led Clémentine out of bed, with a blanket wrapped around her shoulders. She walked toward the boudoir on the other side of the bedroom, after she opened the two gigantic French doors. She noticed Naten standing next to the windows, which were overlooking the backyard. For a fraction of a second, she thought it was Vladislav, but then realized the length of hair wasn't the same and the sunlight would never shine down on his body again.

"Good morning, Clémentine." Naten said, as he turned around with a smile.

"Good morning…but, um, where's Vlad?" Clémentine asked almost instantly. She felt something was wrong and she was worried. Not only wasn't she reliving one of his memories but also she couldn't feel him at all in her mind or around.

Clémentine walked to the wall by her side to touch it. Although the place was empty of his memories, because Vladislav had never lived in the house, now that it had been a few days, some residual of him should be around. It would be stronger in her room since he had experienced some strong emotions there. Something had to have been left behind and Clémentine's extra senses should've been strong enough to pick up on it. But she was getting nothing. Even the house was empty of Vladislav. Something was wrong. Terribly wrong.

"Yes, Vlad told me you were able to read energy, and that you are the last Gravedigger." Naten said, contemplating Clémentine, who was trying to feel the house.

"Yes, I am a Gravedigger, but why am I not picking up a trail leading back to him? Where is he?"

"Vlad is sadly recovering from a brutal attack," Naten said, entirely detached. He kept his eyes on the floor, trying to hide his worries Clémentine guessed.

As Clémentine moved her hand away from the wall, she could see Naten was worried about Vladislav's condition. She felt he needed someone to listen to him for once, as if no one ever took the time to pay attention to him. It felt like Naten had so many emotions locked inside. Clémentine turned around to face him and walked two steps forward, but Naten moved back four steps. She knew something was very different with him. As she glanced at him, only to meet his eyes for a second, she could almost see a presence she should've known was hidden in the back of his mind.

His voice, silvery but worried, reminded Clémentine how she wished she would've gone with Vladislav. She was thinking that maybe she would've been able to protect him, somehow suspecting that another mind reader was at work. The house felt it and Clémentine did too.

"Vlad the Impaler is my best friend. He reigned over the Romanian Vampire Empire and his plans to become the ultimate ruler of the Vampire Empire attracted enemies from the beginning. He somehow always managed to vanquish every attempt made on his life. Throughout the centuries, my best friend has overcome more pain than any other being should have been put through. He stood tall before all his adversaries, never bowed, and never kneeled. Now, the fucking high council knows that to bring Vlad the Impaler to his knees, they must bring in a stronger player, one that can ultimately be the end of the vampire race."

"Judith of Scweinfurt, the one and only Bohemian Necromancer." Clémentine said.

Naten led Clémentine over to the living room, directing her toward the fireplace that separated her room and the boudoir. As he explained to her a little more about the world her lover lived in, he lit a fire and went on with a little history.

"The vampires are a very racist race, but not all are evil. Their people are divided into two clans known as the Conservatives and the Idealists. No surprises there, the Conservatives wish to keep the old ways and rule over the vampire people with fear. The Idealists are the ones trying to change the old ways and help the race evolve into something new."

Naten poked on the logs and added paper to help the fire catch. Clémentine listened to his every word, hoping she would learn something she didn't already know. She had learned some of this, due to the fact that she shared Vladislav's memories. Something as important as politics, had become a part of his nature, and always roamed about in his mind.

"Sadly, the Idealists are growing fewer in numbers, due to the mysterious disappearances of their members. The Conservatives are, of course, slowly taking over the high council. Long story short, a coup is on the rise, and because Vlad is one of the strongest Idealists, he finds himself on the list of one of the most dangerous members of the high council, Elizabeth Báthory."

The room was full of sunlight. The tall rectangular windows let in the beauty of late fall, and made the living room look larger than it usually was. The blanket over Clémentine's shoulders should've been unnecessary by now, but she felt more comfortable with it around her. She listened to Naten going on about politics and he mentioned that it was suspected that Elizabeth was working with Judith.

"When you discovered the remains of that old vampire, the Conservatives realized the plans of all the monsters that were a part of the Belvoir Coven."

"They want to stand against all of us?" Clémentine asked, unfamiliar with the term.

"They don't plan on standing against you; they want to destroy you all. Vampires are territorial and won't forgive humans for what they did to them centuries ago. Vampires were almost extinct, due to the numerous inquisitions.

Not many legends and folklore speak well of them because humans tend to fear what they don't understand. Vampires are done with humans. As for the other monsters, they just decided to eliminate all threats together."

Naten's eyes were fixed on the flames, while Clémentine contemplated him. She remembered how Naten looked different. The paranoia of vampires was true and founded. Now she was made aware of her friends' encounters, and all that was left was figuring out who Naten truly was, because she knew him. It flashed before her eyes. His tan, his hair, his elongated jawline, and the power he possessed, making him capable of scaring even Vlad's adopted son.

"You are King Akhenaten, husband of Nefertiti and the father of King Tutankhamun of the eighteenth dynasty. You are a mummy."

Naten stood up, his eyes rounded by surprise. Clémentine mentioned she had a degree in history and specialized in ancient civilizations. The mysterious pharaoh chuckled, both his hands on his hips. He looked down at her and explained to her that despite not wearing any bandages, he was what her people would call a mummy. "I am in full control of the sand. I have the ability to curse, and at my command, if I touch you, your body could turn to dust. When Vlad told me about the uprising of the Conservatives and his clan growing thinner, I joined his side in a heartbeat. Pharaohs, in other words, ancient Kings and Queens of Egypt, are ranged by his side now. Even though there are few of us left."

Clémentine had studied parapsychology, and when she earned her diploma in history, she combined the two and studied legends and folklore. She was no stranger to paranormal creatures, she just wasn't aware to what degree they were true. Now, a mummy stood right before her eyes. "I feel your doubt about me," Naten crouched before Clémentine and asked her to take his hand in her own. Both her palms facing the ceiling, Naten put his hand in the middle and she felt the warmth of his touch.

He wore an emerald bracelet with gold rims, and a leather braided bracelet. Both hands rested on her palms and his hand turned to sand right before her eyes. She looked into his eyes and saw they were entirely black. Only two gold lights were present in place of his pupils. She still felt the pile of sand in her hands, which was warm and granulated. She felt it moving, almost as if an insect was building a nest. Her eyes stared into Naten's but she glanced down to see what was going on in her hands. As she watched, his hands began to reshape themselves.

Her breathing quickened. She was unaware that mummies could be so dangerous. "There was an insect in there." Naten shook his head, "It was an arachnid." She closed her eyes, "You're saying a scorpion was in my hand?" The mummy laughed, "We do control them as well and scarabs."

The warmth of the fire spread throughout the living room. Still covered by the blanket, Clémentine tried to overcome her fear of arachnids and suddenly, when her eyes closed, she saw Vladislav's fangs scratching his lip. She snapped out of her daydream and asked the ancient king how it was possible for Vladislav to be attacked while a powerful mummy was by his side. She guessed a best friend would defend the

home   of
his friend.

"Also, Vlad has, I don't know how many guards. What the fuck happened?"

"It was friendly fired."

"Damian?"

Clémentine strongly doubted, despite the condescending attitude of Vlad's son, that he would attempt such a move against his own adopted father. Naten confirmed she was right to think so. The lycan had supposedly changed, not long after leaving his residence in Raleigh with his wife, Coralie Bellefleur, who happened to be the last of the Orléans aristocratic family. He reminded Clémentine that nobility was the key to the vampire governmental system. He stated that among many back and forth emails, Damian warned his father about one of his guards, who had turned against him, fearing that Vladislav might have a rat too.

"While Idealists have other 'monsters' allied with them, so do the Conservatives through mindspells, ergo, keeping them under their mind control. That includes people like Judith, who are psychotic sociopathic bitches."

"So you believe all is done by infiltration?"

"It is either that or futile empty promises. The Conservatives never keep their promises to their rats. If you ask me, the one rat that is here must be fond of sadistic torture, because if Vlad or I find him or her, believe me, they will pay for their treachery."

"Is that why I am kept here, instead of bringing him back to the Belvoir Coven?"

"Yes. Guarding Vlad against Judith and finding if the rat is one of the undead. That was the original plan for the medium, until Vlad and I discovered that Damian was under a spell."

"Diversion." Clémentine whispered. Vampires knew that Vlad would pay more attention to his son, than a rat among his people. What they hadn't considered was Naten paying attention to his best friend and Clémentine's abilities. "You're not just a mere Gravedigger, Clémentine. You also have Shamanic healing abilities. You can bring the undead back to life."

A gulp later, Clémentine face palmed herself, "Why do I keep hurting myself like this?" Naten chuckled, and as he stood back up near the window, "Mika said you'd say that."

Clémentine thought about when she met Octavian at the crematorium and the people that were present. Those who lived the vampire lifestyle, or at least some, might have known about vampires and were givers. Octavian was the only being she had ever loved. Vlad never mentioned him and she still wondered if he tasted the blood of another vampire mixed with hers.

"Vampires have a strong sense of detecting intruders. Yet, the attack never awakened his senses. He let himself be taken down."

"Wait. What, why?" Clémentine asked, frowning as she rounded her eyes in surprise.

"Vlad is losing his strength. He has lost what keeps him whole. If it comes to the ears of his enemies, we're all dead. You are what stands between life and death."

Clémentine never thought of her gift being what held the world together at that moment. Naten made sure she understood how being a Gravedigger was both dangerous and powerful. Then it all went back to the night before where Vlad was attacked. Clémentine needed more details on what happened to Vladislav in order to help him. Knowing that he was recovering brought her only little comfort since she doubted the rat had left the mansion. Especially if the creature was still unknown to Naten, Vladislav, and possibly Damian.

"Damian might have been aware of whom the rat was, and that was his reason to visit his father. He gave the false pretense that he wished for his father to meet his wife. He ended up being followed, attacked, and cursed."

"Your theory is exactly what I came up with. However, it isn't a curse because I could break it with a snap of my fingers. It is mind control, and that's where you come in."

Clémentine now understood that Naten suspected the rat to either be undead or capable of mindreading. That would leave traces behind that Clémentine could link back to the rat, and help free both Damian and Vladislav. However, Clémentine doubted it would be that simple. The house was emptied of all memories and residual energies. Whoever was behind it, wasn't working alone.

"Then it is worse than we anticipated."

CHAPTER 28

MR. BLACKWOOD

"Damian is a strong lycan, a true blood lycanthrope, meaning he was born of two lycanthrope parents. However, Vlad, who knew vampires were already trying to become the supreme race, saved Damian. He started feeding the boy his blood to camouflage his lycanthrope scent. Years have passed, and Damian has turned into a hybrid." Naten walked to Clémentine's small refrigerator that she didn't even know she had in her chambers and saw him pick up a bottle of water. "Damian is now more vampire than lycan. He also is his father's right-hand man. Damian has been saving werewolves all around North America by working with SkenderTech to amplify the vampire gene in his blood to hide the scent of the werewolves." Despite Clémentine sharing Vladislav's thoughts, she wondered what the difference was between lycanthropes and werewolves. "Lycanthropes are pure blood. It signifies that a nightwolf's blood came in physical contact with their own creating a DNA mutation. That connection changed them into lycans, i.e., the werewolf makers. Werewolves are the result of a lycan changing them by exchange of blood. Damian is one of the last lycanthropes out there. He's trying to turn werewolves into lycans by modifying his blood, which will give his species a chance at survival and winning the civil war to come."

Clémentine had heard of VitaL. It was a biotechnology company not too far from where she lived in the province of Québec, across the northern borders. She didn't know it belonged to vampires. Of course, Clémentine made quite a few connections, hurting Vlad, but hurting Damian? Maybe his nature is now out in the open and the wrong vampires know about his genetics.

"They do. Damian never changed his name to Tepes. He kept Blackwood, making him a target. What protected him was his blood being camouflaged by Vlad's scent. If they didn't know what Damian looked like, nobody could tell who or what he was. Also, when you are part of Vlad's family, no one dares

fuck
with you."

The room felt colder, and Clémentine wondered if Vlad had anything to do with it. She needed a way to be in contact with him. There was not even a ghost living on the property, no paranormal link at all. Finally, she felt something. She touched the walls, the blanket falling on to the floor. She kept touching the walls and felt a very faint energy. It almost slipped by her, but her desire to save Vladislav took over her mind. She knew she needed to find who orchestrated the attack and how it was done. The old walls of the chambers held quite a history. Clémentine had to push some aside. Because the walls were emptied moments ago, she knew there had been a cleanse, and now, someone was trying to distract her.

"The rats are here."

"Rats?"

"Yes, there are two of them, and some followers. Vladislav is not yet done with treason."

"Who?"

Clémentine felt fear, terror, and a voice. The tone, she had heard it before. She should know whom the voice belonged to but there was too much interference. The white noise, the memories of over two hundred years energizing the walls of the place, put a great distance between her and the puppet master. She told Naten, "One of them is a witch." If only she could contact Mika, she'd know how to disarm the witch. As of now, she could do nothing.

"I'll need to enter Vlad's mind and release him from within. How did the attack occur? Were you there?"

Naten used the wall by the tall French windows to lean on. He crossed his arms over his chest, and his thumb rubbed over his full bottom lip, as he tried to recall the details. Clémentine knew he tried to recall every little detail that happened the night before when Vladislav left her.

"When Vlad left your room, it was to meet with Damian, who was ordering everyone to take you away from the mansion. It was very disrespectful to all of us monsters. I tried to reason with the boy, but he was too far gone. I even tried to un-curse him, but there was no curse to begin with. I had him look into my eyes and saw the vampire part of him being controlled by the dark crimson constantly being gone and replaced by black. Damian's too young to let his lycan side take over his vampire side, so I called his wife. She said he was fine when he left the house back in Raleigh." Naten paced around the room…

The night of the attack...

"Damian! You need to listen to me!" Naten screamed as he shook Damian. The lycan tried to free himself from the Pharaoh's grip, but the Egyptian was too old and his grip too strong. "Damian! Someone is controlling you. This isn't you!"

"Son, what's going on?" Vlad shouted as he zoomed down the stairs. He walked to the entrance where Damian was threatening to kill every guard and human around the property. Naten quickly stated the boy was being controlled by witchcraft. Vlad wasn't a stranger to such activities, having dealt with it his entire life. He had his son moved to the chapel, where a priest was called, one Vlad had trusted for many years. Naten barely recognized him. He had met the man when he first began his career. Now retired, he wondered if Vlad would turn him, so he could stick around longer than would otherwise.

"What kind of witchcraft is it, Vlad?" The old man asked as he took out a Bible and holy water, looking at his friend.

"The eyes are black and the growl is not his. I'm sure you remember Damian's sound, this isn't a wolf. Also, I noticed a branding on him that isn't healing. This, to me, looks like Stregheria, an old witchcraft dating back to the fourteenth century. Its revival happened in the last century, but not many practice it, since it is linked to Catholicism. I thought you'd be the man for the job."

"You did well, my old friend."

Damian was attached to the altar. Naten looked at the priest. His faith was unshakable as he performed an exorcism, with Vladislav at his side. Naten didn't know his friend to be such a believer. Ever since Damian had walked into his life, he had found that believing in something more might allow comfort. He heard Vladislav ask, once the exorcism was done, if Damian would ever be the same again.

"This isn't a demon, my friend. I did all I could." The priest had his arms crossed over his chest. He was looking at Damian, sweating on the altar, as his head was softly turning left to right, whispering some words in another language. "One piece of advice I can give is not to give him your blood."

"How so?" Vladislav asked, a red line forming below his pupils in the inner corner of his eyes.

"You'd feed him what he's trying to fight, what he wasn't meant to be. Your son is a lycan. Right now, that lycan is fighting to survive, while the vampire in him is trying to kill it. What I see is a battle."

"It isn't witchcraft?"

Still looking at the boy, the priest nodded. "Oh, it is witchcraft all right, a mean one at that. The spell is obviously to divide Damian. I tried to take the spell away, but somehow, something is preventing it from happening. Mind you, I'm trained in performing exorcisms and this isn't a demon."

Naten looked at the priest hugging Vladislav, and letting him know that he could call him at any time of the day or night to talk. He said it had been too long since they had caught up and he could use a walk around the cathedral. Naten almost envied his friend's life, his friends, and the respect they had for him. Naten was more of a loner than a social person. He walked to Vladislav, shook the priest's hand, and walked him toward the door of the chapel.

A loud growl, followed by a sound like a full container made of plaster cracking was heard. Naten recognized the sound right away and shouted, "Vlad!" The priest turned around, and both ran to him, but Naten focused on Damian. Quickly, the Pharaoh turned his hand to sand when going through Damian's flesh and rematerialized it when inside. The shout was louder and deeper than he had ever heard. Naten took out his hand and laid the boy back down on the altar.

Once stabilized, Vladislav's men ran into the chapel. Naten ordered them to lock Damian into his father's coffin, while he would see to Vladislav's safety. The priest was holding his friend's hand and Naten knelt at the kind gesture of the priest, who waited until everyone left and leaned over to the Pharaoh's ear. "This isn't Vlad's ring. This one is fake." Naten looked at the ring on Vlad's index finger and he noticed the difference. "His token was stolen from him?" The priest asked but Naten wasn't aware. The Pharaoh knew not many vampires could survive long without their passing token. It was the one object that linked them to their past lives, keeping them alive in the physical world.

The priest said the last sacrament, as Vlad had requested with a very faint voice. His skull was cracked in two and his blood was staining the marble floor. Naten used his scarab necklace to gather Vlad's blood, its purpose being to encompass any precious belongings the Pharaoh desired to possess. At this moment, Naten wished to give his best friend's blood back. He heard the words of the priest and after so many years of hearing the prayers, he surprised himself by reciting them along with him. Once Vlad's blood was safe within Naten's necklace, he knelt by his friend and waited for the priest to end. "Where will you keep him, may I ask?"

"My sarcophagus. It has rejuvenating abilities. It might work… or not. Pharaohs tend to dry with time, vampires just become paler."

"Would you please keep me informed of his health? We've been friends for almost fifty-five years."

Naten smiled. The priest looked younger than he should have. Vlad knew how to take good care of his friends. The Pharaoh nodded and replied, "I'll do better. I'll send some people over. I don't want anything happening to you or I'll never hear the end of it. Believe me, when you're a Pharaoh and friends with a vampire, never really means never." Naten felt a kind pat on his back as the priest chuckled.

They both walked outside and once near the priest's car, Naten was about to walk right past as he heard the priest ask, "Will he survive this time?"

Naten wondered, suddenly shaken by the idea. He held his friend against his torso, Vladislav's skull holding together because of his bicep pressed against it.

"Will I go to hell if I lie to you, Mr. Priest?"

"No need to. I have my answer, son…I mean, Pharaoh."

Again, about to leave, this time Naten stopped the priest, "There's this girl Vlad's been keeping around. She's a special type of psychic, the good kind. She might be able to save him. I'll call you, Sir, I promise."

"Thank you. I appreciate it."

That was all Naten remembered. He lifted his eyes to look into the crystal blue of Clémentine's gaze. "After that, I brought Vlad to my sarcophagus and ordered everyone to leave me alone. No one could get to him. My sarcophagus is kept in a very special place when I visit Vlad and I have stayed with him ever since. I played his favorite music, *Metallica*. I read his favorite book, *King Arthur*. Then I came here to see you, and now I ask that you save my best friend. Mika said
you could."

"His head, you said it bled. Did it crack?" When Naten nodded at her question, Clémentine didn't know if the correct response was to cry, scream in terror, or knock herself out. She tried to imagine the entire scene. She wanted nothing more than to kill Damian. Naten reminded her that the lycan was a good man, and a great son. He was simply being manipulated.

"How is he now?"

"He's still unconscious. I'm starting to believe that my intervention might have cut the link between Damian and the one orchestrating the attack." Naten took a deep breath, "I think at least one of them will be   saved.

CHAPTER 29
BEHINDS THE RAMPARTS

Clémentine knew to help Vladislav that she would have to find a connection. Asking Naten for his blood might be the best way to get into his mind and help him, assuming that his head was back together. Despite being an old vampire, she knew he was different than most and so she wondered if his rejuvenating abilities were strong enough to put his skull back together. She was afraid of bringing the very thought of it into the light.

"I checked on Vlad this morning, and he is getting back together. He might be 'out of order' for a few nights, but he'll get there. The sarcophagus is helping him more than I thought, must be that volcano eruption of his that resembles my ability to turn to sand." Naten said as Clémentine looked at him questioningly. "Well, Vlad turned into a burning lava corpse not long after his skull cracked open. Now, it's like a light layer of volcanic smoke is covering his body. He's reacting the way I would...you know, he's not like any other vampire, right?"

Clémentine nodded. She knew it too well. She did share his memories and parts of his life. She knew his pain, felt the icy mist growing inside of him and any thoughts going through his mind. She knew he was different because she felt it through Vladislav's mind when sharing his memories, and knew that he felt alone. Clémentine shared that feeling because even the friends she worked with didn't share any of the gifts she had. Strangely, the only one who could share her loneliness was Vladislav.

"How do you figure we solve this?"

"First of all, I need to free Vlad from that bitch's grip."

Clémentine knew Vladislav was held captive inside his mind, a prisoner of his own thoughts. Otherwise, she'd feel something. She'd feel him healing. The fire and volcano smoke over his body might be an instinctive protection from his ability. Still, his mind Clémentine knew. She should be able to follow a link like she once did to satisfy her curiosity. However, there was nothing to track.

"The house was cleansed of everything for me to find. When I tried to search for the rat, suddenly two hundred years of history hit my mind. The witch is doing the same to Vlad. Those orchestrating this don't want to be found. I need to know, at the moment of the attack, who got into Vlad's head to have him lose against a lycan."

Clémentine refused to believe Vladislav had been taken by surprise. He would've been looking at his son, holding his hand and talking to him. She knew he wouldn't have turned his back on him knowing he was the victim of witchcraft. Someone had to control him to have him untie his son from the altar and attack him. She knew about remote craft. Clémentine figured that someone was helping Judith of Scweinfurt from inside the house they were staying in. The question remained, "Who?" That's what Clémentine needed to figure out.

"I'll need some of his blood."

Naten took his scarab necklace made of gold and lapis lazuli stones. He held it over Clémentine's hands and asked how much she needed. "One drop will suffice." A single drop fell from the scarab onto her hand, and she licked the red velvet liquid. Afraid, she felt herself trembling. Suddenly her vision blurred and then she felt a warm and large hand holding her own. She turned her head and saw Naten, now sitting right by her side, holding her hand. He was a Pharaoh that she had read about in college. She had been obsessed with his life since her pre-teen years, as Egyptology was one of her first passions. She looked at him, and he turned his head, his bright eyes meeting her own. A coy smile flourished on his face, and she felt better.

Suddenly, she felt pulled into her head, as if her eyes were being sucked into their sockets. She closed her eyes as hard as she could, but a space vacuum inside her mind took her deep into her thoughts. All she heard was a distant echo of Naten's voice, "Clémentine! Clémentine!" It was too late. She was already gone. The entire space was dark and cold and she couldn't see her hand in front of her face. She stood in complete darkness. The smell reminded her of Vladislav's musk and she could breathe easier, knowing it was him, in his healing process. That clumsily grabbed her mind and pulled her into his.

Clémentine knew he was scared; the darkness surrounding her was artificial and maintained by the one orchestrating the attacks. She touched the ground and felt it shaking. Vladislav was fighting and she would help him. Both hands on the ground, she closed her eyes and tried to feel all she could from the ground. Like any other paranormal investigation she would do, she would listen to the walls of the building she was in and feel its residual energy before guiding the spirits to freedom. This was not any different from those cases. She would free Vladislav.

The walls around her were slowly crumbling. Some light tried to come through. Clémentine felt stronger and more confident as she felt Vladislav sturdier every time she would surrender to his energy. "I need to know who got into your head. Show me." Clémentine was there to take down the threat, and she intended to do so. She would hold to her part of the deal, as long as Vladislav would be true to her and she knew, the vampire he was wouldn't lie. He might have felt weak before her, but he wouldn't let his pride overtake his kingdom and his son.

Clémentine searched more in-depth into his memory and found what she needed. That was the night before, in the chapel…

In the chapel…

Naten left the altar accompanied by the priest. Vladislav was unable to leave his son's side. Seeing Damian ill and in pain, reminded him that despite being Lord Impaler and someone seen as the most celebrated monster human history has ever had, he was unable to keep his son safe. *"I could never keep them safe. Someone I love must always die."*

"Eşti slab." Damian was talking with a voice carrying an echo of a female's voice. *"Întotdeauna ai fost."*

Then his son added before ending the sentence, *"Acum veţi plăti."*

Damian's eyes turned entirely black before his appearance changed to a more canine one. He spat in Vladislav's face and when at his weakest, Vladislav looked deep into his son's eyes and felt a massive weight falling over his shoulder. Barely able to stand up, he asked Damian what he had done, but his son said, *"Eliberează-mi tatăl."* Tears were rolling down his face, and Vladislav couldn't stand the guilt, and despite his mind trying to fight his body not to free Damian for his own safety, his body obeyed his son's words. Before he could do anything, Damian sprang forward and his lycanthropian fangs dug into Vladislav's skull.

Vlad was unable to move by the weight holding his body in place, and he was trying to hold himself up with the altar. A crisp hollow crack echoed against his brain, Vladislav felt a horrible pressure against his mind, like nails being hammered into his head. He tried to hold himself together however, the throbbing pain was spreading through his entire body. He lost consciousness and fell to the ground almost instantly.

Everything faded to black. Immobile and incapable of moving, held in place by a paranormal strength greater than his own but Vladislav refused to surrender that easily.

His rejuvenation began he focused on the one ability he had that other vampires lacked his volcano bite. Vladislav relentlessly tried to ignite his smoky wind and mist by contracting his abdomen and muscles in his arms. He felt the volts faintly but he was not becoming any fiercer. His mind felt numb under the grip of someone he knew acted as a conductor.

"Judith, please…you have to let me go," Vladislav whispered inside his mind because talking became excruciating to him, as though his lips were sewn together with fine string. He knew someone had to be acting as a conductor. All he could do was hope Naten would bring Clémentine in so that she could free his mind.

He wanted to wake up and find the one hurting him. Unable to speak, unable to move or think, he was feeling as if every single thought was needles going through his brain. He felt the side of his eyes were damp as tears made of blood fell down his face. He refused to be weak.

"Where am I?" He felt his body warming, rejuvenating faster than it ever had before. He was now able to think without the throbbing pain overtaking his mind, but he didn't have enough concentration to contact Clémentine on his own. As he felt safer, all Vladislav thought about was closing himself and letting his fire take over him. It was as if he was being guided through his healing, and he would continue to do so until someone would find him or save him. Until then, he would hide himself deep in his thoughts. He had

time to spare. He was a vampire; an eternity wouldn't
be   so   long.

CHAPTER 30
THE PHARAOH
AND THE WITCH

Clémentine tuned out of the memory and reassured Naten the best she could, "Your sarcophagus protected him." Clémentine was holding Naten's hand tighter than she ever had with anyone before. "Vlad was able to hide his mind from the attackers." She rubbed her eyes with her other hand, "The bad news is that I still don't know who the master is that planned it. All I know is that someone here is either a fan of Judith or they are working with her and acting as a conductor for her. The witch here might be using Judith's powers."

Clémentine got on her knees and was about to stand up when she heard a loud banging on the door. Naten helped her up and walked in front of her as if to protect her. The door opened and Clémentine felt a strong desire to attack the woman pacing to the room where she and Naten were standing. Clémentine somehow feared the retired prime giver was part of the attacks, yet her love for Vladislav might have been enough to have her stand apart from the plan. Hurting Vladislav would have been too much for Odette to bear and the consequences were too terrorizing.

The prime giver walked past Naten and violently pushed Clémentine against the fireplace and slapped her as hard as she could a few times until Clémentine's head hit the side of the fireplace's metal iron holder and she felt a warm drop following the contour of her face. Digging into her knowledge given to her through Vladislav's blood, Clémentine managed to free herself from Odette's grip by maneuvering a combat move she had learned from Vladislav's mind, and landed Odette in a submissive position with her elbow hooked, unable to free herself.

Clémentine put the woman firmly against the ground, jerked her head to knock her out, and ran to the bedroom where she quickly ran for Vladislav's tank top. She was hoping the scent, once inhaled and inside of her, might be enough to lead her into his mind again, but nothing happened.

Naten walked up to her and Clémentine let him place his hands on her shoulders. As she was about to beg him to help her find a way to get into Vladislav's mind again, she got a glimpse of Odette's face. Clémentine had finally had more than enough of her. She was the whole reason why Vladislav was in pain and carried a lot of guilt in his mind. She had caused him more suffering than good and she refused to let the woman prevent her from freeing Vladislav from his mind, where Judith was keeping him captive.

Clémentine left Naten alone in her bedroom and walked to the other side of the room because she had a few words to say to Odette. Naten followed, and she looked toward the door, where there were guards she hadn't seen before. She turned her attention back to Odette, refusing to let her out of her sight. The more she studied her character, the more she found it strange that she always happened to be at the right place at the right moment. Yet, there were no traces of paranormal emanating from her.

"If I lost the last possible trail back to Vladislav's mind because of your delusions, I promise you, I will impale you myself." She then added with a low, fearful voice as she lowered her brows and walked to Odette, pointing Vladislav's tank top to her. "I pitied you when I first heard your story. Now all I see is a delusional, manipulative psychotic bitch. Leave while I allow you to walk." Clémentine's anger emanated through her body and was felt all around the room. Odette refused to move and she accused Clémentine of being the reason why the prince was attacked. "You were brought here for the sole purpose of serving the prince as a psychic. I come into my guest room only to find you in Naten's arms and I'm the manipulative bitch?"

Clémentine knew that each second she wasn't trying to get under Vladislav's skin, he was falling deeper into the grip of the bohemian necromancer. She might not have known exactly why all of it was taking place, but she knew that Vladislav meant a lot to that necromancer. That was enough to feed her anger toward the one woman who had implanted doubts in her mind as she was about to let the

Romanian prince into her heart. Clémentine knew from the last moments she had spent in Vladislav's mind that his dormant state could eventually fail, and it would allow the attacker back into his mind. If the sarcophagus couldn't protect him long enough, Clémentine feared she was losing precious time allowing Odette, yet again, to separate her from Vladislav.

"I said get out."

"Only my Vlad orders me."

Clémentine felt her vision darkening. She had no more energy in her body and she suddenly weighed a ton. She heard Naten stomping on the woman who caused so many problems since her arrival in Vladislav's life. Clémentine stepped back against the frame of the boudoir entrance, feeling a cold sweat all over her body. She watched Naten and his words made her skin crawl.

"You knew what would happen to you if you stepped out of your bedroom."

"You are not Vladislav! You are nothing but his pyramid friend!" Odette shouted, a horrified expression on her face.

"How dare you disrespect me! I am Pharaoh Akhenaten, King of Egypt!" Naten shouted, as he forcefully grabbed Odette's arm and brought her wrist toward his face. "I will have your hands cut off!" He growled with a gold light in his eyes.

It was clear to Clémentine that in Vladislav's absence, Naten was in charge. She might not have known what Vladislav would do, but she feared his anger towards the silly woman. He might agree with the punishment, due to Odette hitting her, but she decided to interfere and not be the object of a Dark Ages' torture.

"Naten, please…just make her leave. Have her brought back to her chambers and this time, order your guards not to let her leave under any circumstances."

"As you wish, Clémentine."

She held herself up with the framing of the door, her skin was clammy and she had a hard time seeing. She was holding Vladislav's tank top so tight in her hands that she could feel a cramp forming. Then, Odette's whining took over as she ordered Naten to let her go, and that Clémentine had absolutely no power in the house.

"That bitch has no power here! She's not Mrs. Dracula!"

"Maybe not as of yet, but there is a chance and then it would be Mrs. Tepes." Clémentine answered with a grave voice.

Clémentine fought back her anxiety, but then the image of who Vladislav truly hit. He was incapable of love, as hard as a hammer, and she quickly snapped out of her daydream. "Naten, please, get her out of here." Clémentine said as she was slowly sliding down the frame, unable to keep herself up any longer. Clémentine watched Naten forcefully pushing Odette out of the bedroom. He shouted at some guards, and in a flash, four werewolf guards showed up. They took Odette from him and began moving her down the hall. The woman shouted against Naten's orders, saying that Clémentine dared take control but Naten quickly fixed the matter.

"Mrs. Odette Lefebvre is to be kept in her chambers until Vlad is awake again. Until further notice, she is not to be seen anywhere. If she escapes, once found, cut off her hands. Have I made myself clear?"

"Yes,   Pharaoh."

CHAPTER 31
BURRY ME ALIVE

Odette's screams were strident and almost unbearable to Clémentine, whose headache picked up, and a moment later she fell onto the floor, her eyes closed. She only had her hearing to make her aware of her surroundings. "You will be quiet, Mrs. Lefebvre!" Naten shouted masterfully. "You have hurt the one woman my best friend made his. The blood on the side of her face was caused by you, and when I tell the *Printul* about this, you can be sure that there will be hell to pay."

The shout from Odette was loud, her voice cracking and shaking, "Please, please Naten, do not tell him, please."

"I do not keep secrets from my best friend. My role is to rule until he is with us again and then to report every single thing that had happened in his absence, and I will. I am fed up with you taking advantage of the Romanian hero. Now fuck off."

Clémentine heard Naten's footsteps coming toward her, "Clémentine!" Naten shouted, worried as she felt him picking her up from the ground. She quickly felt a cold metallic drop falling on her lips, but she did not have the strength to open her mouth. She then felt Naten's hand behind her neck, moving up to hold her head back. He gently moved her mouth open, and another drop fell in.

Clémentine felt it going down her tongue and touching her uvula, which caused her to choke. When it finally went down her throat, a burst of energy kicked in and she could finally open her eyes. She felt so safe deep in Vladislav's arms, her head against his chest. She squeezed her arms around his waist, but then she noticed there was no long black hair, and the body seemed leaner than usual. It wasn't Vladislav. It was Naten.

"Are you okay?" Naten asked, worried.

"Wait, did you just give me your blood?" Clémentine asked furious, although thankful for a burst of energy.

"No, no, I never would. Pharaohs don't carry that healing factor. It was his blood from the scarab."

Naten softly said, almost fearful of what would've happened if he'd been the one giving her his blood.

Naten explained to Clémentine that Vladislav made it very clear to everyone in the house that when he agreed to give her his blood, he was the one to take care of her. Therefore she would not be fed anyone else's blood. Clémentine found it quite confusing but, still dizzy, she asked how much more he carried in the scarab. Clémentine quickly thought about the fact that Vladislav was merely a ghost of himself at the moment and undead, but Naten answered, "Enough to have you in a trance for days. I cannot give him all of his blood back at once. I must give it back a little at a time so that he doesn't overwhelm himself with all its abilities at once. It would be too overwhelming for him, or anyone else for that matter. When I saw you run to the bedroom to get Vlad's tank top, I thought about letting you know I had his blood. At the time, you seemed quite determined to give Odette a piece of your mind."

The scarab held Vladislav's blood. More than enough to have her reach and save him. The question was if she would be strong enough to survive the entire journey into Vlad's mind. She walked to her bedside table and took out her bottle of gummy multi-vitamins. She chewed on three of them and sat down on the edge of the bed.

She put on some yoga pants and grabbed her zipped hoodie on the chair by the armoire. Naten had his back to the bedroom and asked when the last time was she had something to eat. Clémentine couldn't remember. The Pharaoh said that vitamins might not be enough to save his best friend from the grip of a master necromancer. She saw him walking toward her as she finished tying her hair up into a bun. Naten explained to her that the experience would most likely be exhausting, demanding, painful, and most certainly draining of all energy. She wasn't ready for a battle. In her condition, weak and surviving on only a few drops of vampire blood, as euphoric as it was, it wouldn't be enough against Judith.

"I will not let you risk my best friend's life on an empty stomach."

"Lead the way."

"Good, follow me to the kitchen."

"You're the Pharaoh."

They both walked out of the bedroom and headed for the main staircase where Clémentine recognized the werewolf guards. It was not because of their appearance, but because the sun was slowly going down, and it proved to still be too bright for vampires to walk out of their hidden lairs. She admitted feeling quite dizzy and the Pharaoh explained that her body had adapted to the amount of blood given by Vladislav.

She would now require more to be satisfied, at least until she decided if she would herself become a vampire or stay human. Clémentine had never thought the choice might be given to her. She would say yes in a heartbeat. Naten reminded her that if she became a vampire, the sunlight would forever disappear from her life and so would the people she loved. They would grow old and one day be gone, growing jealous of her staying forever young.

Naten was right, there had to be pros and cons to become a vampire, but her love for Vladislav grew stronger every second. Maybe it was starvation, dizziness, or the heavy load on her shoulders to save him from the grip of the necromancer, but Clémentine felt her heart giving in to the vampire Vladislav was. She thought maybe it was a delusion on her part to think maybe he would, one night, love her back.

Inside the kitchen on the right side of the mansion, Clémentine heard Naten announce as he turned around with a very firm voice, "Waffles, fruits, and English cream for the lady. Pancakes with sausage and eggs for me, and two glasses of ice-cold milk." Clémentine didn't say anything but wondered how Naten knew about her preferences in food. The Pharaoh just smiled and said, "I have my ways."

Clémentine looked at the plate, impressed with the portions and how well it was presented. It smelled fresh and sweet, but her appetite was gone the moment she cut her first bite. Clémentine felt repulsed by the food, and she couldn't understand why, as waffles were her favorite food.

"I will not have you leave the table until you finish at least a third of your plate, Clémentine." Naten said very gravely, as he took a bite off his plate.

"You can't make me!" Clémentine retorted angrily as she stood up.

Quickly two werewolf guards stood next to Clémentine, and stared at her with their mean eyes. They were not about to let her move or even leave the kitchen. Clémentine felt trapped, and she stared at them as she sat back down and wondered what was happening to her. When her eyes were back on Naten, she saw him signal them with his hands to move away.

"What are you doing, Naten?"

"I'm taking care of you while my best friend is captive, yet again." Naten replied hurt and hopeless.

Clémentine wondered how she could nourish her body if the look of it was turning her stomach upside down. She didn't understand what was happening, since everything on her plate looked quite appetizing. She should've been very hungry. Yet, the more she would look at her food, the less she would find it delicious. Something was obviously wrong and she looked at Naten for an explanation, as he was enjoying his own food.

"May I ask, is something wrong with your food, Clémentine?"

"What gave it away?"

Clémentine saw Naten rolling his eyes. His hands above her plate, he cut her a piece of waffle, poked it, and brought it to her mouth. He ordered her to take the bite, but as she got close to it, she felt a burning liquid coming up her throat. Clémentine slightly moved away, and Naten lowered his hand, clearly annoyed by her way of avoiding the inevitable. She grabbed the fork and tried again to bring it to her mouth, but again, it left her feeling nauseated.

"Look, I know what you're going through, Clémentine. Vlad's blood is very empowering and overwhelming. Believe me, I know. I have gone through what you are feeling. If you do not eat while he gives you his blood, you'll simply become addicted, and it'll start changing your own body. You become dependent and think that blood is all you need. However, it's all an illusion. While it gives you strength, energy, and all that you can dream of, it does not nourish your body entirely. You still need physical food and drink. You are a breather, Clémentine."

Naten grabbed the fork and reached out for her hand. There were a few gasps, but Clémentine seemed to be more focused on Naten's touch and his words. She let him know that she wished to eat that she was just struggling. The Pharaoh decided to explain how he knew the reaction of a breather's body to be nourished by a vampire.

"Damian was badly wounded in a battle back when he turned twenty-seven years old. He was brought back to his father in his guards' arms. He was placed at his feet and Vlad knew without him, he wouldn't make it. Silver bullets, silver swords, silver everything had burned his skin and poisoned his blood. Damian was rotting from the inside out."

There was a cold silence in the room. Clémentine could tell Naten wasn't comfortable telling the story of someone he considered his nephew. He explained that his presence was due to the first gathering of a few different monsters. They met to decide the fate of their future, and to see who would range themselves with Vladislav and himself. Naten appeared like a very introverted person, just like Clémentine, and he tried to condense his version instead of creating a story out of a memory.

"Vlad never thought twice. He brought his wrist to Damian's mouth and his son's fangs tore into his flesh. Vlad pulled Damian up against his chest and whispered with his thick Romanian accent; 'Drink Damian! Drink!' He did. The moment his blood fell into Damian's mouth and went down his throat, I could tell by the color of his flesh and his smile that his poisoned body rejuvenated before our eyes. The boy felt what it was like to be a dominant being. He felt invincible, stronger than anyone, and quite powerful. Damian grabbed his father's wrist and held it strongly against his mouth and Vlad never pulled away.

Vlad wanted his son to heal and be healthy again." Naten ended with emotion in his voice. It was obvious all the love that Naten had for his friend. Clémentine decided to put her other hand over his and listened. It was clear to her that Naten needed someone to talk to and care for him in a way that maybe   no one could.

"Later on, Damian was brought to Vlad's personal bedroom. No one is ever allowed in there. Vlad gave him two more mouthfuls of his blood, and the boy was finally healed. You know, it's true that lycanthropes are most likely to heal from anything, but sadly, Damian wasn't at his prime yet. The weapons he was wounded with were almost pure silver or mercury, and it poisons them. What I'm trying to say is that without Vlad, Damian wouldn't be here right now."

Clémentine watched Naten taking a deep breath before he went on, looking outside at the rain. "Because Damian loved the feeling of Vlad's blood so much, he even faked being wounded or sick afterwards. He would cut himself at times with mercury knives, just so Vlad would give him his blood. He   lied   to   him   for   about a year."

Understanding that Damian had grown addicted to Vlad's blood, she feared it could happen to her at any time, especially if given the chance to share a part of her life with him. Clémentine asked him how he had come to know about it. Naten explained that he and Vlad always kept in touch, either by letters or visiting one another.

"I was the one who told him I thought Damian was a night blood junkie."

"What did Vlad do?" Clémentine asked worried, her hand over her mouth. She knew how cruel Vladislav was recognized to be.

"He gave the boy the worst punishment of all."

Clémentine's eyes covered in tears, and she pulled both her sleeves over her hands to cover her mouth in horror. Scenes raced through her head of imagined terrors. Naten chuckled, and she wondered why he would think it was okay for a father to torture his child, adopted or not.

"Whatever you are thinking, you are wrong."

"Then, what did he do to Damian that is worth laughing at?" Clémentine asked worried.

"He took Damian by his arm, pulled him forward, and brought him to the main level of his castle in Romania. He ordered a plate of sweets and porridge with fruits and a glass of milk. He ordered Damian to eat at least a third of his plate before he would be excused." Naten said with a wide smile.

Clémentine looked down at her plate with a shy smile and saw Naten taking the fork back in his hand to lead it toward her mouth. She parted her lips and took a bite. As she was about to spit it out, he ordered her not to. "You must fight the urge,

Clémentine. It's crucial to your detox." He wanted her to chew on it and swallow the bite, despite the taste in her mouth. Clémentine bit down on the sweet dough and tried her best not to taste anything. Naten ordered her to swallow it.

"It all tastes like clay, doesn't it?" Naten said with a grin.

"How do you…I guess Damian told you." Clémentine grimaced. "Why didn't you warn me that it would taste like dirt?"

"Because if I would've warned you, you would've expected that horrible taste. Then you would not have understood how being on a vampire blood diet affects your body."

As Clémentine was about to try another bite, Naten assured her that by the third one her taste would be back, and he also handed her two vitamin C tablets. "You, feeding off Vlad, somehow will leave your body deprived of it. Don't ask me how it happens, it just does. Vlad had Damian eat so much spinach and potatoes back then, before we moved to where they had oranges."

Clémentine chewed on the tablets and after a few more bites, she suddenly felt her stomach starting to scream. Famished, Clémentine tore the waffles apart, and started filling up her mouth like she hadn't eaten in days. Naten warned her not to eat too fast but she craved every single thing in front of her eyes.

The food went down easily, and tasted even better than she remembered. Even the colors seemed brighter and more vibrant. She wondered how it was possible and Naten confirmed it was one of the side effects of having vampire blood in her veins. When Clémentine realized that half of her plate was more than enough, she finished her glass of milk. Naten stood up to go to the kitchen in the back. She looked outside and decided to walk to the glass patio door, which led to a roofed porch. Two of the guards began to   follow her out.

"I just want to step outside, please." Clémentine said, promising that she wouldn't go anywhere, but none of them answered. "They won't talk to you, they only answer me. I'm sorry." Naten handed her a white mug filled up with creamy hot chocolate and small marshmallows on top with a cinnamon stick. It was her favorite drink and she wondered how he would know. "Pure coincidence, it's also my favorite drink," Naten said with a smile.

They were both standing outside and Clémentine asked Naten to help her. "Please, when I was in Vlad's mind, your best friend's mind, I felt his need to be freed as quickly as he could." Naten answered, "Follow me."

Clémentine followed Naten back to the kitchen. Clémentine asked if he judged her ready to go psychic against Judith and he reminded her Vladislav

himself believed in her enough to keep her close to him. Clémentine sensed that Naten was telling the truth. She had skills, and she had been practicing for years. Despite her knowledge of fighting another being like herself, or close to herself, she had to and needed to
show confidence.

"Believe me, Vlad is very protective of innocents. If he didn't believe in you, you wouldn't be here."

"Vlad told me how much you enjoyed sweets and so, I thought you might prefer a white-hot chocolate. I see by your smile that you are enjoying yourself." Clémentine nodded and took another sip. When she put the mug down, she heard Naten chuckle. He grabbed a napkin and wiped her upper lip. "You had some of the marshmallow cream on you." Clémentine felt quite comfortable in Naten's presence and she loved the way his eyes glowed when he smiled, showing just a bit of his Pharaoh side. Their hands touched as Naten put the napkin down.

"Maybe we should go now," Naten said, suddenly uncomfortable as he put both his hands in his front pockets.

"Yes, I think we should. The more time we spend not helping Vlad, the more he falls into this artificial sleep he put himself in."

Naten grabbed her mug, put it on the counter and warned Clémentine about the skillful witch she was about to take down. Apparently, it wasn't the first time Vlad had been attacked by her psychic abilities. Clémentine asked how many times, and he answered four. Each time left a scar in his memory, a constant reminder that he was not capable of keeping her away or defending himself.

"She will show you things so that you will despise him. She will try anything in her power to have you repulsed by him so that you will leave him alone to defend himself. Remember, you know Vlad the Impaler. Most of what was told about him in books was true, not all the details, but most of it. Please, do not be disgusted by his past. He was, and still is a good man."

Clémentine nodded, suddenly wondering what type of memory she would try to have her witness of Vladislav. She could remember all the chapters of Vladislav's life, so many could have inspired horror movies worthy of a rating not proper for even premium cable.

She stared at Naten and saw his pupils glowing brighter. His skin displayed hieroglyphs of an ancient time and she noticed on his skin marks from bandages, while his scarab amulet glowed. Naten turned around and Clémentine could swear she saw a change in Naten's stature. The Pharaoh's voice got deeper and sounded very cold.

"I warned you never to get close to Clémentine again." Naten growled loudly.

"Clémentine, or is it your highness now?" A cocky and challenging voice responded in the kitchen entrance.

Clémentine stood up but immediately felt Naten's hand on the side of her thigh as an order for her to stay behind his back. Naten's stature was very imposing alone and his voice should've been enough to scare the person trying to defy him.

"What do you want, Frederick?"

"I want her, that little bitch of a witch, your motherfucking friend likes so much."

"Go ahead. One more step, and I rip you to shreds, scumbag."

"Stand down, alien face! That's right! To me you'll always be Mr. Nefertiti and the stupid ass who tried to make his people believe he was a god himself."

With a roll of his eyes, Naten answered, "I never did that, UV whore."

Clémentine was astonished. Frederick had been released from his dungeon. He was healed and now back for vengeance against her since she was the reason for his torment. Clémentine then thought about Naten. If they knew he was Vlad's best friend and heard the entire story about Damian, it would mean the end of their immortal existence.

She had to do something.

There had to be a way for her to give Naten an advantage in the inevitable attack to come. Also, she had to know who had freed him, because vampires and werewolves were guarding the room Frederick was placed in. She knew some vampires were Frederick's followers but it would've been too dangerous for him to escape at night. She was certain that none of the werewolves followed him.

CHAPTER 32
THE VIKING KING

Clémentine knew Frederick had the help of humans to get out of his cell. It was apparent to her now that by adding Odette to the equation, the two had worked together. She had made it clear that she wanted Vlad all to herself and that Clémentine was in her way. Frederick obviously desired revenge and so the two of them together could accomplish their goal. They were the only two with something to gain from having Vladislav indisposed. At first, Clémentine thought Odette incapable of hurting Vladislav. However, if it meant having Frederick get rid of herself, Damian, and Naten, then she had nothing to lose. Vlad had already made it clear he had no intention of reconnecting with her at all.

"Where is Odette? Isn't she the one who helped you out of your dungeon? She should be here savoring her sweet victory while she can."

"Who says Odette helped me, bitch? You think I don't have what it takes to free myself from Vlad's antique punishment? Seriously, the old man doesn't have much imagination."

Clémentine saw Frederick slouching, wiping his nose and agitated. She knew she had caught the Scandinavian in a lie. Through his body language, she could tell he was quite unsure of the success of the plan. Odette was clever. She was probably hiding herself away from the scene, trying to stay away from any witnesses.

"When I saw you, Frederick, you were unable to take any more pain. After the burning, blinding, whipping, and impaling, what was left for you to endure?" Clémentine asked as she walked from behind Naten. Her arms were crossed over her chest, acting as if she truly wanted Frederick to reveal his secret.

"You know about my Gravedigger ability but do you know how strong and how deep it goes?" She smiled, winking as she walked toward him. "Let me tell you. I taste one drop of blood and your entire life reveals itself to me. Imagine that! One single drop and I can tell Vlad if you're lying, how you escaped, and how you planned to take over his entire household and kill him in the process."

The Scandinavian raised his hands. "Whoa! I'm not taking the blame for that, bitch!" Clémentine straightened herself, squinted her eyes, and asked what he was to take blame for then. "Odette freed me, all right? The deal was she would free me so I could flee along with my buddies and join Latauro. All I had to do was to get rid of you and Naten. That was it."

There were now four vampires standing in the kitchen beside Frederick. Clémentine saw them by discreetly moving her head to the side, and they looked hungry. Those men might have been lean, but they were vicious vampires. Clémentine didn't know how Naten would handle his own against one vampire. What could a Pharaoh do against four vampires?

The pigmentation in the vampires' eyes were bright red. They were either famished, angry, and most likely aroused by all the blood they were about to get if Naten shall fail to protect her. Clémentine thought about Vladislav. She had to know the truth and now that it was confirmed that Odette had been involved in the plot, she had to get them out of the kitchen. However, by the look on Frederick's buddies' faces, it was very well possible that those vampires would do anything to stop them.

Suddenly, a loud and impressive echo was heard. Once it dissipated, a strong wind, like a tornado, whipped through the room. Clémentine put the hood over her head and squinted her eyes. As she turned, she saw Naten's arms apart, sand coming in from below the outside door. Clémentine didn't hear anything, but when his mouth opened, the vampires quickly changed their stances. She saw that they were covering their ears, while blood was pouring from each ear. At that point, the werewolf guards came barging in the kitchen.

Clémentine feared for Naten and the other two guards who appeared. She had never seen werewolves fight before and wasn't sure how powerful a Pharaoh was against vampires. Despite her time spent in Vladislav's mind, Clémentine couldn't tell how long Vladislav would last without his token, without his mind, or in the sarcophagus.

Her worries grew and she had to find a way to get out of the kitchen before the vampires decided to attack. The room was bathed in a low light, provided by Naten's golden glow, and then everything was silent. The room was cooler than usual, giving it an eerie feel. The house emptied of any sound, only the loud animalistic breathing of the two different creatures could be heard.

Clémentine knew that the moment she stepped forward, they would try and grab her. Clémentine quickly deducted that the reason she was still free was because they somehow feared what Naten could truly do. She decided to take advantage of it.

"Frederick," Clémentine said firmly while all eyes turned to her once again. She walked before Naten and pointed at her ears so Naten would release the same sound as he did before. The vampires couldn't escape the pain of the frequency. This left Clémentine capable of entering Frederick's mind after licking one drop of his blood, which was coming out of his right ear.

His past was filled with anger and hatred. The Scandinavian held Clémentine responsible for the torture he was put through and refused to let her breathe any longer. Frederick did not wish to kill her. He was determined to turn her into a vampire. By doing so, she would be his progeny, and make her suffer, just as much as he did.

Frederick's mind was one of a Viking back in the late tenth century. Clémentine could see his memories of a faraway northern land where the aurora borealis were common. She saw his voyages from Britain to France, from his homeland to other Scandinavian acreages. Frederick had a wife and six children, of which four were boys who grew into young men, but were killed in battles. His youngest son had been tortured to death because of him. His two daughters were taken away from him. One was sent to marry an English king or to marry the English king, while the other went to Paris. Frederick was but a shadow of the man he once was, a servant to the Romanian prince. Vlad the Impaler wouldn't keep his title for long if he wouldn't make an example out of him and give the coup de grace that would end him for good.

"I was a Viking king," Frederick growled. He was held on his knees by the sound Naten produced, torturing his hearing.

Clémentine had no pity for him, but for his family as she answered coldly with a grave voice, "Your greed sold all that you had in shame."

Clémentine saw everything, his cries, and his despair when he lost the ones he loved the most. His precious Anna was the youngest of his children. He protected her as much as he could and was ready to die for her. She had just turned fourteen when she was taken to Paris as a captive.

She screamed his name, she screamed for him to save her, but he was already being chained and beaten to his death. That is when a tall woman with hair as fair as moonlight walked up to him and promised him all that he had been looking for: Immortality.

"*Yet, you didn't save your children,*" Clémentine sent the message to Frederick's mind. The Viking answered back with shame, tears of red rolling down his face, "*She wouldn't let me.*"

Deeper in Frederick's thoughts, in a place he kept as dark as the night, she saw him spying on Anna. Clémentine had a great sigh of relief when she witnessed the happiness as Anna first met her future husband. He was protecting her on the day of their wedding. "In those times, women were violated on the day of their wedding by men, who were trying to claim the bride for themselves. Once Anna's vows were said and she walked to her new bedroom with her new husband, she cried."

Then, Clémentine saw the hand of her husband in hers, ready to take on anyone who would come close to his wife. The memory ended when Anna's husband took her in his arms and ordered everyone out of the room with a loud voice. To Clémentine's surprise, the man was young, barely eighteen years old.

"His name was Constantin and he was to become the ruler of his land. Anna had a long happy life with him, bearing four children. He loved her, and he had to, because I would've killed him."

Clémentine felt his pain when unable to reach his child, "I believe you."

Clémentine refused to look into the lives of his other children. She knew most of them had not been so lucky, the pain on Frederick's face was clear. She used her skills to dig deeper into Frederick's mind, to control his thoughts and keep him off balance. She wanted to see what he had planned for Naten, Vladislav, and herself. She might even discover who held

Vladislav's token.

Frederick dreamed of the night he could sit on the throne again. He worked his way up the vampire hierarchy to become a potential candidate to replace the Scandinavian Queen, but sadly Vladislav had other plans for Frederick. He wanted him to become his general, trusting in his Viking skills to defend his realm, and instead named Damian next in line for his throne.

Frederick never trusted Damian to be a true vampire, as he had never witnessed him walk to a lair to hide himself from daylight. The Viking couldn't even recall the last time he saw Damian fed on someone and the idea of serving Vladislav's son repulsed him to the point that he agreed to end him by Odette's orders.

"I will have them both dead, Vlad and Damian, a death worthy to be passed down generations. I will keep their heads and hang them above my bed so you, Clémentine, can see it every time we lie down to remind you of your hero's fall."

Frederick's mind was dark from years of pain and sadness. His past took over his entire body and created the monster Clémentine witnessed that night. What she needed to understand was why. All she saw was a greedy king, who would've done anything to save his family, but lost it all.

Three breathing women had played Frederick throughout his vampire life. There may have been centuries in between each, but all three used him for the same reason. They had wanted to become Vladislav's givers, hoping to become his next wife. Although the Viking refused to admit he had feelings for them, as they reminded him of his wife, he did love them. His trust in women died along with the last shred of humanity he had ever had.

He gave in to the vampire instincts of a bestial ravaging scavenger and once Clémentine entered Vladislav's life, he knew it would wreck his plans of taking over the throne. He felt her psychic abilities were stronger than anyone he had ever encountered. He knew Vladislav suspected something was wrong and he blamed Naten. He had always been by Vladislav's side every time an attack occurred, keeping his friend safe.

"I will have you as mine," He said with a low voice, fighting the urge to cover his ears.

"I do not belong to anyone, Frederick. Never have, and never will."

"Is that so? Do you think Vlad will not own your freedom?" The Viking asked with a smile. "If you think I am a psychopath, wait until you see what Vlad is truly capable of when he loves a woman. He owns what he loves, and he loves you."

Red lines were forming under Frederick's eyes. The pain of the frequency was damaging his hearing. However, Clémentine had finally heard what Vladislav wanted to say; yet it was from the lips of a vampire that couldn't be trusted. Trying to put everything together, she wondered what he told Odette to have her believe that getting rid of her would cause Vlad to fall back into her arms.

"Odette might be delusional. I should know, as I've witnessed her in Vlad's life until she was moved here without so much as a thank you for her services. She wants him and will stop at nothing to have Vlad love her. Yet what Vlad has planned for you is more than owning your freedom. He'll make you his for eternity, without any means of escaping, except…you know."

Yes, Clémentine knew, falling to her final judgment. She was not about to listen to someone who wished nothing but to avenge his pain and ally himself with a nutcase. Clémentine had given enough time to delusional people to create doubt and fear in her mind.

As she was about to try and extract the scene between him and Odette from his mind, she heard Frederick choking, "So, how does it feel to be in total control? Exquisite isn't it, Clémentine? You decide if I am to give you what you wish or to terminate me. Go ahead, do it! Let me see the evil a true woman can do."

CHAPTER 33
THE GLASS SLIPPER CUT

Anger, terror, and disgust took over her thoughts and she lost all control over Frederick's mind. As she released her grip, she felt the Viking grabbing onto her legs, forcing her down. Naten stopped his frequency, and the scene changed from them having the upper hand, to angry vampires ready to attack. Quickly, before Clémentine could be kidnapped, Naten grabbed Frederick by the throat and threw him out the window. The glass left a strident echo in the building as the body of the vampire violently flew through it. The moment Naten stepped outside to walk in Frederick's direction, Clémentine ran out of the way, but not without a wooden stake that was given to her by one of Naten's guards. He stayed by her side to protect her from the two remaining vampires.

Clémentine saw the last two vampires running after Naten, who had suddenly become a worthy adversary. Like a predator, his dominant stature and strength startled both vampires. Naten, violently held down by one of the traitors, got a mean punch across his face by the biggest one there. The big goon made the other vampire hold Naten up as he pounded on his abdomen as hard as he could. Clémentine could barely watch, and it all became blurry once her vision watered up. The Pharaoh seemed to have given up.

"Clémentine!" The guard shouted. She shouted in her head, *Stop!* The vampire fell to his knees, and Clémentine remembered, *"Vampires are undead."* The vampire was young enough to be easily commanded, unlike Frederick who required most of her energy. She was the last Gravedigger, and that also meant feeling the dead. Once the younger vampire was bound in silver chains, Clémentine thanked the guard for his help. He mentioned that her abilities did not go unnoticed and that despite not being a necromancer, she was close enough to one to be feared by all beings alive or dead. Thinking about leaving the house altogether, she realized she could never leave him behind. There was too much she loved within the building to escape.

"You will save Vlad, won't you, milady?"

"That's all I want to do."

The guard let go of the silver chains, and kicked the young vampire onto the ground to keep him there. Clémentine tried to run to Naten but felt an arm pulling her back, preventing her from going anywhere. "Naten!" Clémentine screamed, but the big vampire opened his mouth wide and closed in on Naten with his fangs, ready to suck him dry. Clémentine screamed as loud as she could but Naten wasn't done.

She watched one of the two vampires being thrown into the back of the garden, deeply wounded as thick black froth spilled out of their mouth and vomiting as they tried to get back up. "Incapacitate him now and bring him back to me!" Naten shouted at his two guards.

Clémentine then witnessed one of the most violent acts right before her eyes. What she had seen from Vladislav's past, although cruel and barbaric, was nothing unexpected. As Naten stared down at the vampire, he was ready to bleed him like an animal. Clémentine realized then that the Pharaoh wasn't the kind soul she thought he was. He was a man that was at the head of all the Pharaohs of his league. He would be a strong partner to join sides with Vladislav in the civil war that was coming between the monsters.

Clémentine watched as Naten grabbed the vampire by the throat, forcing him on his knees before tearing both his arms off. With his arms swirling in sand, Naten violently plunged them into the vampire's torso, only to reform in the flesh as he pulled out the pancreas and stomach before he finally decapitated the poor creature. Naten held the head up in the air in front of the vampires, guards, givers, and helpers that had gathered. They all wanted to witness Naten's greatness in one of the bloodiest battles they had seen in   a long time.

"This is why in Vladislav's absence, I, King Akhanaten, am on his throne." Naten stated with the deepest, coldest voice Clémentine had ever heard. "Who will challenge me?" A river of blood was running off Naten's mouth from the head losing its fluids. His eyes menacing reflected the moonlight as he was standing tall and proud in the middle of the backyard. His body was covered in red and dirt, with bite marks all over his chest and neck.

Clémentine wondered if she would be better off back home, afraid of both Naten and Vladislav. She stared at the Pharaoh tearing his shirt off, as it was falling to pieces. He then threw the vampire's head away like a quarterback would with a football. He stepped over the body after spitting on it. Clémentine witnessed it changing into a gruesome pool of blood in the blink of an eye and then magically reduced to nothing but a pile of ashes.

As Naten was about to step back inside the kitchen, she considered a million scenarios to try and get away from him. Naten quickly turned around and tightened his grip around the last of the vampires and held him at arm's length. It was Frederick. Clémentine could see Frederick grasping Naten's forearm, trying to free himself. It was like a déjà vu, as she remembered Vladislav doing the same to him back in New Orleans. "I will have your head," Naten growled as he loosened his grip, letting Frederick fall to the ground. As Damian was about to order his men to bring Frederick to a secret location, the Viking spoke up, with a cracking voice.

"Whatever you do, it's over. Vlad has lost! His token is gone, his mind belongs to the pikey, and Odette will get what she wants. Your best buddy is gone, and there's nothing you can do. Even your sarcophagus cannot keep him alive endlessly, because without it, you'll turn to sand."

"I warned Vlad about you long before he accepted you. I said not to trust kings of the past as his guards, because they would envy his throne. Once a king, always a king."

"He wanted Vikings as guards. He got most of them because of the Scandinavian Queen but he won't get me and my followers. Never."

"Then so be it."

Naten's strength was fading. Clémentine noticed that the glow in his eyes was dissipating. She walked to the Pharaoh and looking at Frederick, said that she wouldn't keep it a secret if Odette ever asked about who spat the entire truth about their plan. With a smile she added, "I would fear a Pharaoh of over three thousand years old with the capability of cursing not only you, but your entire company. Hell would sound rather marvelous compared to having both King Akhenaten and Vlad the Impaler on your ass for eternity. Don't you agree, Frederick?"

Naten smiled and squeezed a little harder around Frederick's throat. As his voice cracked, and gasping for air, he said "Don't think because you're Vlad's bitch, Naten, that I won't come after you if you do anything to me."

"Name calling bores me. I'd rather see what Vlad will do when he gets his hands on you."

Clémentine stood unable to move, thinking about the hours that had passed since she had last tried to infiltrate Vladislav's mind. She was hoping it wasn't too late to save him. Afraid of what Odette might do, and terrified of the bohemian, Clémentine wished she just ran to Vladislav and hugged him out of the nightmare.

Clémentine tried to hide against the wall, hoping Naten would leave the kitchen with Frederick. But she was going to be disappointed. "Take him. You know where, and have him guarded around the clock. Your men only, Arnold."

The werewolf agreed, and calling eight of his guards, left kitchen which had turned into a battlefield. Naten walked to Clémentine, who noticed his body was covered in bruises. She saw that many of them were old, but some were new, covering his chest and abdominals. Naten's mouth was covered in blood, as was the rest of him, and Clémentine realized what a Pharaoh could truly do to other beings, such as vampires.

"Humans aren't at the top of the food chain, are they?"

"Humans don't turn to sand after a week without their sarcophagus. Humans don't burst into flames when walking in the sun. Humans don't explore new life, they conquer it. I'd say you're fine, but I'd be lying. I do not wish to lie to you, Clémentine."

"Why would you say I'm not fine?"

"Because you're more than just human. You're the one who will save Vlad from that fucking pikey and her puppet."

His eyes were barely glowing and Clémentine knew she had to help him too, so that he could rejuvenate. He needed his sarcophagus that was keeping Vladislav alive. She took his hand and stood up. Thanking him for his protection, she confessed that she had never thought that the power of a Pharaoh could be so great. He chuckled and said, "I can't wait for you to meet Nefertiti." Clémentine covered her mouth with awe. "She is quite a Pharaoh herself." Despite revealing that he was no longer with his original wife, he reminded Clémentine that he lived in a different time with a few problems. "You would call it schizophrenia. I actually have a human friend bringing me the medication I need. I'm not as strong as   I   seem, mentally anyway."

Clémentine felt as if Naten had read her mind about her doubts. Suffering from anxiety was a burden on her shoulders and she did fear the memories she would see. She knew Vladislav's life, and she could scare easily. Naten held her hand and said he would be with her every step of the way.

Clémentine shifted her weight, getting ready to leave the kitchen, and her right ankle felt like a strong sting went through her flesh and hit her bone. Naten caught Clémentine right before she hit the ground. He held her up before sitting her on the kitchen island where he looked down at her ankle. Clémentine gazed at Naten, staring down at her foot, handling it delicately. He gently asked her not to look, that it was swollen, but nothing that he wouldn't be able to take care of with a little of Vladislav's blood.

However, just the idea of living through another of Vladislav's memory wasn't at the top of Clémentine's list. She feared another brutal encounter with the Romanian's prince's past because she feared she would be pulled into his mind at the same moment.

"Look at me, Clémentine," Naten said with a soft smile on his face. As she was about to look down, he held her head with his left hand. "Argh!" Clémentine shouted at the top of her lungs, feeling something being pulled out of her flesh. It created a sensation of a thousand razors grating on her skin. "It was a large piece of glass. I guess the adrenaline gave you a high, but now that all has calmed down, your high did too."

Naten grabbed a kitchen knife and slowly cut the slipper off Clémentine's foot to see the damage. The fur inside the fuzzy boot was stuck to Clémentine's skin and made her cry. Naten carefully peeled it off. He tried to have her look away but her desire to see the damage overtook her and she glanced down.

Her Achilles tendon was severed, and blood still dripped from her leg. Naten leaned it against his shoulder and said, "You have no choice. You need Vlad's blood now, before we have an entire crowd of vampires barging in the kitchen ready to dry you out. Without Vlad to protect you physically, and me at the lowest I've ever been, I can't promise your safety. Unless Damian comes in, we're both in deep shit right now."

Clémentine, scared and helpless, begged for a thread and needle. She added that she needed some disinfectant, and then it would be fine. Naten disagreed and reminded her, "There might be glass dust in the wound, or some residual glass and you want me to stitch you back together cold-turkey? There's no way I'm doing that, you wanna know why? Because I need you at full strength to save my best friend and me. I'm dying, Clémentine."

The pain felt like a constant burn mixed with a heavy beat. Her foot was entirely wet now, and Naten was about to help her lie down, so he could hold her leg up to stop it from bleeding. There was rumble coming from the outside of the kitchen door. Soon, a clan of vampires, probably those following Frederick, would come in and ravage Clémentine, leaving nothing behind except her bones. There was no way Naten would let that happen and Clémentine knew it the moment he took the scarab in his hand.

"I will be with you every single step of the way. I'll hold your hand and protect your body while you're away. Use this as a test to see if you and he are meant to be together."

"Naten, may I ask why you aren't with Nefertiti anymore?"

"Because I was meant to be with someone else, and so was she."

Clémentine wanted to know. She had always thought they seemed perfect together. Her beauty and his mysterious appearance, they were part of a fairy tale. Now, she was about to see if her own *Printul* would be part of her story. Trembling inside, afraid, and suddenly cold, she knew there was no way around it. All there was left for her to do was to win against the bohemian necromancer. Then she could bring Vladislav out of his coma, out of Naten's sarcophagus, and get the token from whoever is holding it.

"I will save you both. I promise." Clémentine said, holding Naten's hand.

"I know Vlad would've wanted it another way. This wasn't what he wanted."

"I know. It never happens the way we plan, but I'll save you both. I promise."

"All right. Here we go."

One drop touched Clémentine's heel, and someone barged in through the door, leaving a strong gust of wind behind. Naten turned his head, his golden pupils shining. Clémentine was afraid she was too vulnerable to attempt any other psychic attack. She knew deep down she needed Vladislav's blood to go into a trance and save him.

Afraid vampires came in, she moved her head and saw a surprise visitor. "Damian, please tell me you're normal again, Naten said as the boy nodded. He guaranteed safe passage to Clémentine's chambers, where she would be safer than in a broken kitchen with broken windows and doors.

A crowd of vampires was surrounding the outside of the mansion. In Naten's arms, Clémentine felt safe. She wrapped her own around his neck and held on tight. She was afraid the drop of blood would soon go into full effect and pull her back into Vladislav's head. She closed her eyes as she didn't want to see who wanted her dead. Instead, she trusted the Pharaoh to bring her to safety. Never in her life had she ever felt this weak and dependent on someone else's strength.

"I've never met a strong woman like you since Nefertiti."

"Really? Because right now, I feel like shit."

"You shouldn't. You are about to save an entire kingdom, and mine as well. Many people depend on our safety, Clémentine, and saving us, means saving them."

When they finally walked up the stairs, Clémentine felt each step like a hit of a hammer on her foot with in harmony with Naten's body. One drop had not been enough she feared she needed more and the more she needed, the more she would see and the deeper she would get. That's how it worked, at least from the experiences she has had so far. New to the blood reading, Clémentine deducted by logic and feared the worst was yet to come.

"Don't worry. It will be over soon."

"What a fraction of a second is to you is an eternity for me. You're immortal, I'm not."

"Yet."

The door opened and Clémentine could smell her chambers. Vladislav's smell, still emanating from her bed sheets, reminded her how much she missed him. Her mind was lonely and her body was craving him. Her arms were missing his skin and she hoped to be strong enough to face the memories of a man who had brought so much terror to human history.

CHAPTER 34
SAY HIS EVIL NAME

Back in her bedroom, Clémentine lay down on her bed and she opened her mouth when Naten took his scarab amulet and brought it to her lips. A few more drops of Vladislav's blood, Clémentine let it sit on her tongue before slowly swallowing. She closed her eyes and focused on the one she promised to save. Clémentine could smell his mossy scent and then felt the cool breeze roaming through her mind, followed by a small static shock. Clémentine felt her body getting heavier and she knew it was about to hit her head. It was a strong, heavy memory of his past that he did not want her to see but it was already emerging through his mind. Someone obviously wished for her to fear him.

"Naten, I'm already scared. It's like—"

"Don't fight it yet, Clémentine. Let it take place and remember, everything happens for a reason."

Clémentine knew she could take the bohemian necromancer down but she wasn't sure about the memory that was about to unravel before her eyes. Vladislav had a life that most would consider monstrous and barbaric. She feared that seeing it all through his mind would affect the way she would see him after it was all said and done. She tried to push the fear aside and call for him to come to her. She needed to free him from his mind and reanimate the vampire that had been dormant for too long. Vladislav was not like any other vampire; he was unique, and lonely, alone with his demons. She had to help him and by doing   so,   save a Pharaoh.

Ready or not, Clémentine was being absorbed and a memory of Vladislav was unfolding before her eyes. Clémentine understood that his memories were being spied on. The necromancer was obviously attempting to scare Clémentine so that she would flee Vladislav's protection. It was clear to her because she could feel Vladislav trying to resist and keep that memory away from her at all costs.

Clémentine felt the need to defend Vladislav, so she took possession of his shield and warned him to let go. Nothing would make her leave him, especially not a memory. Clémentine decided it was time for her to take over the bohemian's mind, just like Vladislav had done with her countless times. The shield of ice slowly melted and Clémentine imitated his frequency, leaving the bohemian unaware of her presence. Clémentine tried her best to act as confident as Vladislav would within his mind but she didn't feel as if she was entirely fearless either.

Clémentine accessed a little more of Vladislav's memory, wanting to know what this Judith of Scweinfurt looked like so she could know what to use against her. Knowing her appearance would play against the necromancer if she could draw her and look for her in a databank or on the web. Learn from Vladislav's memory who was this witch and what she caused.

In one memory, Judith had a thin little body dirty, long brown hair, and caved-in, dark eyes. Tattoos going down her legs, she wore a dirty linen dress and was barefoot. It was evident to Clémentine that the last time Vladislav saw the bohemian, she was locked in the dungeon. Clémentine then tried to find a trace of her, not by using Vladislav's abilities, but his senses. She refused to tire him out more than he already was. Clémentine was not about to take possession of his vampire skills that required energy, only what could be easy to use without hurting him any further.

In the back of Vladislav's mind, Clémentine heard the necromancer's nasally voice. She focused on it and because she heard her speak English, Clémentine decided to make sure she would use Vladislav's maternal language. It was all like a dream to Clémentine. When she was in Vladislav's mind, she shared all his knowledge, right down to the language he would use. Clémentine posed as Vladislav and presented herself as him when the necromancer walked before her to attack the prince yet again. A strong anger hit Clémentine's body like lightning from the sky. She fell on her knees, fighting to keep the image of Vladislav alive and not reveal herself.

Clémentine wondered how the necromancer was able to command her, a breather. She wondered if it was because she was in another body and it weakened her. Clémentine was not out of tricks. Knowledge was power, and she intended to use it all.

Clémentine decided to access the other part of Vladislav, the one everyone seemed to fear the most, the burning wind. She focused on Vladislav's body instead of his mind and she slowly felt her own colliding with his to become one. She let Vladislav wrap himself around her residual energy and take control. She let herself fall into him and once she felt the volcanic static, she gave it a reason to be. She ignited the passion, the emotion, and the raw desire to fight.

She felt it strong and so she aimed it toward the necromancer, who stepped back when facing the dark smoky wind. Clémentine could see a whirlpool of embers with ashes dancing around. She felt a strong powerful presence taking over and a freezing sensation burned her entire body from the inside out.

She wouldn't be able to keep going much longer. It was devouring her mind and it wanted to possess and eat her alive. It felt so overpowering, filled with anger, desolation, and torment. It wanted her to give herself to it and Clémentine tried to resist the ice because it wasn't Vladislav. It was someone, or something else, that he alone controlled.

The necromancer was backing away and the icy wind undoubtedly scared the traveler. Clémentine decided to try to order it to push her out but she heard her nasally voice say, "This is impossible. You cannot resist me!" Clémentine found the strength deep inside, while her eyeballs were burning in her skull and her throat and lungs were filling up with a coat of embers to the point of burning her flesh away. "There are many things you do not know about me."

"I know you were given the rare ability of being a Gravedigger and you are of Shamanic descent. I know about your knowledge of history and what you are capable of against the undead, and me. However, what you might not know yet, young girl, is that while other vampires and creatures will fear you, this one that you're in, right this moment, will set you ablaze."

Clémentine refused to listen and tried to use the icy wind to chase the necromancer away. She was almost out of reach, almost ejected out of Vladislav's mind, when she heard the words that would imprint doubts in her mind forever. "You know his name, yet you are afraid to say it. You love him. I know you do, because I feel it too. You might be out of reach for me, for now, but keep in mind, that what I am about to force him to show you is for your own good. I will not disrespect the gift that has been given to you through a long, strong line of witches. So please, Clémentine, see this as a warning I am giving you, to show you who your
heart loves."

Clémentine let go of the ice the moment she felt Judith completely gone. She let go of Vladislav's spirit and let herself breathe. She was exhausted and in more pain than she had ever felt before. Many questions surfaced in her mind, but the moment she was about to whisper to Vladislav to wake up, a rumble was heard. Everything around her changed and Clémentine noticed she was now a ghost in Vladislav's past, a past that she could feel he was still fighting for her not to see. Then, the voice of Judith was heard one last time...

"Only when the memory is over, will you both be free of his mind."

Vladislav was walking outside. It was in the early hours of dawn and the body of a man accused of treason and witchcraft was brought to his feet by two of his best soldiers. The metallic armor of the men was darker with red embellishments, which proved to be somewhat unique.

The man at his feet grabbed onto Vladislav's ankles and begged him for forgiveness. The prince recognized the gentleman; he was one of those who had started rumors about his condition, which brought terror to his people. If only the rumors would've been about him being a vampire, Vladislav would've learned to live with it. Those would have been true. However, that person also claimed that he would drink the blood of virgin men and women until they were dry and impaled those opposed to him.

So many lies were told about Vladislav that he could barely stand looking at the man. He felt betrayed, deceived, and hurt. The man begged for him to set him free, "I have a wife and she's pregnant. Please let me go!"

The prince stepped back, kicking him away, but the man crawled forward. One of the guards stepped on the victim's hand before piercing it with his sword. The scream was loud and frightening, but nothing compared to what was coming. Through his lamentations, the victim made one more mistake that cost him his life. "You are a vampire, we all know it..." If only he had stopped there. "I might have spread lies but that's because I can't trust a monster and a traitor."

Vladislav, in a vampire second, rushed towards the man and lifted him off the ground. Fangs out, he shouted, "I have defended our land for years! I have been wrongfully imprisoned for your safety, and you call me a traitor? You and your men have crossed the line. Your blood will be spilled to pay the debt, for it won't be crossed any further."

The memory moved forward, the sun was not yet about to rise but the colors in the sky changed, becoming more vibrant and in harmony with Vladislav's fury. "Get all of his men, I want them all." Guards ran out into the court and Vladislav let the victim fall, his face hitting the pavement in a puddle of mud. The prince turned to walk away, when yet again, he felt the liar's arms around his ankles.

The beginning was pitiful. "My wife, my child...please, have a heart, my Lord." Vladislav crouched before him, anger burning through his body. "You should've thought about her before telling lies and calling me a traitor. They will speak of me in books. My name will be on everyone's lips centuries from now. You, however, will be rotting in front of my castle, mounted on a wooden stick for a month before we all forget about your name. No one will remember that you ever existed."

The screams were horrifying as the knights were dragging the victim to the square where his torment would begin. The prince had heard them all before; the shouts, the begging, the cursing and finally, the insults. Vladislav had always thought that it was in moments like this, he could see the true face of people. Walking in the opposite direction of the victim, Vladislav felt a violent hit on his back and he stumbled forward. Quickly, one of the knights helped him up, confused, as no one ever touched Vladislav.

"Are you alright my friend?" The knight asked, obviously worried.

Vladislav tried to nod, but his knees seemed to be heavy, and he felt blood coming out of his mouth, nose, ears, and eyes. Vladislav tried to stay up, using his friend to level himself, before he finally hit the ground.

"Something's wrong. I'll go get your giver right away."

Vladislav was now leaning forward, his hands on the ground. A hysterical laugh was heard and the prince suddenly looked toward the man he had condemned to impalement. He stared at the man with disgust for a short while, promising himself that he would pay to have made him kneel in his direction.

"Wait, I'll help you do it," Vladislav said to his men about to pierce the man's body.

Gasps were heard all around but mostly coming from the one who had him kneel. Vladislav found the strength deep inside him to stand up and resist the man's command. For the first time, Vladislav felt a strong current passing through his body. He might have known about the burning sensation he would have deep in his chest, but never the static it would create in his arms and abdomen. He took off his linen shirt and looked at his skin. The change in his flesh was undetectable to the human eye, but clear as day
to Vladislav.

"Now I see it, Vlad! I see it."

"What's happening, Atanase?"

"I wish I knew, my friend," Atanase said, hoping Vladislav would be all right.

The hysterical laugh from the condemned man returned and the humiliation was enough that now, Vladislav felt a strong burning sensation taking over. He was in full control of this newfound power. As he looked upon his friend's face, he saw fright and could smell fear in the air.

Vladislav didn't understand. Atanase was his closest friend, why would he be scared of him? Vladislav looked over his shoulder and noticed a thick black smoke circling around him. What he thought was only a fire burning inside of his body was, in fact, a way to command an entire entity. When the prince finally stood tall and strong, slowly understanding how to rule the smoke, he turned to look at the liar in the eyes.

Vladislav felt the smoke following him and obeying his command. Like a sword, it was an extension of his body, so he guided it forward to push the quisling down on his back as he got closer.

"You can't resist me," The man said, trembling and shaking. Sweat was pouring off of him in terror.

"I just did, necromancer." Vladislav said with a mean grin slowly passing his tongue on his right fang.

"I was reborn as a vampire but not just any vampire. I am stronger, capable of greater things that your mind can never understand."

Vladislav ordered his men to put the man in position. Once the victim was upright, Vladislav lifted the pointed pole and maneuvered through the man's body with vampire strength. There was no resistance as it broke through the man's organs and bones and then spear through his clavicle.

"Plant him in front of the others and bring nourishment to my guards."

Clémentine screamed so loud, one would have thought her vocal cords would burst. The moment her cry came out of her mouth, she opened her eyes in horror. She thought she was finally out of this nightmare, but was drawn back in as she realized Vladislav wasn't free yet. After all, Judith said, *"Only when the memory is over, will you both be free of his mind."*

She wished Vladislav had closed his eyes when the man had violently been tortured. Watching from his final place of torment, to the location where he would slowly become food for the crows was horrifying.

"What was the charge, my prince?" asked one of the men coming his way with a paper and a quill.

"Witchcraft," Vladislav coldly answered.

Vladislav stared at the body, as blood dripped from the pole. The man, his eyes full of tears, unable to cry, scream or even move.

"Let it be a lesson to any necromancers crossing my path," Vladislav shouted, before spitting at the foot of the pole. His knights approached with the remainder of the group. "Say your last words now," he growled, looking down at each of them. They were all brought to the same place but it all went black when Clémentine closed her eyes.

She thought she was scared enough, but there was still a wish for Vladislav to be a good being. The fear of seeing another man being tortured was more than she could take.

She heard another horrifying scream echoing from the background. Just before Vladislav turned again she shouted, "Please! Make it stop!" Clémentine was only a ghost, unable to be heard.

Through her tears, she saw Vladislav quickly turning in her direction, his hand forward. He crouched by her side and took her hands away from her face, "It's okay, my little *înger*, I'm here now. Close your eyes." There was a burning sensation in Vladislav's belly, and his arms were warming up. Clémentine felt the prince gently pushing her out of his mind. Clémentine resisted, despite the horror that she had witnessed from his past, she had promised she would save him and she tended to hold her promise.

Clémentine was about to take over the icy wind but she turned over to her right where she felt a set of eyes spying on them. Judith had never entirely disappeared. While Clémentine's senses were focused on what was happening around her, as she had never witnessed anything so brutal and barbaric, she heard the voice of the unwanted presence.

"Do you see the monster you have fallen for?" Judith asked.

"It would take more than this memory to have me walk away from him."

"Won't you? By all means, say the name we all know him to have. If you love him, you have to love all of him," Judith's voice, so suspicious yet so real, Clémentine somehow felt frightened.

When she turned around to face Vladislav, she saw his eyes were crimson red, his arms were flexed, and his fists clenched. His current was at full capacity when the fire was ignited in his chest. Clémentine could see the fire from under his skin. Vladislav was a mean man. He was a mean breather and vampire.

He was to be feared. When the current was discharged, the fire enveloped Judith entirely. Vladislav shouted at the top of his lungs, "Get out!" The energy charge acted as a lightning strike when it got to the necromancer. She was violently and brutally propelled out of his mind.

Clémentine was now emptied of all energy. When she finally opened her eyes, she actually heard Vladislav in her mind, telling her the end of the memory he now shared with Clémentine.

"One of my guards came to me. I looked at him, and with him, I saw a young woman sitting on the cold stone ground. She had long hair, dark eyes, and a dirty dress. Regardless of the temperature, her feet were bare and she was covered in soot. Her eyes were filled with tears and terror. I asked my guard if she was a witch but he said she was the liar's wife, and possibly, his own daughter. I gently took her hand, and helped her up. I asked her as softly as I could if she was scared of me and she said yes. I asked why, and she said it was because of all the lies her husband told her, the brutal killings, and the confusion as to what I truly was."

There was a small pause before Vladislav continued his story. Clémentine was begging for him to stop but he wouldn't, and the prince's voice cracked.

"I told my guard to bring her inside my home, to ask one of my servants to give her food, clothes, and a

place to stay. I promised her that she would be cared for and that she had my permission to stay for as long as she wanted. She asked me what I would demand in return, knowing what I was. I told her nothing but a smile. I know it sounds horrible, even tacky, but that is what I said. When she walked into the castle, my friend asked why I did what I did; pointing out that she was not pregnant. I said I knew, but as I looked at her I saw that she had been terribly abused. I could not tolerate one of my people being tortured this way and not pay for it."

Clémentine wanted to know what happened to her. Vladislav answered, *"She married one of my knights and lived happily ever after."*

CHAPTER 35
WAKE UP! I'M POUNDING ON THE DOOR

Clémentine put her arm over her eyes but the moment she closed them, she saw the men being tortured. She saw a glimpse of the darkest past someone could have and was horrified by it. She thought she wouldn't be able to sleep ever again. As she was about to scream, she felt two hands grabbing her wrists and moving them off her face. "Wake up, Clémentine!" A strong voice shouted.

Clémentine opened her eyes and wondered if all had been a dream. She was lying in her bed and saw

Naten holding her hands. His knees were on both sides of her legs and he was holding her wrists apart above her head. His body was leaning toward her. She looked around, then at herself and noticed she was in her pajamas. She couldn't recall how she got in bed, or even how she changed clothing.

She stared at Naten as he slowly moved away from her. The moment he let go of her wrists, she wished he had stayed next to her. She could see his eyes turning back to a normal dark umber brown as he moved. He brushed his hair back and stood by her side. Vladislav crossed her mind and she felt a cool breeze in her thoughts that made her think that he was awake
and well.

"Naten, what happened?"

"After you freed Vlad, you fell into a deep sleep."

"How did it happen? I ate and I was feeling alright when I entered Vlad's mind."

"I believe Vlad made you." Naten sighed before revealing to her what really happened. "You kept screaming, Clémentine. I mean you were crying hysterically and trembling like a leaf. I think he had no choice but to make you sleep so you could let go of what you saw. I've never seen anyone so traumatized in my life. I tried to calm you down. I even held you in my arms but you suddenly got scared. When you looked at me, you were terrified. I kept repeating who I was but you rolled away from me. Once you hit the floor, you crawled into the corner, next to the hearth, and grabbed one of the log pokers."

Clémentine tried to remember but it was like a page was missing in a book. It was gone. She stared at Naten and pointed at him with her index finger. She frowned.

"Did Vlad mind spell me or did he voluntarily erase what I did and what I saw?"

"No, he would never do that to you, Clémentine. Whatever happened after you fell asleep, your mind suppressed it all on its own, which is better I guess. I felt so bad for you Clémentine. I wanted to take your place, but I didn't know how. I had tears in my eyes the entire time you were in there alone." Naten's finger followed the line from the middle of Clémentine's forehead and down her face. Naten moved closer and Clémentine looked at the bed sheets. She felt his hand moving her chin up so she would look into his deep dark eyes.

"I am broken too," Naten said. Then he stopped, taking a moment to think. "Clémentine, I wished I could have faced this memory instead of you." It seemed so hard for him to say anything so she took his right hand in hers.

"I wished what you saw would have been something to make you stronger, and not something scar you for life. I want you to know that you were never alone," Naten leaned in and kissed her forehead before another comforting voice was heard. Clémentine moved to see who it was.

"He actually held your hand the entire time. I asked him many times to go lie down and that I would watch you, but he ordered me out." It was one of the female givers that made sure Naten and Clémentine wouldn't need anything during their rescue mission.

"Thank you. That will be all." Naten said, after clearing his voice and quickly moved away from the bed and Clémentine. The woman left a platter of fresh water bottles and a bowl of grapes, Clémentine's favorites, and closed the door. Clémentine looked back at Naten and smiled.

"Thank you. I do not remember what happened at all, but—"

"It's for the better," Naten stated, as he moved a lock of Clémentine's hair away from her face. "Come, I'll cook some waffles for you." When Clémentine got out of bed, she looked at her pajamas and recalled the giver saying that Naten stayed with her all night. With that reasoning, he was the one who undressed her.

"No! I wouldn't dare do that for a hundred reasons that don't involve you! Forget I ever said that, it came out wrong. I meant that Lore changed you. I wasn't even in the room at that time," Naten answered horrified, standing as far away as possible from Clémentine. "No problem. I believe you."

CHAPTER 36
YOU WILL LEARN
ME RIGHT

As she was about to follow Naten out of the room, they heard the door opening. Clémentine had a smile radiating on her face, knowing who it might be. There was a giant fireball building up at the back of her throat, tears coating her eyes as she realized she had succeeded. She had saved him.

Clémentine looked at his face. He had a huge black eye on the right side, and bloodstains on his cheeks. The river of blood around his mouth was almost dry, with small streaks going down his chin to his chest. Her nails were digging into his forearm. As he turned around, she noticed his lightly-haired athletic torso, with its well-defined abdominals.In the center of his stomach, there was a fine line of dark hair going down his lower abdomen beneath his belt buckle, disappearing into his pants.

"So many scars," Clémentine murmured as she delicately touched a significant mark.

The scar was where Vladislav had been stabbed alongside his V line. The torn flesh had been sewn back together, with the hope of stemming the bleeding. Clémentine could see the stitch marks, and as she followed it down, Vladislav grabbed her hand.

"What are you doing, Clémentine?"

"What does it look like I'm doing?"

She saw the loneliness in Vladislav's eyes. He gently brought her right hand to his mouth, kissing her palm. He moved his body close to hers, revealing his fangs. His eyes looked dark, although no red showed in them. His pain danced with hers as they embraced
each other.

Clémentine caressed his face, thinking by now he should have been entirely healed. She didn't know how long she had slept and how much time had passed. No matter the amount of time or how strong a vampire Vladislav was, he would never entirely heal from
the wounds.

"Vlad, I can't let you go," She cried, tears streaming down her face.

"I'm not derailing from my destiny anymore. Because now I know you are my road, my fate…my path." Vladislav's eyes fixed on hers, a red line of tears ready to fall.

"And you are mine," Clémentine whispered.

"You are my path, my own." Her whispered answer came as she caressed his face.

A voice came from a dear friend who, without his help, Clémentine might have found the fight to keep Vladislav alive harder.

"Clémentine is the bravest woman I have ever seen, Vlad. Take good care of her, as she did with you. Without her, you would have remained lost. As you said, she is your path. Follow her and you just might remain safe." Naten said as he closed the door.

Clémentine thought of Naten as he walked away. She hoped he would not leave her life forever. In Naten, she had found a friend, someone she could be close to and trust.

Clémentine rested her head against Vlad's arm. She tried to remember the memory that disappeared. She knew she should be afraid, but *"Everything happens for a reason."*

"I was afraid I would never see you again. You saved me, my son, and my best friend."

"What I did, I did for the hero I know you are."

He lifted her chin with his fingers, "My intentions never were to put you in danger. So, please, my hero Clémentine, tell me what you would have me do."

"I want to know what happened. I want to remember. Would you do that for me?" Clémentine asked, trembling at the idea of being Vladislav's hero.

Vladislav's breeze penetrated Clémentine's mind, and his voice released a fresh wind. She could almost see it glow from inside her head. Then, in an instant, it was all revealed to her. The horror that Vladislav had tried to protect her from when she fought the traveler inside his mind.

They were impaled. They had been pierced through and placed on a wooden beam one by one, so every person walking by would see. So many horrifying screams and cries, and then it would all come to silence.

Words would fall down their bleeding lips here and there, but soon, they, too, would be forgotten. Clémentine's vision blurred, her skin shivered, and she could barely hold back her cries as the need to scream appeared. Her mind suppressed it, and she was no longer trembling.

"Clémentine, please remember you wished to know the real me." Vladislav's voice caressed her mind.

"I don't know if I'm strong enough. See, I thought I was tough, a paranormal psychic, and now, I wonder if I'll ever be strong enough again."

Clémentine said, finding the strength to speak the words aloud.

Vladislav's voice reminded her why she quickly fell for him. In her mind, she saw his arms wrapped around her as she fell unconscious. She recalled his kiss when they were on the bed, crawling toward one another, wishing it would never end. She remembered his icy wind enveloping her, protecting her from any malevolent entity.

But, the memory surfaced yet again, and they had all been impaled by Vladislav. It seemed to be a never-ending forest of horrifying views.

"I don't know if I'll be able to protect you again," Clémentine's voice was faint, and she wished to run away. It was a dim hope, but she knew Judith was just as intrigued in her as she was in him. "I must find a way."

"Don't do this. Don't do something you might regret one day."

Clémentine couldn't believe it. She could hear the tears through his words. She wiped her eyes and looked up. Vladislav's eyes were covered in blood as tears dripped down his face.

He stood tall, in silence, only tears of blood falling. She was the weakness of his strength, the one who could bring his entire world down if she was taken away from him.

"Please. I was locked in a sarcophagus for days. I was incomplete without the strength of the look in your eyes and the science in your mind. For the longest time, I've prayed for this hole in my chest to close. I do not wish to hold you against your will, but forgive me if I cannot let you go. I refuse to have you face this cruel, broken world alone. I want to let you go. I just can't."

Clémentine's eyes blurred again as she touched his face. She put her hands in his hair, pulling him toward her as close as she could. "In my head, I tried to move on as though we had never met. It was for your safety, Vlad. But the pain was too much, and my heart shattered to pieces. I was weak. It felt as though glass was cutting my soul. I can't let you go." She whispered.

"Please, don't leave me. You are my path. I would be lost in this world, haunting a space that means nothing to me without you. Just tell me what you need me to do." His hands closed on her wrists, both hands on his chest now he held her tighter.

"I am not leaving you," Clémentine said. "I never could, even if I would. I just need to know who your Donor—"

An intense noise filled the mansion. It sounded as though a bomb had exploded. They looked down, but suddenly, Clémentine lost Vladislav's grip. When she looked up, there was nothing but the echo of a laugh.

"Vlad!" Clémentine kept screaming his name over and over again as loud as she could. She ran outside her room, but there was no one there, not even the guards who protected her chambers. She huffed out a breath in anger.

Clémentine ran to the banister overlooking the entrance hall where the voice seemed to have emerged. Vladislav would not be lost to her again. Her blood was boiling, and her thirst for blood was growing.

With her core turning into ice, Clémentine was livid. The gravedigger that she was would soon have all the holes needed for each soul who dared hurt Vladislav, ready in her cemetery.

"I will scratch your heart out and eat it in front of your face!" The voice screamed with rage as it cracked, turning raspy.

But, Clémentine knew who had orchestrated it all, and with whose help.

"Then so it begins…Odette." Clémentine said with a strong voice, her hands on her hips. "I am coming for you. *Vin după tine.* I'll be speaking my tongue of old, and you'll learn me right. Test me all you want, but my love for Vlad is not fragile."

ANNEX

NAME – PLACES - TRANSLATIONS

The spelling of place, names, and translations from their original linguistic to American English was uncertain research done to the best of my capabilities. Adaptations were accomplished with the help of fellow authors, including Andreea Pryde (@andreeapryde) and various online translators, as well as the Oxford English Dictionary. As I am French from the French-Canadian province of Québec, I was capable of doing the French translation myself.

I recognize that history is a great and wonderful beast filled with secrets and mysteries when it comes to a bloodline such as Tepes and The Order of the Dragon. The research done on historical figures, as well as places and dates in history were accomplished with the help of written encyclopedias, Wikipedia, Britannica, BBC, History, Published Work, among other reliable   sources.

NAMES

Vladislav Tepes III: Vlad III, also known as Vlad Tepesh, i.e., the Impaler, saw the light of day for the first time between the year 1428 and 1431. No one knows his actual birth date and can only estimate it to be around those times.

Vlad III was born Roman Catholic and would eventually become the voivode, ruler, warlord, of Wallachia, today known as Romania.

Although Vlad III's bloodline is a noble one, the truth is, due to Romania's history, it was hard for his father to maintain his reign. The era Vlad lived in was unstable due to the constant attacks from Matthias Corvinus and other Muslim-based countries invading countries such as Romania.

Matthias Corvinus: King of Hungary and Bohemia from 1469-1490. Vladislav marched to Transylvania to seek assistance from Matthias Corvinus, King of Hungary, in late 1462, but Corvinus had him imprisoned. Vladislav was released in 1476 and had to fight for Matthias.

Elizabeth Báthory: Let's dig in Elizabeth Báthory, the Blood Countess. Elizabeth Báthory, born on August 7th, 1560, was a noble Hungarian woman. She reigned over the Kingdom of Hungary that now is part of Hungary, Slovakia, and Romania.

When young, the countess suffered from many seizures that led historians to understand those were probably from epilepsy and possibly transmitted from inbreeding from her direct parents. Between the years 1585 to 1609, Elizabeth lived a secret life as a murderer. Some believe that the number of murders she committed goes up to six hundred and fifty. However, it is not official to this day.

Ragnar Lodbrok: Lived in the 9th century and was a Norse King. He is a historic character, as well as a legend at the same time. His life was not as documented with precisions as other later Vikings of his caliber.

Cennétig mac Lorcáin: Dál gCais dynasty and maintained sovereignty by becoming king of Ireland. In 1002.

Akhenaten: Pharaoh of the 18th dynasty and known for bringing Egyptians under the reign of one god. Because of his strange ways during his reign, once he passed, statues and monuments were destroyed.

Nefertiti: Queen of Egypt, she reigned alone for a short period after her husband, Akhenaten, passed. She is known for the revolution of worshiping the Aten god, i.e., sun disc. She also lived in the wealthiest Egyptian period.

Tutankhamun: The young king of Egypt was the last of his dynasty and became most famous due to the discovery of his tomb in 1922 and the curse surrounding his treasure and sarcophagus. King Tut is also believed to have died between the age of 19 and 21.

Lycanthrope: Also known as werewolf developed in the parallel belief of witches. In the Middle Ages, like witchcraft trials, werewolves were also perceived as witches. The most popular place being Switzerland, most likely, Valais and Vaud.

Viking: Scandinavian people from the 8th to late 11th centuries, Vikings were known for raiding, trading, and explored Iceland, Greenland, and Vinland. Northern European were known to be the place for Vikings to go and originate. The Viking Age is between   793-1066 AD.

Stregheria: It is a form of Catholic-rooted folk magic having little if any relationship to other types of Italian   Witchcraft.

PLACES

Moosham Castle: One of the most haunted castles in the world is Moosham Castle in Unternberg, Austria. Also known as Witches Castle. Moosham has been the site of not only gruesome witch trials in Austrian history but werewolf hunts as well. If you *Google* Moosham Castle, you'll find story after story of witch trials and werewolf hunts.

Moosham was first deeded in 1191. Before that date, not much is known. It's believed to be built on the foundation of a Roman Fortress. Austria was part of the Roman Empire up until its fall in 476A.D.

Poenari Castle: Vlad III ordered for one castle's construction, the Poenari Castle. However, it is almost sure that he never walked inside the Poenari Castle.

It is at the top of a mountain overlooking a large part of Romania, strategically placed, like most fortresses at the time. It was easy to stand guard and see anyone coming their way. Nevertheless, Vlad most likely, himself, never set foot in the Poenari Castle and had prisoners sent to the location to build it for him.

The castle is highly placed and looked overly gloomy and terrifying for anyone daring to attack the homeland of the Impaler.

Wallachia: Found in the early 14th century by Basarab I. It was after the rebellion against the King of Hungary, Charles I. The first mention of Wallachia dates back to 1246 by Béla IV of Hungary.

Battle of Posada: The battle took place November 9th, 1330, to November 12th, 1330. The fight occurred between Basarab I of Wallachia and Charles I of Hungary, i.e., Charles Robert. Despite the numbers of the Wallachian army being small, they defeated 30'000 Hungarian knights.

Montréal: Founded in 1642 named Ville-Marie or City of Mary, is named after Mont Royal or Mount Royal, which is the triple-peaked hill right in the heart of the city. The French island itself took the name after the   mountain.

TRANSLATIONS

<u>Romanian</u>

Printul: Prince.
Voivode: Warlord.
La revedere: Au revoir.
Îngerul meu mic: My little angel.
Îngerul meu frumos: My beautiful angel.
Înger: Angel.
Fiu: Son.
Dă-i drumu: Let go.
Dute din cale: Get out of the way.
Pulă: Dick.
Ești slab: You are weak.
Întotdeauna ai fost: You always have been.
Acum veți plăti: Now you will pay.
Eliberează-mi tatăl: Release me, father.
Vin după tine: I am coming for you.

<u>French</u>

Au revoir Madame Lefebvre et bon voyage: Goodbye miss Lefebvre and have a good trip.
Madame: Miss.
Mademoiselle: Young lady.
Révolution Française: French Revolution.
Général: General.
Ma   belle: My   beautiful.

ABOUT ARIELLE LYON

Arielle Lyon grew up in the artistic and publishing world. She studied visual art as well as imaginative literature, classical ballet, acting, and storytelling.

Despite her introverted personality, Arielle decided to realize one of her secret dreams to create a gothic magazine that would reach out to all who had a passion for the tales older than time. That is when **Gothic Bite Magazine** was born.

Lyon's first dream achieved, she then desired nothing more than to publish her novels series. Torn between two passions, she found a way to mix together fairy tales and history.

She made her place in the author world by believing she could do it as long as she never stopped writing and believe in her stories.

Made in the USA
Monee, IL
21 December 2021

86815916R00223